The
Road
to
Stillwater

Philip Mazza

Also by Philip Mazza

From Under a Tree
Book One; The Harrow Saga

Shadow in the Flame
Book Two; The Harrow Saga

Children at the Gate
Book Three; The Harrow Saga

The Child of Fire
Book Four; The Harrow Saga
(Coming 2025)

The Neon Hive

The Quantum Gardener

At the End of it All

Beneath the Ashen Sky

The Never-Ending Road

The Road to Stillwater

Philip Mazza

⬡MNI PUBLISHERS

www.philipmazza.com

Omni Publishers of New York
ISBN 979-8-9924526-1-7
Printed in the United States of America

First Printing: April 2025

To my parents, whose love and support have always guided me. And to all those who have ever felt the pull of home.

From the author

The Road to Stillwater is more than just a novel; it's an intimate exploration of the fragile, intricate web of human connection. I've always been captivated by the way the past lingers beneath the surface of the present, quietly shaping our identities and influencing the choices we make - sometimes consciously, often without us realizing it. Writing this book allowed me to delve into the echoes of history, both personal and shared and to consider how those echoes can guide or hinder our paths forward.

As a writer, my goal has always been to illuminate the extraordinary within the ordinary, and to find beauty and meaning in the everyday moments that make up our lives. In *The Road to Stillwater,* the quiet Vermont town of Stillwater becomes more than just a setting; it transforms into a stage where the profound plays out amidst the seemingly mundane. The story centers on the Keller family, their tangled relationships, and the small community that serves as both backdrop and catalyst for their personal transformations. Through their lives, the novel explores universal themes of love and loss, the enduring grip of regret, and the healing power of forgiveness.

Family is at the heart of this story. I've sought to portray its complexities in all their raw, unpolished forms - the ways we misunderstand one another, the ways we fail and hurt those we love, and the ways we come back together despite everything. In Ashley's journey, in particular, I found a way to weave these threads into a narrative of self-discovery. Her path isn't just about making peace with others; it's about finding compassion for herself, about embracing the messiness of her past and the imperfections that make her whole.

Writing this book was, in many ways, an act of vulnerability. I wanted to create a story that doesn't shy away from the difficult questions: How do we reconcile with the things we cannot change? How do we learn to forgive - not only others but also ourselves? And how do we find meaning in the face of life's inevitable losses? By charting Ashley's journey, I hoped to give readers a mirror for their own introspections, a chance to confront the weight of their histories while embracing the possibility of hope and renewal.

At its core, *The Road to Stillwater* is a celebration of resilience, of the human spirit's capacity to endure and to grow. Through the lens of this one family's struggles and triumphs, I hope to offer a story that resonates deeply, one that lingers long after the final page is turned. My wish for readers is that Ashley's journey - and the town of Stillwater itself - might serve as a reminder that healing is possible, that the past does not have to define us, and that even in our darkest moments, the light of understanding and connection is never far away.

1 The Return

Ashley parked her car on the quiet main street of Emberton, Vermont, the engine's thrum fading into the stillness of the late afternoon. The town seemed frozen in a moment of postcard perfection, with its white-steepled church, brick storefronts, and a row of maple trees shedding their amber and crimson leaves. She stepped out of the car, stretched her back, and inhaled deeply. The air was crisp, laced with the faint scent of woodsmoke, the kind of smell that made her think of home, though she hadn't quite decided where that was anymore.

A small café caught her eye - a weathered sign hanging above the door read *Hearth & Table*. Its windows were fogged, the warm light inside a contrast to the chill creeping into the late October day. Ashley crossed the street, the soles of her boots scuffing against the uneven brick sidewalk, and pushed open the door. A bell jingled overhead.

Inside, the café was cozy in a way that felt intentional. Mismatched chairs surrounded wooden tables, and a stone fireplace crackled in one corner. A chalkboard menu hung behind the counter, its letters curling slightly at the ends as if the handwriting couldn't quite stay still. The air smelled of brewed coffee and something sweet - cinnamon, maybe.

Ashley hesitated for a moment before stepping up to the counter, where a young man with a flannel shirt and an easy smile greeted her.

"What can I get you?" he asked, his pen poised above a notepad.

"Just a coffee, black," Ashley replied. She paused, glancing at the display case filled with pastries. "And one of those pumpkin muffins."

He nodded, ringing her up and sliding the muffin onto a small plate.

"Passing through?" he asked, making small talk as he poured her coffee.

"Something like that," Ashley said. She slid a bill across the counter and took her change without further elaboration.

Scanning the café, she spotted the only empty table tucked away in a cozy corner. Carrying her cup and plate to a corner table, she sank into one of the chairs and wrapped her hands around the warm ceramic cup. The first sip of coffee was bracing, cutting through the lingering fatigue of the long drive. She allowed herself to settle, letting the café's soft hum of conversation and the clatter of cups wash over her.

The door opened, letting in a burst of cold air as a man in a heavy coat stepped inside. He stomped his boots on the mat, shaking off the chill, and made his way to the counter. Ashley glanced at him briefly before returning her gaze to the steam rising from her cup.

Her thoughts drifted to Stillwater. It had been years since she'd been there, the kind of time that stretched so long it almost felt like another life. The place carried a weight for her, the kind that came with unfinished conversations and memories she hadn't yet made peace with. But the pull was undeniable.

She picked at the edge of her muffin, the crumbly texture flaking beneath her fingers.

"Excuse me," a voice interrupted her thoughts.

Ashley looked up to see a woman standing near her table, balancing a plate of cookies and a steaming latte. She looked to be in her forties, with kind eyes and a slightly frazzled energy.

"Mind if I join you? Every other table's full," the woman said, gesturing to the café, though it wasn't quite true as a couple was just leaving.

Ashley hesitated but nodded. "Sure."

The woman slid into the chair opposite her, placing her plate and cup on the table. "Thanks. I hate eating alone in places like this. Makes me feel like people are staring, even though they probably aren't."

Ashley managed a small smile. "I get that."

"I'm Claire, by the way," the woman said, extending a hand across the table.

"Ashley," she replied, shaking it briefly.

"Passing through?" Claire asked, echoing the barista's earlier question.

Ashley nodded. "On my way to Stillwater."

"Stillwater," Claire said, her brow furrowing slightly. "Beautiful place. Quiet. You have family there?"

"Kind of," Ashley said, her tone carefully neutral.

Claire studied her for a moment but didn't press further. Instead, she took a sip of her latte and changed the subject. "I'm here for a book club retreat. A whole weekend of discussing *Middlemarch* and drinking too much wine. It's indulgent, but it's my little escape."

Ashley chuckled softly. "I have a friend who loves books. Sounds nice."

"It is," Claire said, smiling. "What about you? What brings you to Stillwater?"

The question just dangled there for a moment, fragile as a golden leaf clinging to an autumn branch, quivering with unspoken possibilities. Ashley wasn't sure how to answer, wasn't sure she even had an answer.

"Just some loose ends to tie up," she said finally.

Claire nodded, seeming to sense the conversation wasn't meant to go deeper. "Loose ends can be tricky," she said, her tone lighter now. "But sometimes, it's worth the effort."

Ashley didn't reply. Instead, she lifted her cup to her lips, letting the rich aroma of coffee envelop her senses. The silence that settled over them was not uncomfortable, but rather a shared moment of contemplation, each woman lost in her own thoughts.

Time seemed to slow in the little café, the world outside fading away until there was nothing but the gentle clink of cups against saucers and the soft rustle of turning pages from a nearby patron. When Claire finally took the last sip of her coffee, the sound was almost startling in its finality.

"Well," Claire said, her voice carrying a note of reluctance as if she were leaving behind more than just a brief encounter. "It was nice meeting you. Good luck in Stillwater."

Ashley looked up, meeting Claire's gaze. "Thank you," she replied simply.

After Claire left, the café felt quieter, and emptier, though it seemed the same number of people occupied the space. Ashley stayed a while longer, nursing the last of her coffee and watching the fire in the corner as it crackled and spit.

The drive ahead felt both distant and immediate, the miles stretching out like a path she had no choice but to follow. Still, she couldn't deny the flicker of anticipation curling in her chest. Whatever awaited her in Stillwater, she was ready to face it.

Leaving a few crumpled bills on the table, she stood, tucked her scarf more tightly around her neck, and stepped back out into the cold. Emberton was already slipping into twilight, the edges of the day softening as the streetlamps flickered to life.

Ashley climbed into her car, the engine sputtering to life as she adjusted the heat. She sat there for a moment, watching her breath fog the windshield, before pulling onto the road and heading toward whatever came next.

Ashley gripped the wheel, her gaze moving from the road to the dense stretch of trees pressing in on either side. Maple and pine crowded together, branches tangled, trunks standing like a barrier against the outside world. She rolled down the window. The air held the scent of damp earth and leaves beginning to break down, a sharp contrast to the city she had left behind.

"It's been a long time," she murmured, though no one was there to hear.

The road curved ahead, each turn revealing something half-remembered. She had forgotten how Vermont folded itself around you, the hills rising and falling like a breath, the silence deep enough to make a person uneasy. Manhattan had been easier in that way -

its noise left no room for second thoughts, no space for memories creeping in.

When the attorney had called, she had listened without interrupting, her pen scratching out details that suddenly mattered in a way she hadn't expected. An estate. The shop. The apartment. The necessary arrangements. She had thanked him, her voice even, her hand steady. And then, when the call ended, she sat at her kitchen table, staring at the pattern in the wood, tracing it with a fingertip.

Now, with every mile bringing her closer, the past grew sharper. The last time she had driven this road, she had been eighteen, a bus ticket in her pocket, a burning certainty in her chest that she would never come back. But places had a way of holding on, of waiting. The trees had grown taller, the roads had worn down at the edges, but nothing had truly changed.

Her father was gone. That was the fact she had come to face. The man who had once filled their small house with stories, who had possessed a patience she hadn't appreciated until it was too late, had disappeared from the world without her permission.

Ashley tightened her grip on the wheel. She wasn't that eighteen-year-old girl anymore, but Stillwater wasn't letting her slip in unnoticed. The town was waiting, just ahead, unchanged and unyielding, offering no softness to cushion her return.

Ashley eased the car down Stillwater's quiet main road, past buildings that seemed untouched by the years. The storefronts stood just as they had when she was a child, their colors softened by time. The river ran steady beyond the trees, and the hills framed the town like old hands cupping something fragile.

She slowed near McDowell's hardware store, where the same "Closed on Sundays" sign swayed in the window. Next to it, Kimball's Bakery still listed its specials in careful chalk strokes— blueberry scones, apple turnovers, lemon tarts. The words might have been written yesterday or a decade ago.

At the town square, a small market had taken shape, just like the ones she remembered from childhood. Mrs. Garner sat behind a folding table covered in hand-knitted scarves, a deep purple hat perched on her head. Ashley could hear the rise and fall of easy conversation, neighbors catching up, exchanging small news that mattered only here.

Stillwater had never been a place for spectacle. It endured in the way a well-built house did, standing firm even after the years had worn grooves into its floors. Some towns remade themselves to keep up with the world, but Stillwater remained as it had always been, certain of itself.

Just beyond the square, the diner's door stood open. The neon coffee cup in the window blinked in a slow, steady rhythm, casting a familiar glow onto the sidewalk. "Breakfast Served All Day," the sign declared, the promise unchanged since before she was born. Ashley pictured the cracked vinyl seats, the scent of bacon clinging to the air, the scrape of forks against plates. She knew, without stepping inside, that the moment she walked through the door, conversations would pause, heads turning in quiet recognition.

She slowed the car further, passing faces she half-remembered. Some had aged into versions of themselves she could almost place; others were young, familiar in a way that suggested they belonged to people she had once known. A group of women on the sidewalk broke their conversation just long enough to glance at her out-of-state plates.

A low unease stirred in her chest. This town had claimed her once, stitched her into its fabric in a way she had spent years trying to undo. Yet here it was, holding her in place, its grip gentle but sure. She pulled into a parking space, cut the engine, and stepped onto the gravel. The air smelled like autumn—crisp, sharp, edged with woodsmoke.

She had come because there was no other choice. Her father was gone, and Stillwater had called her back, the past opening its doors whether she was ready or not.

2 *The Shop*

The antique shop sat wedged between the hardware store and a stationery shop, its facade almost swallowed by the surrounding buildings. It seemed to have settled into the ground over years of being forgotten, a quiet relic among louder lives. Its windows were darkened, filled with shadowed relics that seemed to press against the glass, as though eager to escape but held back by the grime. A small, faded sign above the door read *Keller Antiques & Curiosities*, the paint chipped and weathered from years of harsh winters and hot Vermont summers. Her father's name was painted in that old-fashioned type - black letters on a white-washed board, the kind he'd always liked, that to him held a kind of gravitas, as though it were a mark of authenticity from an era no one remembered anymore. She could almost hear his voice now, the gruff mutterings as he'd scrape away any new rust or dirt that dared to touch those letters, rubbing at them with a kind of rough affection until they gleamed under the streetlight's solitary glow each evening.

She opened the door and a bell jingled from above. Inside, the smell hit her immediately - musty, stale, a mix of dust and wood rot, overlaid with the faint tang of old leather and iron. She wrinkled her nose, stepping cautiously into the shadowy maze that had always been his kingdom. It was as if time had stopped here, freezing the place in some perpetual twilight, where the objects rested in their stillness, untouched since the last time she'd been here. The shelves were thick with dust, each layer carrying the years like a quiet witness to their passing, and as she moved, the faint light streaming through the grimy windows cast long shadows over the piles of vases, ancient clocks, cabinets filled with silver spoons, and tarnished jewelry. There was a sadness in these objects, an abandonment that seemed to echo in the empty spaces between them.

She let her fingers drift over a small, ornately carved box on the counter, the wood cool and gritty beneath her touch. She remembered her father leaning over it one evening, squinting at the delicate carvings as if they held some long-forgotten secret. The box hadn't moved since then, and she wondered if anything in this place ever had.

A voice pulled her from her thoughts, cutting through the quiet hum of the shop. She turned to see her father's attorney stepping toward her from the back, his presence as incongruous as a ship moored in the shallow stream of Stillwater. He held a worn manila envelope in his hand, the kind that looked as if it had traveled through time, accumulating the faint smudges and creases of countless desks and drawers.

The attorney was not a man of Stillwater but of Burlington, a place that felt both near and impossibly far in its bustling energy. He was in his late fifties, his suit bearing the marks of a long day a faint sheen on the elbows, a wrinkle along the lapels, and a weariness in the way it hung on his shoulders. His glasses teetered precariously on his nose, threatening to slip with every step he took, and his hair, graying in an even, respectable pattern, had been combed back with the precision of someone who believed in order, even if the rest of the world did not. A single strand, however, had defied him, curling rebelliously at his temple as if to remind him that control was never absolute.

There was something about him that seemed to belong to Stillwater, despite his city roots. Perhaps it was the way he carried himself, the quiet gravity of a man who had spent years navigating the waters of other people's lives. His posture was slightly stooped, not from defeat but from the cumulative weight of stories, secrets, and burdens that were not his own. He moved with the unhurried rhythm of someone who understood the futility of rushing, who had learned to let the world unfold at its own pace. This man, she thought, seemed tethered to his past in a way that felt almost familiar, as though history clung to him - not as a shadow, but as a badge he wore with reluctant pride.

"You must be Ashley," the attorney greeted her, his tone soft, balancing cordiality with a hesitance that felt almost rehearsed. It was as though he wasn't quite sure how much he was supposed to know about her - about the life she'd carved out far from Stillwater or the one she might've left behind. "It's good of you to come back. I am sorry for your loss."

Ashley gave a tight smile and extended her hand to take the envelope he offered. "Thank you."

The paper felt rough against her fingertips, thick and almost ceremonial, the kind of envelope that carried the weight of something unspoken yet undeniably final. Her eyes flicked to the man standing before her, his hands retreating into the deep pockets of his coat, as if he hoped to find words hidden there, words that might fill the silence stretching between them.

"Your father . . . " he began, hesitating just long enough to suggest he'd rehearsed this too many times on the way over and still hadn't landed on the right phrasing. "He was a unique man. Different." The statement hovered between them, soft and careful, an attempt to frame the past in terms gentle enough not to disturb the dust that had already settled. "He left everything to you. Though, I imagine you might have suspected as much."

Ashley's lips tightened into something that wasn't quite a smile. "Not sure why he'd do that," she murmured, glancing down at the envelope, her voice thick with the mix of resignation and weariness that only comes from reopening a door you thought was closed for good. "We really didn't see eye-to-eye. But it doesn't matter now, I suppose."

The words lingered between them as Ashley's gaze drifted around the shop, her father's shop, each item seeming to hold a fragment of his presence as if he were still somehow embedded in the crevices of this place. She could see him there still, bent over an object of mysterious origin, turning it over in his hands, cradling it with a reverence he'd never shown for her report cards or school plays. He'd turn the item this way and that, lips pursed in concentration, lost in a world of his own making where every chipped teacup and tarnished locket held secrets meant for his decoding. It was a patience Ashley had never known from him, a tenderness reserved for the voiceless things that filled this space, leaving her to wonder if she too might have earned his undivided attention had she been born of porcelain or brass instead of flesh and blood.

The ticking of the clocks came back to her then - not one clock, but all of them, a chorus of competing rhythms that never quite synchronized. It was the sound of her childhood, of hours stretching and contracting in this strange little corner of the world.

The attorney cleared his throat, breaking the spell. "There are keys to the shop and the apartment upstairs in that envelope," he said, his voice gentle but purposeful now. He adjusted his glasses, the gesture almost nervous. "There's also a set of bank statements you'll want to review. The inventory records too. He kept meticulous notes, of course. But you should check the inventory."

Ashley looked up at him then, her expression caught somewhere between bemusement and disbelief. "He wanted me to have all of this?"

The attorney nodded. "He did."

"Why?" she asked, though she wasn't sure if the question was for him or herself.

The attorney hesitated, glancing around the room as though the answer might be written in the worn leather bindings of the books stacked haphazardly on a nearby shelf. "Maybe he thought you'd understand it better than anyone else," he offered quietly. "Or maybe . . . he just hoped you would."

Ashley exhaled, the air leaving her lungs with a weight she hadn't realized she'd been carrying. "Well," she said, her voice steadier now, though no less conflicted. "I guess I'll find out."

The air seemed heavy as if the walls themselves had leaned in to listen. She held the envelope close, feeling the life her father had left behind condensed within it. For years, she had imagined this moment, her return to the place that had been her childhood home, but now that she was here, it felt as though she were standing at the edge of a chasm, staring into an unknown that had once been so familiar.

The attorney sensed her hesitation. His gaze lingered on her, his expression thoughtful, probing, and perhaps even curious. "If you don't mind my asking," he began slowly as if he were treading on delicate ground, "what happened with your mother? He never spoke of her. No one in town that I spoke to seemed to know."

The question dropped between them, heavy and unexpected, as though he'd opened a door she had long since bolted shut. Ashley felt the words sticking in her throat, years of silence making them feel foreign and unwieldy. She looked up, meeting his gaze, seeing in his eyes that quiet curiosity that came with the territory of small-town life, where stories lingered like ghosts, unresolved and whispered about in hushed tones.

"My mother left one day," she said finally, her voice brittle, as if it might break under the weight of the memory. "I was fifteen. She just . . . disappeared. My father didn't seem to care where she went, and so, neither did I." The words sounded strange, even to her, but they were true. She had never known why her mother left, only that she had woken up one morning to an empty house, the echo of her mother's absence filling every corner.

The attorney adjusted his glasses, his gaze lingering on Ashley as though weighing her carefully chosen words. He tilted his head slightly, an almost imperceptible nod that seemed to signal both agreement and an unspoken caution. "It's a lot to take in, isn't it?" he said softly, his voice threading through the quiet room.

Ashley didn't answer immediately.

He hesitated, then rested a hand on her shoulder. The touch was tentative, awkward even, as though he wasn't quite sure if it would be welcome. "You've got questions," he said, withdrawing his hand and letting it fall to his side. "More than I can answer. But if you need help - sorting through the estate, finding records, anything at all - you call me."

She looked up at him, her expression guarded but grateful. "Thanks," she said, her voice barely above a whisper.

He stepped toward the door but paused with his hand on the frame. "Stillwater's a good town," he added, glancing back. His tone carried a hint of reassurance, though the faintest shadow flickered across his features. "It might take some time, but things have a way of finding their place. Just . . . don't rush yourself."

"Oh, and my brother," she said.

The attorney let out a quiet breath. "He knows. I'm sure you'll see him soon."

Ashley gave a small nod, her throat tight as she watched him leave. The door creaked shut, the bell jingling once more, leaving her alone in the dim light of her father's world. She stood in the silence, feeling the weight of it settle around her like a second skin. The shop seemed to close in on her, each shadowed corner a reminder of the years she had spent avoiding this place, avoiding him, and now there was no one left to tell her what any of it meant.

She moved deeper into the maze of antiques, her fingers grazing the edges of a tarnished mirror, a set of porcelain dolls with faded faces, and brass candlesticks that felt cold and unyielding beneath her touch. There was an intimacy in these objects, a quiet fellowship in their presence. They seemed connected to him, holding fragments of his essence within their worn and weathered forms. They were fragments of a man she had never fully understood, a man who had held his secrets close, guarding them as fiercely as he had guarded this shop.

Her gaze drifted to the staircase at the back of the shop, the steps worn smooth from years of her father's footsteps. She remembered the nights she had crept up those stairs, careful to avoid the creaking boards, desperate not to wake him as she slipped back into her room after a night spent anywhere but here. It felt strange now, standing here alone, with no one left to judge her, no one left to care where she went or why she had left. The silence was almost unbearable, pressing down on her like a weight she hadn't known she was carrying.

Slowly, she made her way up the staircase, each step echoing in the emptiness. The apartment was small, cramped even, with a single window overlooking the street below. The air was stale, tinged with the faint scent of pipe smoke and the musty odor of unwashed clothes. She could almost see him there, sitting in his worn armchair, his gaze distant, his mind fixed on some relic or memory she would never fully comprehend.

There was a pile of books stacked by his chair, each one dog-eared and well-worn, as though they had been his only companions in those last lonely years. She picked one up, running her fingers over the cracked spine, feeling the faint indentations of his fingerprints on the cover. The realization struck her suddenly, with a force that left her breathless: she would never know him, not in the way she had once longed to, and now, standing in this empty apartment, surrounded by his forgotten treasures, she realized that perhaps she had never truly wanted to.

With a sigh, she placed the book back on the stack, her hand lingering on the worn cover. The apartment felt hollow, empty in a way that transcended the physical. The walls seemed steeped in his loneliness, his regrets, and now they returned to her in silence, an unspoken presence she hadn't prepared for. She closed her eyes, letting the memories wash over her, memories of the man he had been, the man she had once loved and resented in equal measure.

As the sun dipped below the horizon, Ashley found herself back down in the shop, drifting about, her fingers trailing over the delicate edges of porcelain teacups and the rough grain of oak tables worn smooth by countless hands before hers. She traced the rim of a small saucer chipped just slightly along one side, and as her thumb ran over the jagged edge, she remembered the old, unyielding caution her father had drilled into her - no elbows on tables, no careless fingers smudging the glass. Each item in this shop had been preserved under his precise and watchful eye, preserved as though by protecting these things, he was holding back time itself.

The dim light spilling in through the dusty window cast a sepia tint across the cluttered room, turning everything into a haze of browns and grays, shadowed corners thick with dust like shrouded memories. Ashley could hardly believe how little the shop had changed since she was last here. It was all exactly as she remembered, yet cloaked now in that unfamiliar layer of neglect. Dust lay like a fine frost on every shelf and surface, settling into corners and crevices, veiling the shapes of porcelain figurines and tarnished silverware, casting a dimness over it all. Her father would've never let things fall into such disrepair. This abandonment was a reminder that he was gone, that his hands would never again be here to fuss over a scratched clock face or adjust the angle of a delicate, hand-painted vase. She was alone, inheriting the small universe he had curated, a collection that had once held no meaning to her at all.

The shop had been her father's entire life, an obsession she had never understood. His devotion to these things, to objects she'd once dismissed as useless clutter, had stood between them for years, an invisible wall that had blocked him from ever truly seeing her. He'd cared for these relics - this bric-a-brac of no particular meaning to her - more than he'd ever cared for people, more, it seemed to Ashley, than he'd ever cared for her. She felt a deep melancholy settle over her, something both unyielding and somber, its presence lingering on her like the persistent dust that seemed impossible to brush away.

As she wandered further, her eyes landed on an old clock on a narrow table near the back of the shop. It was a brass contraption, polished to a deep, uneven shine, its face yellowed and the numbers slightly faded. Intricate designs swirled across its base, patterns too fine for most people to notice. It was ticking steadily, the rhythmic sound deep and resolute, as though it too, had absorbed something of the shop's age and her father's resolve. She reached out and let her fingers rest against its cool, worn surface, the steady pulse of it vibrating under her palm, like the faintest heartbeat.

He had had a sharpness about him, she thought. It was a kind of exacting intensity that had scared off almost everyone he'd ever known.

She could remember him scowling as he meticulously arranged a set of china dishes, adjusting each cup and plate until they were in perfect alignment. He'd had an eye for detail, a stubborn commitment to precision that made his world small, even forbidding. It had kept most people at a distance, including the rare customers who happened upon his shop, more curious than they were interested in buying anything. And though she'd tried to leave that stubbornness behind, tried to become someone entirely different, she could hear a small, biting voice inside her wondering how much of him she'd unknowingly carried all these years. She could see it now, in her own carefully controlled life, in her need for order, in her habits that had gone unexamined for so long. Her father's legacy had lingered, hidden in her all this time.

Something behind a glass display case caught her eye, and she leaned down to look more closely. There, tucked into the shadows, was an old photograph she hadn't seen in years - a faded black-and-white picture of a young couple standing in front of this very shop. Her father, impossibly young, his eyes earnest and soft, stood beside a woman Ashley barely recognized.

"Mom," she whispered.

Her mother's arm was looped through her father's in the photograph, her head tilted slightly toward him, smiling in a way Ashley hadn't seen often enough to think of it as natural. There was a softness to her mother in that moment, something unguarded, unspoiled, captured before life seemed to grow heavier for all of them. She stared at it for some time, trying to reconcile the happiness frozen there with the woman she remembered - someone who, toward the end, before she suddenly left, had become distracted, forgetful, and at times so far away she might as well have been in another room entirely.

"Ashley, where are the keys?" her mother would ask, her voice tinged with confusion.

"Mom, you just had them," Ashley would reply, a knot of worry forming in her chest.

And then, that summer in Silver Birch – "Have you seen your mother?" her father's voice had asked, rising in panic. "She's gone. Again."

They found her by the dock, sandals in hand, staring out at the water. "What are you doing here?" Ashley had asked, her heart sinking.

"I don't know," her mother had answered softly, as though she'd forgotten entirely.

Later, the arguments started. "You never pay attention to anything, do you?" her father would yell, his voice harsh with frustration.

"I can't do everything, George!" her mother's voice would tremble. "I can't keep up with it all!"

Ashley buried her face in the pillow, the words cutting through her, leaving marks that wouldn't fade.

It was only later, after her mother left, that Ashley began to wonder if the forgetfulness had been more than just a distraction, more than the ordinary burden of a busy life. But by then, the questions felt too big to ask and too late to matter. Her mother had slipped away from Stillwater like a tide retreating, leaving her father behind to anchor himself in the shop, in the quiet, predictable world of things that did not leave.

There was another moment that drifted into her mind, the one when he'd been showing her how to help in the shop.

"Ashley," Dad said, his tone even, "everything has its place. There's a time for everything. That's how we live."

Ashley glanced at him, sensing the same familiar distance. "You need order. Control."

He nodded, his gaze steady. "That's where I find peace."

"And Mom?" she asked, her voice softer.

"She's different. Always lost in her thoughts. Kind - until she forgets. And when she does . . . " His voice trailed off, leaving the rest unsaid.

Ashley exhaled slowly, her eyes drawn back to the photograph. "She couldn't meet your expectations. Not with her mind so often somewhere else," she whispered.

As she thought of her father, anger surged in Ashley, sharp, stinging. He had become angry with her mother, blaming her for everything - the missed appointments, the misplaced keys, the weight of their lives that he carried as if it were his alone. And now, looking back, Ashley realized he had never tried to understand. He had never asked why her mother seemed distant, why her memory slipped, why the warmth in her eyes had dimmed.

But why had the anger started? Why so suddenly and with such force? She wrestled with the question, knowing it wasn't as simple as her father's impatience or her mother's forgetfulness. Deep down, Ashley understood that her father had loved her mother, just as she was certain her mother had loved him. Their love had been real, tangible - something she could feel even now in the ghostly echoes of their life together. So what had gone wrong? What had shifted, snapping the thread that bound them? What could've sparked the anger that had unraveled everything? The questions felt like shadows moving just out of reach, teasing her with answers she might never find.

Then again, this was the same man who had never understood her, either, who dismissed her aspirations as a teenager with a quiet shrug or a curt reminder that dreams didn't pay bills. She remembered the conversations she'd started with so much hope, trying to explain her ideas about her future, about leaving Stillwater, about what her life could look like beyond the walls of their small, suffocating apartment. His responses had always been the same: practical to the point of cruelty, shutting her down before the words had even fully formed. "The life you want, Ashley," he said, his voice calm but unyielding. "It doesn't belong here. Not in this house."

But she pushed those thoughts away, unwilling to revisit them. She wasn't ready to untangle all the knots he had tied inside her, all the small ways he had made her feel less-than, tethering her to a life she hadn't chosen. It was easier to focus on her mother's absence, on the questions left unanswered, than to wade into the murky waters of her father's failings. That anger was cleaner, sharper - something she could carry without it breaking her entirely. Or so she told herself.

For a moment, the anger Ashley had felt for him softened, the familiar bitterness toward her father dissolving into something gentler, something almost mournful. There had been so many years between them, years marked by words left unsaid, by long silences and misunderstandings that had grown and festered until she'd finally left. The shop had always been a wedge between them, his love for it a constant source of conflict she could never overcome. She would never understand why he had chosen to cling so fiercely to this place, why he'd held onto these objects as though they were lifelines.

The chime of the clock as it struck the hour jolted her from her thoughts, each gentle toll filling the silence, settling over the shop with a sad resonance. She looked around, taking in the worn, dust-coated shelves, the narrow aisles, the crooked stacks of oddments and keepsakes. She felt the quiet closing in around her, the kind of quiet that felt as though it had been waiting for her all along.

In the dim, muted light of the shop, she realized that her return to Stillwater would be more than a passing week, more than a simple farewell to her father. She was bound to this place now, tied to the ghosts of memories she'd spent so long trying to forget. Her father's death had left her with questions she'd never wanted to ask, questions she now knew she could not avoid.

3 The Brother

Ashley's fingers were smudged with ink from her father's bank statements. She'd read through them again, scrutinizing every line. A tidy balance sheet was the norm for Charles Keller, who had, much like everything else in his life, long excelled in financial precision. The records were blunt and clear: no debt, and nearly half a million dollars stashed in savings. As she sifted through the final pages, the questions began to mount. The man who had once scolded her as a child for wasting her "hard-earned allowance on trifles like candy and dolls" had, in time, amassed a modest fortune of his own.

Her eyes were heavy, but she couldn't leave the work unfinished. It was strange, sifting through his life from an upstairs bedroom that still felt like it belonged to the girl she'd once been - a girl she had worked hard to leave behind. The scent of cedar drifted from the old wooden dresser, mingling with a faint trace of lavender from her mother's perfume, and suddenly, she was swept back to age sixteen, to summer nights when the sounds of Stillwater drifted up through her window. In those days, she'd plotted her escape from the quiet Vermont town and the confines of the family business that was both her father's pride and his prison.

As she held the metal keyring, she could feel its weight, tangible and symbolic. She held the keys to the shop now, a shop that had been at the center of her father's world, and which now rested in her reluctant hands. She glanced around her childhood bedroom - pale blue wallpaper, scuffed floors, an old stuffed bear on the nightstand. It had all remained untouched. After so many years away, everything seemed smaller, trapped in amber like the things her father had collected downstairs.

Exhausted, she slipped beneath the worn quilt and fell into a dreamless sleep. When she woke, pale light slanted through the blinds. Morning had settled around her, bringing that peculiar moment of disorientation when memory lagged behind awareness.

In the kitchen, she started a pot of coffee and cut two slices of bread for the toaster. There was butter in the refrigerator, and it was soft and glided across her toast like a memory. Soon, the smell of coffee filled the apartment, oddly grounding her in a place she barely recognized as home anymore. As she ate her breakfast, her mind began to drift to the work that awaited her, the odd task of sorting through her father's life - a life that had felt almost as foreign as it had familiar.

With a final sip of coffee, she steeled herself and made her way downstairs.

Pausing at the foot of the stairs, Ashley took in the cluttered expanse of the shop. Her father had always kept his store in what he called "organized chaos." It was still crammed with relics and artifacts that spanned decades, possibly even centuries - hand-painted china, mahogany cabinets, lamps with yellowed shades, and tarnished silverware lying in heaps. It was a time capsule of a place, unchanged since the last time she'd been here.

Ashley made sure the sign on the door was flipped to *Closed*. She wasn't ready for Stillwater's residents to come knocking, their curiosity about Charles Keller's legacy thinly veiled as condolences. For now, the shop was hers alone, a little world where she could unpack whatever her father had left behind.

She ran her hands over the dust-coated countertop, then paused to look around. Strangely, it felt as if her father was still there, shuffling behind the counter or cursing at the creaky register. She could almost hear his voice - a low rumble of irritation with the world that he'd never managed to change, his loyalty to this store the one constant in a life full of complicated relationships. Especially with her.

The papers rustled beneath her fingers, ink-smudged ledgers whispering secrets of the past. Then there came the knock at the door, a thunderclap in the quiet shop, and Ashley's heart leaped to her throat as she turned. Through the glass, she saw him - Owen, her little brother, now a man with hard eyes and hands buried deep in his pockets. Time had carved lines into his face, etching a map of the years they'd spent apart.

For a moment, Ashley hesitated, her mind a tangled web of memories and uncertainties. The boy she'd left behind - all gangly limbs and crooked smiles - seemed impossibly distant from this stranger at her door. His face was lined with unfamiliar creases, his eyes clouded with secrets she couldn't penetrate. She wasn't ready, not yet, to bridge the chasm of years between them.

Her lips shaped the words instinctively, a rhythm learned from years spent observing her father during those countless evenings when the lights dimmed and the doors were locked. "We're closed," she mouthed through the window, a slight smile, fragile and transparent as spun sugar, barely concealing the tremor in her heart.

But Owen wasn't deterred. His face tightened, muscles working beneath the skin as if trying to contain an explosion of emotion. He tried the door, its resistance only fueling his determination. He rapped against the glass, each strike sharp and urgent, a desperate staccato rhythm that matched the sudden pounding of Ashley's pulse.

"Ashley, it's me. Owen," he called, his voice a rasp of urgency. "Open the damn door."

She felt cornered, a sparrow trapped between the warmth of her carefully constructed nest and the wild, unpredictable world beyond the window.

She turned the lock with a click, its sound unnervingly loud, and as she swung the door open, the cheerful jingle of the bell above seemed absurdly out of place, a discordant note in this unfolding drama. She had imagined this moment a thousand times over the years - a tearful embrace, perhaps, or at least a tentative smile, a gentle rekindling of what once was. Instead, Owen brushed past her, his shoulder barely grazing hers as he entered. He brought with him the chill of sixteen years of absence and a sense of finality that seemed to settle over the store like a heavy fog.

Ashley secured the door behind him, the deadbolt sliding home with a finality that echoed through the cluttered antique shop. The sound seemed to reverberate off the dusty shelves, laden with the detritus of their father's life - ornate clocks frozen in time, tarnished silver candlesticks, and faded photographs in gilt frames.

Owen's gaze swept the cluttered shop, taking in the detritus of their father's life before landing on her. His eyes were a maelstrom of emotion - anger, frustration, and something deeper, more raw, like an old wound reopened.

"So," he said, each word sharp as broken glass, "you finally made it back."

"I guess you're not too glad to see me," Ashley replied coolly. She crossed her arms, leaning against the weathered oak counter with a stance of casual defiance, her fingers absently tracing the grooves worn smooth by decades of transactions and conversations. "Are you here to help me sort through all this."

Owen's laugh was a bitter sound, as bitter and acrid as day-old coffee left to stew. It was a laugh that had no place in Ashley's memories of the freckle-faced boy who once chased fireflies with her on warm summer evenings. "No," he spat, his voice rough with resentment. "Why should I? He left everything to you. I thought I'd been handling things just fine. But I guess I wasn't."

"Handling things?" Ashley's tone grew sharp, slicing through the musty air like a paper cut. Her eyes, once warm with nostalgia, now glinted with steel. She felt cornered. "You mean looking after him for your own benefit? Hoping that you'd get the store?" She gestured around at the cramped space.

Owen's eyes narrowed. "What are you talking about? I took care of him while you were off – in the big city, doing whatever you do there." His words dripped with disdain, each syllable a pebble tossed into the widening rift between them.

"Working, Owen. Working and building a life, while you were here, acting like there wasn't another way." Ashley's voice softened a bit, tinged with a sadness that surprised even her. She thought of the life she'd carved out for herself, far from the suffocating small-town air that seemed to cling to Owen like a second skin.

He looked away, his jaw clenched. "It's not like that," he muttered, his voice barely above a whisper. "I was here because he needed me."

"Or maybe you stayed because you needed him - because this was the only life you ever let yourself know." Her words landed with an unyielding force, stark and final, the way the last leaves hold fast to a tree long after they should have let go. They held each other's gaze, an ache rising between them, steeped in years of separation and the sharp pang of things left undone.

After a tense silence, Owen let out a long breath, rubbing his eyes with the heels of his palms. The gesture reminded Ashley of their father, and for a moment, she saw the family resemblance she'd always denied.

"Look, Ashley," he said, his voice thick with exhaustion. "This isn't about you or me. It's about what he left behind. There's more to sort through than you might think, and it's not just paperwork. I have a life here, whether you believe that or not. There are people here who need me. And there are people here who needed Dad." He swept a hand toward the clutter that filled the shop.

"Owen, all that's just an excuse to stay here, tied down by obligations you pretend are necessary." She could feel her own anger slipping from her grasp, its heat lingering in her chest like embers from a dying fire. The familiar scent around her suddenly felt stifling.

Owen raised his hands, fingers splayed in a gesture of frustration. "What are you talking about, Ashley? Some of us actually care about this place, this town. We're not all eager to escape the moment we get the chance." His words hung in the air, carrying with them a history neither of them could ignore.

His words hit harder than she expected, their barbs sharp and undeniable. She looked away, her gaze trailing over the objects around her, things she could no longer see as mere relics of a bygone era. They were symbols, remnants of a life she had never fully understood, that perhaps she had never wanted to.

Owen, too, had fallen into a kind of stillness, his gaze lost among the clutter, his body heavy as though the very air in the room had grown too thick for him. His fingers lightly brushed a shelf nearby, gathering dust that seemed to mirror his thoughts. His voice softened, losing its edge. "You know, he didn't tell me much about you. No reason for why you left. It was like you'd vanished." He paused, meeting her eyes with a look of weary curiosity. "Sometimes I wondered if you'd ever come back."

"Maybe that's how he wanted it," she said quietly. "Out of sight, out of mind."

He looked at her, something unreadable flickering in his eyes, like shadows dancing on water. "Is that how you wanted it?" he asked so quietly it might have been a thought accidentally spoken aloud.

She felt the familiar sting of regret, sharp and unmistakable, a thread she had woven tightly into the fabric of her indifference. For years, it'd been simpler to relegate her father to the backdrop of Stillwater, as unchanging as the mountains or the river - something she could turn her back on when she left. Yet here he was, not in the flesh but in the echoes and dust of this shop, a legacy she couldn't outrun. The walls seemed to hold him, to breathe his name.

Then, as if sensing that the silence could shatter at any moment, Owen squared his shoulders and let out a low, sad laugh that seemed to scrape against the quiet.

"You know, Ashley," he began. "I always thought if you ever came back, you'd have a little more respect. For him. For me. I was the one who was here. I was the one who watched him fade away, day by day, while you were off living your life in the city. You . . . you just . . . left."

Ashley drew in a slow, steadying breath, feeling the air fill her lungs like a shield against his words. "I had my reasons," she said, her voice steady despite the tremor she felt in her hands. "You were too young to understand what happened. What it was like for me here."

Owen's eyebrows rose, his voice laced with a hint of something that might have been pity. "Then why don't you explain it to me?" His hands spread out in an invitation, his stance daring her to step into that past she'd locked away, a past that seemed to loom larger with each passing second. "Go on. Tell me. Tell me why you left without so much as a goodbye."

She met his gaze, and for the first time since he'd arrived, there was a flicker of vulnerability in her eyes, a subtle crack in the defenses she'd carried for years. Then she shook her head, her voice barely above a whisper. "Not now, Owen. Not here, and not like this."

His shoulders dropped, frustration simmering just below the surface like a pot about to boil over. He took a step back, his eyes lingering on her, hard and searching, like he was trying to excavate the truth by sheer force of will, to peel back the layers she'd carefully constructed over the years.

"Of course," he said, his voice thick with resignation. "It's never the time. Even when I had reached out to you in the past. Do you remember those letters? Even when Dad was sick and told me I shouldn't bother, I reached out again. But it's never the time. You shut down. You keep everything to yourself, and you don't let anyone in. It's like you'd rather burn everything to the ground than . . . than just let someone understand you."

Ashley's mouth tightened, a familiar tension settling into her jaw. "I had a life beyond Stillwater, Owen," she said, her words clipped and precise. "I had to. And I didn't owe you . . . or anyone else an explanation for that. Not then, and not now."

Owen's voice rose, his face flushing with a familiar anger that Ashley remembered from their childhood. He gestured wildly at the cluttered shop, a haphazard collection of oddities and curiosities their father had amassed over decades.

"Of course. It's always about you, isn't it? Your freedom, your life. Meanwhile, I'm the one picking up the pieces left behind. You think I wanted to stay here forever?" Owen's words came out in a rush as if he'd been holding them back for years. "I had plans too, Ashley. Big plans. I was going to travel and see the world beyond this little town. But someone had to take care of him. And in case you forgot, someone still has to take care of this place." He ran a hand through his hair, leaving it standing on end, making him look younger and more vulnerable than Ashley was prepared for.

Ashley laughed, a short, humorless sound that seemed to bounce off the cluttered shelves. "Listen, I don't know why you stayed. But don't act like you're some kind of martyr, Owen." She could feel the old resentment bubbling up, hot and familiar in her chest. "You know he needed you, and you stayed. Maybe because it made you feel needed, or something. But don't blame me for that." Even as the words left her mouth, she could taste their bitterness, could see the hurt blooming in Owen's eyes.

He blinked, stung as though her words had struck him. For a moment, his features mirrored their father's so precisely that Ashley felt her footing shift beneath her. "You don't know anything Ashley, and you can't possibly know what it was like." His voice was low, worn thin by something unguarded and familiar, an ache that gnawed at her resolve. Ashley felt a pang she didn't want to acknowledge. "He was so ill. Not just his body - his mind, too. Some days, he'd look at me with a vacant stare, as if I were nothing to him. The man you remember - the one who taught us to ride bikes and helped with science projects - that man left long before you did." Owen's eyes carried a heaviness that went beyond words, a mirror of their father's weariness. "He needed help. He needed us. Both of us."

"I'm sorry," Ashley said, her voice breaking against the confines of the shop. She glanced down at her hands, clasped tightly as if to tether herself. "I couldn't come back. I had to leave it all behind - everything he expected, everything he wanted me to be. You don't understand what it was like to feel trapped by him. You were too young."

"Too young?" Owen echoed bitterly. His laugh was a hollow thing, reminding Ashley of the sound antique music boxes make when the mechanisms are winding down. "That's what you tell yourself, isn't it? That I was just some clueless kid who didn't understand. Well, I did. I understood enough to know what it meant when you left. And I grew up, Ashley. Faster than you could imagine."

The look he gave her was searing, a flash of pain that seemed to cut through the defenses she'd so carefully constructed over the years. Ashley felt herself waver, felt the temptation to explain, to bridge the divide that had yawned between them for so many years. But she could already feel the words slipping away, like sand through an hourglass, a reminder of just how deeply buried her own regrets had become.

"If I could go back," she said finally, her voice trembling just enough for Owen to hear, "maybe I would've done things differently." Ashley's gaze drifted to a faded photograph on the wall – their family, years ago before everything had fallen apart. She could almost smell their mother's perfume, and could almost hear their father's laugh. "But I can't turn back time, Owen. None of us can." She turned back to her brother, seeing the years etched on his face. "And frankly, I'm not too sure I would've done things differently if I'm being honest."

For a long time, Owen didn't respond. His face softened, the anger ebbing away like the tide retreating from a rocky shore, leaving behind a kind of resignation that seemed to age him before Ashley's eyes. He looked away, his gaze tracing the familiar shapes of their father's possessions - the old brass cash register with its worn keys, the delicate porcelain figurines that had always fascinated Ashley as a child. These fragments of their father's life were scattered across the shop like breadcrumbs leading back through time.

"Maybe you can't go back," he said, speaking more to the room than to anyone in particular, his voice blending with the steady rhythm of the grandfather clock in the corner. "But that doesn't mean you have to keep running."

Ashley swallowed, an ache settling deep within her chest, as familiar and unwelcome as an old injury flaring up. Her fingers traced the edge of an ornate picture frame, feeling every ridge and curve of its intricate design. Her eyes fixed on a point somewhere beyond the dusty glass, seeing not the faded photograph within but the memories it evoked - summer days spent chasing fireflies, winter evenings huddled around the woodstove, listening to their father's stories.

"I'm not running," she said softly, the words drifting between them, delicate and unanchored. "Not anymore."

Owen shifted his weight, the floorboards creaking beneath him with a sound as familiar as a lullaby. It was a sound Ashley remembered from childhood, the way the old shop seemed to speak with every step as if the very bones of the building were sighing with the weight of memories.

"What about the shop, then?" he asked, his tone carefully neutral, though Ashley could hear the undercurrent of tension, of hope and fear intertwined. "You going to keep it?"

The question was simple, but Ashley knew it was loaded with a thousand unspoken implications, like a deceptively small box filled to bursting with springs and coils, ready to explode at the slightest touch. Keeping the shop meant staying in Stillwater, facing the ghosts she'd spent years outrunning - the whispers of small-town gossip, the expectations she'd never quite managed to meet, the disappointments she'd left in her wake. It meant reconciling the person she'd become with the girl she'd left behind, the one who'd known every nook and cranny of this shop, who'd dreamed of adventures beyond the town limits. But selling it, walking away again — that meant trading one kind of regret for another.

She turned to face her brother, really looking at him for the first time since she'd arrived. The years had changed him, slight lines around his eyes and mouth that spoke of laughter and worry in equal measure, like the rings of a tree telling the story of seasons past. He was no longer the boy she'd left behind, all gangly limbs and mischievous grins, but a man shaped by the very absence she'd created, sturdy and grounded like the many oak trees that surrounded Stillwater.

"I don't know what I'm going to do with the shop," Ashley admitted, her voice steady despite the uncertainty churning inside her like a storm-tossed sea. "It's not just about keeping it or selling it. It's about . . . everything. This town, our family, the life I left behind. It's about who I was and who I've become, and whether those two people can exist in the same space anymore."

A flicker of understanding passed across Owen's face like a cloud momentarily obscuring the sun. "You know, Dad always said you'd come back someday," he said. "Even though you never called or wrote. He never gave up on you. He'd sit in that old armchair of his, by the window, watching the street like he was expecting you to walk by any minute. I think . . . I think he knew you'd find your way home eventually, even if it took his passing to bring you back."

A wave of remorse overtook Ashley, sharp and sudden. Her father's unwavering belief in her return, untouched by years of silence or the distance she had created, was a love so steady it defied time. The realization struck her with the force of a physical blow, leaving her momentarily breathless.

"I didn't know that," she murmured, her voice fragile as spun glass, trembling with a complex mixture of grief and a sudden, devastating understanding.

"There's a lot you don't know," Owen replied, but there was no bitterness in his tone now, just a quiet sadness. "Maybe it's time you learned."

He moved to the shop's front window, pushing aside a heavy velvet curtain. Sunlight streamed in, illuminating the dust motes that danced in the air and casting long shadows across the floor. Outside, Stillwater's main street was coming to life, the first stirrings of the day's business beginning to unfold. The familiar scene was both comforting and disorienting, like stepping into a beloved photograph only to find it subtly altered.

"Remember when we were kids - how we used to sit here on Saturday mornings?" Owen asked, a hint of nostalgia creeping into his voice. "Watching the world go by, making up stories about the people we saw?" His words conjured the ghost of their younger selves, two small figures perched on the window seat, noses pressed against the glass, breath fogging the pane.

Ashley nodded, the memory washing over her with unexpected clarity. "Mrs. Hendricks and her secret life as a spy," she said, a small smile tugging at the corners of her mouth. "Mr. Peterson and his collection of rare butterflies." The names felt strange on her tongue, like speaking a half-forgotten language.

"Dad would bring us hot chocolate," Owen added. "And tell us we had the most wonderful imaginations he'd ever seen." The memory of their father's voice, warm and encouraging, filled the space between them, bridging years of silence.

For a moment, they stood in silence, both adrift in the shadows of a shared past. Ashley felt something shift inside her, a gentle unfurling in her chest that had been tightly coiled since she'd first set foot back in Stillwater. It was as if a key had turned in a long-rusted lock, opening a door she hadn't realized was closed.

"Maybe you need to see this place," he said, turning to face Ashley. "To really see the people in it. It might change you." His eyes held a mixture of challenge and hope.

Ashley reached out, her hand hesitant at first, then steady as she squeezed her brother's fingers. It was a small gesture, but it felt like the first step on a long journey home. The warmth of his skin against hers was a reminder of all the years they'd lost, and all the possibilities that still lay ahead.

"Maybe, I do, Owen," she said, her voice finding its strength. "Maybe, I do."

His face brightened with a genuine smile, the first she'd seen since her return. "Good," he said. The single word held forgiveness, a promise of a new beginning.

And then he was gone, the bell over the door singing his departure. Ashley stood alone in the shop, surrounded by the ghosts of her past and the whispered promises of her future, feeling for the first time in years that she might be exactly where she needed to be.

4 The Friend

Ashley stood in the middle of the antique shop, the silence settling around her like dust on the shelves. The jingle of the bell over the door had long since faded, taking Owen with it. She took a deep breath, inhaling the familiar scent of aged wood and forgotten memories.

Her fingers trailed along the edge of an ornate mahogany dresser as she made her way to the back of the shop. The inventory list was where she had left it, tucked away in the top drawer of her father's old desk. She pulled it out, the paper yellowed and curling at the edges, a relic of a time when things were simpler.

As she began to count and catalog, her mind drifted to Owen's words. Her father had always believed she would return home. The idea settled in her chest, both a reassurance and a quiet pressure, like something pressing just below the surface. She paused for a moment, her hand hovering over a delicate porcelain figurine, a dancer poised in mid-pirouette, suspended in time.

"Did you really think I'd come back, Dad?" she whispered to the empty shop. The figurine offered no response, its painted eyes staring blankly past her.

Ashley shook her head, trying to focus on the task at hand. But as she moved from shelf to shelf, each item seemed to carry a memory, a whisper of the past. The old clock that never kept the right time, the collection of mismatched teacups, the weathered leather-bound books – each one a piece of the life she'd left behind.

She found herself in front of the large mirror that dominated one wall of the shop. Her reflection stared back at her, familiar yet strange. She looked older, of course, but there was something else. A weariness in her eyes that hadn't been there when she'd left Stillwater all those years ago.

"Maybe you do need to see this place," she murmured, echoing Owen's words. "To really see the people in it."

As she turned away from the mirror, her gaze fell on her father's old computer, tucked away in the corner of the shop. It was an outdated model, its bulky monitor a relic of a bygone era. She hesitated for a moment, then walked over and pressed the power button. To her surprise, it hummed to life, the screen flickering before settling into a soft blue glow.

Ashley sat down in the worn leather chair, her fingers hovering over the keyboard. She wondered if her father had kept any records on this old machine. As she navigated through the folders, she stumbled upon a spreadsheet labeled "Inventory_Current".

Curious, she opened the file. It was a meticulously detailed list of every item in the shop, complete with descriptions, purchase dates, and prices. Ashley scrolled through the list, marveling at her father's organization. Of course, she was not surprised.

But as she read through the entries, she noticed something odd. Many of the items had notes attached to them, little snippets of memory or history. "Vase - blue and white, reminds of Owen trying to lift it," one note read. Another said, "Antique clock - Ashley loved to wind this up as a child."

Ashley's throat tightened. These weren't just inventory notes; they were pieces of her father's heart, carefully cataloged and preserved. She continued scrolling, each entry revealing another facet of the man she thought she knew.

Suddenly, a new idea struck her. Instead of using the old paper inventory list, she could update this digital version. It would be more efficient, and she could add her own notes, creating a bridge between her father's memories and her own new experiences.

With renewed energy, Ashley began the task of updating the inventory. She moved through the shop, carefully examining each item, and comparing it to the list on the computer. Some pieces were missing, sold in the years since her father had last updated the file. Others were new additions, waiting to be cataloged.

As she worked, Ashley added entries. "Silver tea set – used to play pretend with this as a child," she typed, the memories flooding back. "Vintage camera - Dad taught me how to use one just like this."

Hours passed unnoticed as Ashley lost herself in the task. The shop around her seemed to come alive, each object whispering its own story. She realized that this wasn't just an inventory; it was a living history of her family, of this town, of the life she had left behind.

The afternoon sun began to slant through the dusty windows, casting long shadows across the floor, Ashley sat back in the chair, stretching her stiff muscles. She had made significant progress, but there was still so much to do. The task that had initially seemed overwhelming now felt like an opportunity, a chance to reconnect with the past and perhaps find a way forward.

She saved the updated file, feeling a small sense of accomplishment. This was just the beginning, she knew. There were still boxes to unpack, shelves to organize, and countless stories to uncover. But for the first time since she'd returned to Stillwater, Ashley felt a spark of excitement about what lay ahead.

As she stood up, her gaze fell on a small wooden box she hadn't noticed before. It sat on a high shelf, partially hidden behind a stack of old books. Curious, Ashley reached for it, her fingers brushing away a layer of dust.

The box was intricately carved, its surface worn smooth by years of handling. Ashley smiled. She remembered it – it was her grandmother's jewelry box, a piece she thought had been lost years ago. With trembling hands, she opened the lid.

Inside, nestled on a faded velvet lining, was a collection of old photographs. Ashley's breath caught in her throat as she lifted them out. There she was, a gap-toothed seven-year-old, grinning widely as she sat on her father's shoulders. Another showed her mother, young and radiant, laughing at something off-camera.

But it was the last photo that made Ashley's heart skip a beat. It seemed recent, the colors still vibrant, the edges crisp. Her father stood in front of the shop, his familiar smile bright and genuine. But it was the woman beside him that made Ashley pause. Long, grey hair framed a face that time had touched gently, leaving beauty in its wake. Her father's arm was draped comfortably around the woman's shoulders, and they both radiated an almost palpable contentment.

Who was this woman? What was her name? She studied the photograph, searching for clues. The woman's hand rested lightly on her father's arm. Was it a gesture of intimacy that spoke of a deep connection? How long had they known each other? What role, if any, had she played in her father's life?

Ashley's mind raced with more questions. Had this woman been a source of comfort to her father in his last days? Did the woman know about her, about the daughter who had left and rarely looked back? What stories could she tell her about her father?

She carefully returned the photos to the box. The inventory suddenly seemed trivial compared to the mystery that had unfolded before her. Ashley looked around the cluttered shop, seeing it with new eyes. Each object now held the potential for revelation. What other secrets were hidden among these shelves, waiting to be discovered?

Ashley realized that the inventory was just the beginning. There were deeper mysteries here, stories waiting to be uncovered. She carefully placed the box back on the high shelf, behind the stack of old books.

She thought about asking Owen, but something held her back. Strangely, this felt personal, a puzzle she needed to solve on her own. Besides, would Owen even know? How much of their father's life had remained hidden from both of them?

But for now, she had a shop to put in order, a legacy to understand, and a father to rediscover. Ashley looked around the cluttered shop, seeing it with new eyes. This wasn't just a collection of old things; it was a treasure trove of memories, secrets, and untold stories.

With a deep breath, she turned back to the computer. There was still work to be done, and Ashley was finally ready to face it head-on. As she began to type, Ashley felt a shift within herself. The shop was no longer just a burden she'd inherited, but a bridge to a past she'd left behind and a future she couldn't yet imagine. Coming back to Stillwater had seemed like a step backward, a retreat from the life she'd built. But now, surrounded by these echoes of her father's life, she wondered if it might be the beginning of something entirely new.

The bell over the door sang out, its cheerful jingle a stark contrast to the quiet that had settled over the shop. Ashley's heart performed an acrobatic feat, leaping into her throat as she realized her oversight – she'd forgotten to lock up after Owen's departure. Who would just come in when the sign at the door said *Closed?*

She spun around, ready to face whoever had wandered in, only to find herself arrested by a familiar yet impossible sight. There, framed by the doorway and backlit by the golden afternoon sun, stood the woman from the photograph. She was a vision, her long grey hair cascading down her back like a silver waterfall, her features still holding the echoes of a beauty that time had refined rather than diminished. She carried herself with an easy grace as if she'd stepped out of the frame and into the shop, claiming her place in this world of antiques and memories.

Ashley blinked, her mind struggling to reconcile the image before her with the reality she thought she knew. Words seemed to have abandoned her, leaving her mouth dry and her thoughts scattered. When she finally managed to speak, her voice sounded distant and uncertain, as if it belonged to someone else.

"I'm sorry," she said, the words tumbling out awkwardly. "I inadvertently left the door unlocked."

It was a ridiculous thing to say, she knew. The notion that a shopkeeper, a creature of habit and routine, would simply forget to lock the door seemed absurd, a glaring omission in the intricate choreography of their days. Yet it was all she could manage as she stood there, caught between disbelief and a strange, growing curiosity about the woman who had stepped out of her father's hidden history and into her life.

The woman smiled - a warm, enigmatic smile that made Ashley feel like she was hovering just outside the edges of a story she couldn't quite grasp. "Oh," she said, her tone soft and assured, "I'm not here to shop. I'm Miriam Ryan. I knew your father. You must be Ashley."

Her smile held layers — a quiet confidence, a hint of shared secrets — that made Ashley feel simultaneously intrigued and unsettled. It was the kind of smile that suggested entire volumes of unspoken narrative, a complexity that hinted at depths Ashley had yet to plumb.

Ashley blinked, momentarily unmoored. Their hands met in a brief, tentative clasp, her fingers cool against the unexpected warmth of this stranger's grip. "Yes . . . yes, I am," she heard herself say, the words a delicate thread. A pause stretched out, soft and uncertain.

"I'm so sorry about your father," Miriam said, her voice soft but sure, as though her words were meant to carry not just sympathy but a gentle truth. "He was a good man. Stillwater won't be the same without him."

Ashley tilted her head slightly, her voice tinged with a fragile kind of wonder. Her voice, when it came, carried a tentative warmth. "I'm sorry," she said, "but I don't think we've met before."

Miriam's smile held steady, warm and undemanding. "No, I don't suppose you would have," she said. "I own *The Stillwater Reader*, the little bookstore a few shops down. Your father and I - well, we were friends."

Ashley's mind churned, a quiet chaos of thoughts skittering, trying to find their place. This woman – Miriam - existed in a space of her father's life she'd never imagined. "Good friends?" she asked, her voice edged with a careful skepticism that betrayed her uncertainty, her disbelief hovering just beneath the surface of her carefully modulated tone.

Miriam nodded, moving further into the shop with a familiarity that made Ashley uncomfortable. "Oh yes. We'd often close up our shops during lunch and share a meal. Your father often visited my bookstore. He loved to wander through the shelves."

There was something in Miriam's tone, a warmth that hinted at more than just friendship. Ashley felt a flicker of . . . something. Not quite jealousy, not quite anger, but a complex emotion she couldn't quite name. She pushed the thought away, focusing instead on the practical.

"That's . . . nice," Ashley said, her voice sounding strained even to her own ears. "I'm sorry, but I'm in the middle of taking inventory. Perhaps we could talk another time?"

Miriam's eyes sparkled with amusement. "Of course. I'm sorry to intrude, but I thought you might like some help. There's quite a bit about your father's life in his later years that you might not know."

Ashley hesitated, torn between her instinct to politely dismiss this stranger and her curiosity about the life her father had led in her absence. "I appreciate the offer, but -"

"Did you know," Miriam interrupted, her hand resting on an old record player, "that your father started collecting vinyl again in his sixties? He said the sound reminded him of his youth."

Ashley turned her gaze to the record player, its smooth casing worn down to a subtle shine, the way things do after being touched so often. Something tightened in her chest, unexpected and unwelcome. She hadn't known that. She wondered what else had slipped past her, the fragments of her father's life she'd never thought to ask about.

"I . . . I didn't," she admitted softly.

Miriam's face softened. "There's a lot you didn't know," she said gently. "About your father. About this place. Maybe even about yourself." Her smile came slowly as if coaxed into being by the thought of what remained unsaid. "He talked about you often, you know."

Ashley's fingers traced the edge of the record player, feeling the smooth wood grain beneath her skin. "Really?" she asked, her voice barely above a whisper. "He talked about me?"

Miriam nodded, her eyes warm with memory. "Oh yes, dear. He talked about you often. About your youth, your dreams, your adventures. He always hoped you were doing well."

Ashley felt a tightness in her chest, a mixture of guilt and longing that threatened to overwhelm her. She turned away, pretending to examine a nearby shelf of knick-knacks. "I . . . I didn't think he'd want to talk about me. Especially after how I -" The unfinished thought just hanging there between them.

Miriam's laughter was soft, almost tender, carrying a weightless understanding that seemed to fill the space where Ashley's words had faltered. "You were about to say 'after the way you left,' weren't you?" she said gently, her eyes kind. "But that didn't change anything for him. Your father never stopped thinking about you. Never stopped loving you. He knew where you lived, you know. What you were doing."

Ashley spun around, her eyes wide. "He did? But how?"

"He asked his attorney to look into it for him," Miriam explained. "He wanted to make sure you were doing alright, if you needed help." Her words slowed, caught on the cusp of something more. She glanced at Ashley, her expression shifting into something gentler, more deliberate. "And . . . he wanted to be certain he could leave you the shop."

Ashley felt her knees go weak. She leaned against the counter. "So . . . he wanted me to have the shop? Even after everything?"

Miriam nodded, moving closer to place a comforting hand on Ashley's arm. "He believed in you, Ashley. He believed you'd come back someday."

Ashley closed her eyes, fighting back tears. She could see her father so clearly in her thoughts, puttering around the shop, telling stories about her to anyone who would listen. It was a version of him she'd never known, a life she'd missed out on.

"I don't understand," she said, opening her eyes to look at Miriam. "Why didn't he tell me all this himself?"

Miriam's smile was tinged with sadness. "Oh, honey. He wanted to. So many times. But he was afraid."

"Afraid?" Ashley echoed, incredulous. "Of what?"

"Of driving you further away for good," Miriam said gently. "Your brother sent you letters but you never responded. That made your father believe that if he tried to draw you back into his life, you might slip away even more. So he chose to wait. He held onto hope. And he made plans."

Ashley's gaze swept around the shop, seeing it with new eyes. Every item, every dusty corner, suddenly held a new meaning. This wasn't just a collection of antiques. It was a legacy. A gift. A bridge between the past she'd left behind and a future she'd never imagined.

"I don't know if I can do this," she whispered. "Or, if I want to."

Miriam rested her hand lightly on her arm, the touch steady, reassuring. "No need to decide anything just yet. Your father understood that this might take time. He wanted you to have space, to find your way to it in your own time. That's why he did his best to leave everything in order - or as much as he could manage. The shop was meant to be here, waiting for you, ready when you were. But those last days were difficult for him. Owen did his best to keep it running, but antiques were never Owen's strength."

Ashley nodded, feeling the comfort of Miriam's words settle over her. She exhaled slowly, trying to calm the torrent of thoughts that swirled in her mind. There were so many things she wanted to ask, so many questions that felt heavy on her chest. But she wasn't sure if she could voice them, or if Miriam would even be able to answer. Still, she found herself speaking. "Tell me more," she said finally. "Tell me about the father I didn't know."

Miriam's face lit up. "Oh, where to begin? Did you know he took up baking in his seventies? Said he wanted to learn how to make the perfect apple pie."

Despite herself, Ashley felt a smile tugging at her lips. "Dad? Baking? I can't imagine it."

"Oh, it was quite the sight," Miriam chuckled. "Flour everywhere, muttering curses under his breath. But he was determined. Said it reminded him of when you were little, how you'd always beg him to make cookies on rainy days."

The memory cascaded through Ashley like the opening chords of a familiar song she hadn't heard in years. She could almost catch the bittersweet aroma of chocolate chips melting into dough, blending with the damp freshness of a rainy afternoon. "I had forgotten about that," she said softly, her voice carrying the fragile wonder of rediscovery. It felt as though she were touching something long hidden, a fragment of herself she hadn't realized was missing.

"He never did," Miriam said. "Those memories, they were precious to him. He held onto them, nurtured them. They were his way of keeping you close."

Ashley moved away from the counter, needing to put some distance between herself and the emotions threatening to overwhelm her. She wandered over to a bookshelf, running her fingers along the spines of old volumes.

"What else?" she asked, not turning around. "What else did he do?"

Miriam followed her, her voice warm with affection. "Oh, so many things. He joined a book club at the library. Said it was high time he caught up on all the classics he'd missed. He volunteered at the animal shelter on weekends. Claimed it was just to get away from the shop, but we all knew he had a soft spot for those strays."

Ashley's hand paused on a worn copy of *To Kill a Mockingbird*. She remembered reading it in high school and discussing it with her father over dinner. Had he reread it in his book club, thinking of her?

"Was he . . . happy?" Ashley asked, her voice thick with unshed tears.

"He was," Miriam confirmed. "Not always, of course. He missed you terribly. Grief can be a persistent companion, and your father carried his disappointments like carefully wrapped packages, some too heavy to set down, some tucked away in quiet corners of his heart. But he found joy in his life here, in the shop, in his friendships. In the hope that someday, you'd come back."

Ashley turned then, facing Miriam with a vulnerability she hadn't allowed herself to feel in years. "I wish I had . . ." she whispered, ". . . I wish I'd known."

Miriam's smile was gentle, and understanding. "You're here now, Ashley. That's what matters. Your father believed in second chances. In new beginnings. That's why he left you the shop. He wanted you to have the opportunity to reconnect, not just with him, but with yourself. With the part of you that belongs here."

Ashley looked around the shop again, seeing not just the dusty antiques and forgotten treasures, but the life her father had built. The legacy he'd left behind. For her.

"I don't know if I can live up to all that," she admitted softly.

Miriam reached out, taking Ashley's hand in hers. "You don't have to live up to anything. You just have to be here, open to the possibilities. Your father gave you this gift not as an obligation, but as an invitation. An invitation to rediscover the part of yourself you left behind all those years ago."

Ashley nodded, feeling something shift inside her. A loosening, an opening up to possibilities she hadn't allowed herself to consider before. She didn't know what she'd find as she delved deeper into her father's life, into the town he'd loved so much. But for the first time since she'd arrived in Stillwater, she found herself looking forward to the discovery.

"Thank you," she said to Miriam, squeezing her hand. "For telling me all this. For . . . for being here. For being here . . . for him."

Miriam's smile lit up the room. "It was truly wonderful. He was a remarkable man."

Ashley inhaled deeply, feeling the warmth of possibility wrap around her like a cherished quilt.

"Well, I'll leave you to it," Miriam said, her voice carrying the balance of kindness and practicality that Ashley had always admired. "You've got plenty to keep you busy. And if by some chance you know anyone who's always dreamed of running a bookstore, let me know. There's a very nice apartment upstairs, similar to your shop. Managing it isn't coming any easier for me these days."

As Miriam turned to go, the soft chime of the doorbell followed her, a sound so light it seemed to linger, marking the moment with a delicate finality.

Ashley needed to breathe, and she knew just the place. Maple Creek Park sat at the edge of Stillwater, a quiet embrace of nature that felt impervious to time. The creek itself was its heartbeat, a ribbon of water weaving through the green expanse of lawn and maple trees, carrying with it the soft murmur of flowing currents and the faint, rhythmic splash of fish beneath the surface. Visitors moved along the banks as though drawn by an unspoken promise, their steps falling in tune with the whispering water and the rustle of leaves overhead.

At the heart of the park, a modest picnic area offered its welcome: simple wooden tables nestled under the shade of maples that seemed as old as the town itself. It was a place that invited both the gentle chaos of family outings and the contemplative solitude of a lone visitor cradling a book. Just beyond, a play area stood in quiet anticipation, its swings creaking in the breeze, as though waiting for the echo of children's laughter. It was a corner of Stillwater untouched by the demands of change, a constant in a world that refused to sit still.

Ashley paused at the entrance, her hand resting on the cool iron gate. The air was crisp, carrying the faint scent of woodsmoke and decaying leaves. As she stepped onto the gravel path, a woman holding the hand of a little girl passed by, nodding a polite hello. Ashley returned the nod and kept walking, her boots crunching softly in the stillness of the morning.

But the woman slowed her steps, turning back toward Ashley. "Excuse me," she called, her tone warm but curious. "I don't think I've seen you here before. Are you new to Stillwater?"

Ashley hesitated, caught off guard by the directness of the question. "No," she replied, her voice softer than she intended. "Well kind of, I suppose. I was born here. I've been away for a while, but I've come back. I live in New York City now."

The woman smiled, shifting the stroller slightly as her toddler peeked out, clutching a stuffed rabbit. "Oh, so you're just visiting family then?"

Ashley's stomach tightened at the assumption. "Kind of," she said carefully. "My father was George Keller. He passed away recently, so I'm back for a while, tying up loose ends."

The woman's smile faltered, replaced by a quiet sympathy. "I'm sorry to hear that," she said. "Your father was a good man. I didn't know him well, but he always had a kind word whenever I saw him around town."

Ashley nodded, swallowing the lump that rose unexpectedly in her throat. "Thank you. He loved Stillwater and the people here."

The woman tilted her head, studying Ashley for a moment. "If you don't mind me asking, why'd you leave?"

Ashley froze, the weight of the question pressing against her chest. She didn't want to share the tangled history between her and her father, the rift that caused her to leave. Instead, she gave the easiest answer. "It just felt too small," she said, her words cautious. "I needed something bigger, more room to grow."

The woman nodded thoughtfully, her expression kind but unreadable. "Well," she said after a pause, "it's good to see people coming back, even if it's for a visit. Stillwater's better for it."

They exchanged goodbyes, and Ashley watched her walk away, the little girl giggling as she ran toward the playground.

Ashley smiled as she watched the little girl. The swings, their chains worn shiny from years of small hands, swayed gently in the breeze. The slide, once a towering challenge in her childhood eyes, now seemed smaller, its metal dulled but still gleaming faintly in the filtered sunlight. The benches stood where they always had, scattered like old friends waiting patiently for her return. She made her way to the one nearest the maple tree, the same one she had sat on countless times before, and ran her fingers over the wood. It was smoother now, the years softening its surface, but the grooves and knots still lingered, traces of all it had withstood. Here, her memories waited like old photographs tucked in a drawer. The play of sunlight through the leaves seemed softer now, the park's familiar rhythms more soothing.

"This is where it happened," she murmured. The thought came unbidden, a whisper from a time she hadn't revisited in years. She let herself sink into the memory, her breath catching as it unfolded with startling clarity.

She had been ten, her limbs gangly and her hair wild, a child more comfortable in movement than stillness. Her father had taken her to the park that day, his expression serious in a way that made her fidget. He had always been her anchor - steady, dependable, the kind of man who could make you believe in the world's goodness even when it seemed hard to find. But that day, there had been something different in his eyes, something weightier.

"Ashley," he said, lowering himself onto the bench beside her, "do you know what makes a good life?"

She shrugged, swinging her legs as they dangled over the edge of the bench. "I guess . . . doing what you love?"

He smiled at her answer, but there was a sadness in it too, as if he knew she wouldn't fully understand what he was about to say. "It's the connections we make," he said, his voice soft but firm. "And the stories we share. That's what matters. Not the things we have, not the places we go. People, Ashley. It's always about people."

She didn't know what to say. The words felt heavy, their meaning just out of reach, but something in his tone made her nod. She had filed it away, a seed planted deep within her, not realizing it would take years to bloom.

Now, here she was, so many years later, sitting on the same bench, her hands folded in her lap. The memory felt like a gift, one she hadn't appreciated enough when she was younger. She could almost see him there beside her, his strong hands resting on his knees, his presence as solid and certain as the oak tree behind them.

Then another memory nudged its way forward - Owen, lanky and awkward at eight or so, his face blotchy from crying. She had brought him here after some of the boys in school made fun of him. He had been inconsolable, his shoulders hunched in defeat as he buried his face in his hands.

"What do I do now?" he'd asked her, his voice cracking with despair. "I've no friends."

She had hesitated, searching for the right words. And then, as if her father were speaking through her, she had said, "You let yourself feel it. And then you move forward. Connections, remember? You'll make more of them. You'll find more friends."

At the time, she wasn't sure he believed her, but he had looked at her with something like hope, a flicker of trust that maybe she knew what she was talking about. And now, thinking of Owen and the life he had built here in the smallness of Stillwater, she realized he had carried that lesson with him.

Ashley leaned back, letting the smooth wood of the bench press against her shoulders as her gaze wandered to the canopy of leaves above. Above, the maple branches swayed gently, their leaves catching the sunlight in shifting patterns that danced across the ground. Each breeze brought a faint rustle, a soothing, unbroken rhythm that matched the unhurried pulse of the park. She closed her eyes, and the symphony of sounds filled the quiet corners of her mind: the crackle of dry leaves tumbling along the gravel path, the distant squeal of a child on a swing, and the steady hum of Stillwater stirring to life beyond the tree line.

For a long moment, she let herself sink into the embrace of the park. It was a feeling she hadn't realized she missed, this seamless blend of stillness and motion, of solitude and connection. The faint scent of woodsmoke drifted through the air, mingling with the earthy aroma of damp soil and decaying leaves, a perfume that felt uniquely tied to this place. She hadn't planned to come here today, but now that she was, it felt inevitable, as though the park itself had called her back.

When she opened her eyes, her attention was drawn to a little girl, her dark curls bouncing as she attempted to climb the slide backward. Her small hands gripped the edges of the metal, her sneakers squeaking against the surface as she tried to hoist herself up. From a nearby bench, the girl's mother called out, her voice teetering between amusement and mild exasperation, "Lila, come down the right way!" The girl ignored her, undeterred, her brow furrowed with determination.

Ashley smiled, the corners of her mouth softening as she watched. There was something achingly familiar about the girl's grit, her refusal to be thwarted by a challenge. She could see herself in that small figure, remembering her own childhood battles against the slide, the swings, and even the stubborn creek when she'd dared to test its icy shallows in spring. She had once been that girl, full of fierce energy and relentless curiosity.

The words her father had spoken so many years ago came to her then, carried on a memory as vivid as the sunlight: "What makes a good life is . . . the connections we make . . . the stories we share." She could almost hear his voice beside her, steady and warm, the cadence of a man who had learned to value simplicity and meaning over the noise of the world. Those words had seemed so abstract to her at the time, a lesson she wasn't ready to learn. Now, they resonated with a clarity that brought both comfort and ache.

Ashley stood, brushing the back of her jeans and taking one last glance at the park before turning toward the path. She noticed the details she'd missed earlier - the faint imprint of initials carved into the maple tree, some so worn they were almost whispers, others freshly cut and sharp against the bark; the scattering of stumps near the creek where old trees had once stood. This park, like the town itself, held its stories in quiet layers, a patchwork of moments and memories stitched into its soil and shade.

The little girl, Lila, finally gave up her conquest of the slide and bolted toward the swings, her laughter ringing out as she propelled herself into the air. Her mother followed more slowly, hands tucked into her coat pockets, her face lifting to catch the warmth of the sun. Ashley watched them for a moment, a flicker of something bittersweet blooming in her chest. She turned back toward the park's entrance, her steps measured and deliberate.

The day ahead would be full - the antique shop on Main Street needed organizing, and there were always customers with stories to share, and memories to unearth. She hadn't come to the park to search for anything, yet it had given her something anyway, the way it always seemed to. It was a reminder, a tether to the past, and a gentle nudge toward the present. As she reached the iron gate, Ashley paused, looking back one last time at the play of sunlight on the creek and the steadfast maple trees. Then, with a quiet resolve, she walked on, carrying the park and her father's words with her, woven into the fabric of her day and the ones to come.

5 The Letters

Ashley stood before her father's rolltop desk in the small office. The massive oak piece had been rooted in the shop for as long as she could recall. Her fingers moved over the wood's uneven grain, each ridge and dip a quiet chronicle of years gone by. The surface held its own story: a faint coffee ring from late nights, a deep scratch from a pen wielded with too much force. The air in the antique shop surrounded her, a mixture of scents that pulled her instantly back to childhood - the musty fragrance of aging books with fragile pages, the sharp bite of lemon polish on brass fixtures, and the faint trace of lavender from sachets her father tucked away to keep moths at bay.

Her hand hovered over the brass handle of the center drawer, cool and inviting beneath her palm. She hesitated, her breath catching in her throat. Opening this desk felt like breaching a barrier, crossing a threshold into a part of her father's life – and by extension, her own past – that she wasn't sure she was ready to confront.

"Do I really want to do this?" she thought, biting her lower lip. "What if I find something I don't want to know?"

With a deep breath, she pulled open the drawer. It creaked in protest, revealing a jumble of papers, pens, and odds and ends. Ashley began to sift through the contents, her mind racing.

"Why did you leave everything to me, Dad? After all these years, after everything that happened . . . why?"

Her fingers grazed a bundle of envelopes held by a brittle rubber band. Then her breath hitched at the sight of another stack, tied neatly with a red ribbon. With trembling hands, she pulled out the stack.

These were the letters he had written to her but never sent - birthday cards, Christmas wishes, the occasional postcard - all meticulously bundled and kept. Ashley eased into the chair nearby, her knees unsteady, a faint tremor running through her limbs.

"Why? I thought you didn't care."

She untied the bundle, spreading everything across the desk's surface. Her eyes fell on a Christmas card. The message was brief, almost impersonal:

"Dear Ashley, Hope you are well. Heard about your job. That's great. Hope you have a wonderful holiday. Merry Christmas, Dad."

Ashley thought, a lump forming in her throat. "Why didn't you send them?"

As she continued to sort through the letters, a pattern emerged. His messages grew shorter, and more infrequent over time. Yet he had kept every single one.

"You held onto every word you wanted to say." She began to cry.

She leaned back in the chair, closing her eyes to her memories. The day she left Stillwater, her father's face was a mask of anger and disappointment. The years of silence that followed, were broken only by the recent communication from his attorney.

"We were both so frightened," she realized. "Both of us too scared to make the first move."

Ashley's gaze drifted to the shop around her, seeing it with new eyes. Every antique, every dusty shelf, spoke of her father's life – a life she had chosen to step away from. And yet, he had never truly let her go.

"Was this your way of reaching out?" she wondered. "Leaving me the shop, the money . . . was it an olive branch I'm only now seeing?"

Her thoughts turned to Owen, his anger still fresh in her mind. She could understand his resentment now, seeing how he had stayed while she had run. But there was more to the story, more that Owen didn't know.

Ashley's fingers brushed against a small, leather-bound book tucked away in the back of the drawer. Curious, she pulled it out, recognizing it as her father's journal. Her heart raced as she opened it, unsure if she was ready for what she might find inside.

The first entry was dated just after she had left Stillwater:

"Ashley's gone. I don't know if I'll ever see her again. I said things I shouldn't have, let my anger get the best of me. Now it might be too late to make things right."

Ashley's vision blurred with more tears. She blinked them away, forcing herself to continue reading. Entry after entry revealed a side of her father she had never known – a man filled with regret, longing for reconciliation but unsure how to bridge the gap he had helped create.

As she read, Ashley's mind drifted to the conversation with Miriam, whose words echoed in her memory: "He missed you terribly. Grief can be a persistent companion, and your father carried his disappointments like carefully wrapped packages, some too heavy to set down, some tucked away in quiet corners of his heart."

"Was Miriam the one who helped you change?" Ashley wondered. "Did she show you a different way to see things?"

The journal entries revealed a gradual change in her father's outlook, his thoughts turning more inward with each passing page. He wrote about the town, about Owen, and always about Miriam, whose presence seemed to brighten the corners of his life.

Ashley felt ashamed. "I should be grateful someone was there for you," she chided herself. "Even if it wasn't me."

She kept reading, the hours slipping by unnoticed, drawn deep into the quiet pull of her father's thoughts and confessions. The final entry, written in a faltering hand and marked a mere week before his death, stopped her cold.

"I hope Ashley comes home. I wanted to tell her how sorry I am, that what I did was wrong, that I understand now. I want her to know I've always loved her, even when I didn't show it. Miriam always told me I should write to her, but I thought it was too late. I thought she never wanted to hear from me after all this time. Who would, after what I said."

Ashley closed the journal, her hands shaking. She looked around the cluttered shop, seeing it now as her father must have — not just a collection of antiques, but a life's work, a legacy he wanted to pass on to her.

"You were waiting for me," she realized. "All this time, you were hoping I'd come back."

The weight of missed opportunities settled heavily on her shoulders. Years of silence, of fear on both sides, had robbed them of the chance to reconcile. And now, it was too late.

"Or is it?"

Ashley stood up, a new determination filling her. She couldn't change the past, but she could honor her father's memory. She could try to understand the man he had become, the man who had kept every letter and waited patiently for her return.

Her gaze fell on a framed photograph on the desk – a picture of herself as a child, sitting on her father's lap in this very shop. They were smiling, surrounded by the antiques that had been such a big part of their lives.

"I can't bring you back, Dad," she thought, "but I can try to understand. I can try to make things right, even if it's just in my own heart."

With renewed purpose, Ashley began to truly look at the shop around her. Each piece held a story, a memory, a part of her father's life. She realized that by leaving her the shop, he had given her more than just a business – he had given her a chance to reconnect with the parts of him she had never truly known.

As the afternoon light filtered through the dusty windows, Ashley made a decision. She would stay, at least for now. She would sort through the antiques, learn their stories, and in doing so, perhaps learn more about the man her father had become.

"And maybe," she thought, "I'll learn something about myself too."

She picked up the journal and letters, carefully placing them back in the drawer. There would be time to read more later, to piece together the years she had missed. For now, she had work to do.

Ashley stood, brushing the dust from her jeans, and looked around the shop with new eyes. It was more than just a collection of old things – it was a bridge between past and present, between the father she had known and the one she was just beginning to discover.

As she began to straighten up the nearest shelf, Ashley felt a sense of peace settle over her. The past was beyond her grasp, irretrievable, but the present - the tangible, real moments her father had entrusted to her - offered a path forward. Then, she came upon a wooden box.

Ashley reached for the box, her fingers tracing the intricate floral pattern etched into its weathered mahogany surface. It was heavier than she expected as if weighted with secrets. She placed it on the desk with a soft thud, disturbing a thin layer of dust that swirled in the late afternoon sunlight streaming through the shop's grimy windows. The brass hinges creaked in protest as she lifted the lid.

The box held a collection of letters, their pale envelopes striking against the deep, somber hue of the interior. She reached for the one on top. The date, written several years ago, seemed almost immediate, the paper still holding its original stiffness, untouched by time. Ashley's pulse quickened as she slipped her thumb under the seal, feeling the resistance of adhesive yielding in a soft, deliberate tear. She unfolded the letter slowly, the faint rustle of the paper offering a quiet, intimate voice.

The handwriting moved fluidly across the page, a delicate dance of loops and curves, speaking of a time when writing was not merely functional but an expression of care and craft. Ashley traced the flow of the ink with her eyes, imagining the unseen author leaning forward at a desk, the deliberate movement of a fountain pen across the page. Every letter seemed alive with meaning, bearing the essence of the hand that had guided it and the mind that had chosen each word so deliberately.

As she began to read, her father's world unfolded before her in his prose.

"My dearest George,

The autumn leaves are turning, transforming our sleepy town into a canvas of impossible beauty. Maples blaze crimson, their edges tinged with fire; oaks stand resolute in burnt orange as if holding fast against winter's approach. I wish you could see it through my eyes, George – the way the late afternoon sunlight filters through the canopy, turning ordinary sidewalks into rivers of gold and shadow. Each step I take disturbs this delicate artwork, sending leaves skittering and twirling, nature's own confetti celebrating our absent reunion.

It reminds me, with an ache so sweet it's nearly unbearable, of that day we spent in the park. Do you remember? The air was crisp, carrying the scent of woodsmoke and promises. You took my hand – your fingers rough and warm against mine – and said the world had never looked more beautiful. But I knew then, as I know now, that it wasn't the world that had changed. It was us, seeing everything anew through the lens of what we'd found in each other.

I carry that day with me always, George. It's a talisman against loneliness, a reminder that even in separation, we are bound by something greater than distance. Until we meet again, I'll walk these gilt-edged streets and whisper your name to the falling leaves, trusting the wind to carry my love to you.

Yours, with all my love, in every season,
Miriam"

The world around Ashley seemed to fade away, leaving only the whisper of paper and the weight of unspoken truths. The letter's words, so tender and alive, wrapped around her heart like a bittersweet embrace, pulling her into a moment frozen in time. She felt the crisp autumn air on her skin, saw the dappled sunlight dancing on the sidewalk, and heard the rustle of leaves in a gentle breeze. For a fleeting instant, Ashley wasn't just reading about her father's past - she was living it, breathing it, feeling the depth of a love she had never known existed. The shop's dusty silence pressed in around her, a stark contrast to the vibrant world pulsing within those carefully penned lines, leaving her caught between two realities - the faded present and a past suddenly, achingly alive.

She read the letter again, her eyes widening as she absorbed the depth of feeling expressed in Miriam's words. It was clear that this wasn't just a fleeting romance or a late-life dalliance. This was something profound, a connection that had spanned years.

"How long?" Ashley murmured, rifling through the stack of letters. "How long were you keeping this secret, Dad?"

As she sorted through the correspondence, a pattern emerged. The earliest letters dated back so many years ago – right around the time her mother had left. Ashley's heart clenched as the realization hit her.

Then, nestled among the shorter notes and hastily scrawled postcards, she came upon an envelope that stood out from the rest. It was thicker, the paper of a higher quality, as if its contents demanded a more dignified vessel. She slid her finger under the flap and unfolded the pages within, she was struck by the sheer volume of words that flowed across them, a torrent of emotion captured in Miriam's elegant script.

"My dearest George,

The wind whispers through the trees tonight, carrying with it the scent of rain and secrets. I sit here at my desk, pen in hand, my heart heavy with the weight of our love and the fear that threatens to overshadow it.

I saw your wife in town today. She was at the grocery store, picking out apples with such care, each one inspected as if it held the key to some great mystery. For a moment, I allowed myself to imagine it was me there beside you, our hands brushing as we reached for the same piece of fruit. But then reality came crashing back, and I felt the guilt wash over me anew.

George, my love, what are we doing? This passion we share, it's like a flame that burns so bright it threatens to consume us both. Yet I can't bring myself to extinguish it. Every stolen moment, every hushed conversation in the back of your shop, they're etched into my soul like the rings of an ancient tree.

But I worry. Oh, how I worry. What if she suspects? What if the truth comes to light and shatters the careful life you've built? I couldn't bear to be the cause of such pain, to see the hurt in her eyes or the disappointment in your children's faces.

Sometimes, in the dark of night, I wonder if we're being selfish. Is it wrong to grasp at this happiness, knowing the cost it might exact? But then I remember the way you look at me, as if I'm the only person in the world, and I know I could never willingly let you go.

I don't have the answers, my love. I only know that my heart belongs to you, come what may. Perhaps that makes me a terrible person. Perhaps it simply makes me human.

Be careful, my darling. Guard our secret well. For now, it's all we have.

Forever yours,
Miriam

P.S. I've left a book for you at the shop. Page 143 holds a pressed flower – a reminder of that perfect day by the lake. May it bring you comfort when we're apart."

Ashley's fingers ran over the desk, tracing the nicks and scratches in the wood. Her eyes skimmed over the clutter until they landed on a book - set apart, almost deliberately. It was a first edition of *A Canary for One*, its leather binding cracked with age. She picked it up gently, conscious of its fragility. The spine creaked when she opened it, a faint protest. She turned the pages until she reached 143, where a pressed flower lay hidden between the lines of Hemingway's sparse prose. Once vibrant yellow, the petals had faded to a soft parchment hue, but their beauty remained, and Ashley's breath caught. She touched it lightly as if brushing a butterfly's wing. In that moment, everything she had wondered since childhood came into focus.

"Oh, Mom," she whispered, her voice barely audible in the dusty quiet of the shop. "Is this why you left? Did you know about Miriam all along?"

The flower seemed to hold all the answers, yet remained stubbornly silent, a fragile sentinel guarding decades of secrets.

More questions ricocheted in Ashley's mind, rapid and disorienting. They were unrelenting, each one opening a door to another, each more troubling than the last. Had her father been unfaithful? Was his relationship with Miriam something that had grown after her mother left, or had it been there all along, hiding behind the ordinary rhythms of their everyday life?

She could see her father in her mind, retreating further into the small, quiet spaces of his life, a man who had always been difficult to understand, but now, more than ever, seemed like a stranger. And then, buried beneath all the questions, were more letters - letters that spoke of pain, sorrow, and something that seemed far too intimate for a man who had spent his life hiding his heart behind a stoic, unyielding exterior.

"My Dearest George,

I hope this letter finds you in some measure of peace, though I know the times we find ourselves in have made such a thing rare. I cannot begin to express how deeply sorry I am for what has come to pass. It is with a heavy heart that I write to you now, knowing that no words I offer could ever ease the pain you are bearing.

Please know, my love, that I am here for you. In this uncertain world, I am the constant you can rely on. Whatever comfort you seek, you will always find it in me. I will be with you, in the stillness and in the times of sorrow, as you navigate your way through this storm.

I know that strength can seem elusive in times like these, but you have a well of it within you that is deeper than you realize. You must hold on to it, George, for yourself and for those who depend on you. You have faced trials before. Please know that this, too, will pass. It is in these darkest hours that the light of resilience shines the brightest.

I can only hope that in time, the weight of what we have experienced will lift, leaving room for peace and healing. Until then, I am yours, always, ready to support you with everything that I am.

With all my heart, I am always here for you,
Miriam"

Ashley set the letter down, the paper trembling slightly in her hands. Miriam's words held a quiet force, their tenderness startling in their honesty and transparency, offering a view of her father she had never known. She had never known this side of him. The man who had taught her how to ride a bike, the one who presided over family dinners with a practiced distance, was not the one Miriam described. That man had been a figure of formality, a silent presence who gave nothing of himself except what was necessary. This man, though, was different. He was someone capable of love so deep it almost seemed to ache in the telling. There was a sadness too, a longing that stretched through time, and with it, a tenderness Ashley had never imagined. The realization stung - how many years had she spent thinking she knew him? How many years had she spent locked out of a life that, it turned out, had been far more expansive than the one he had ever allowed her to glimpse?

The letters spoke of a life she had never been part of, a connection that had lived in the shadows, influencing him in ways Ashley struggled to grasp. She thought of the boxes still unopened, their contents waiting to reveal more pieces of a life she never knew, and felt both a rush of need and a quiet hesitation. To understand him like this would mean letting go of the version she had held onto, losing him in one sense, but finding him in another.

She leaned back in the chair, letting her eyes close, allowing the memories to come back. She could still feel the tension in the house before her mother left, a kind of quiet that was too loud. She remembered the hushed voices, the sharp edges of words she pretended not to hear, each one cutting through the silence, each ·one creating a rift she couldn't understand. Then her father, after everything fell apart, retreating further into his work, burying himself in the shop, as though the endless hours there might somehow fill the space left behind.

"I thought I knew you," Ashley whispered, her voice thick with emotion. "But maybe I never really did."

She stood, needing to move, to process this new information. Pacing the length of the small office, Ashley's thoughts tumbled over one another like leaves in a swift autumn stream. She'd come back to Stillwater expecting to wrap up her father's affairs quickly and efficiently, to close this chapter of her life once and for all. But now, it seemed, she'd stumbled upon a mystery that was slowly beginning to unfurl before her, its tendrils reaching into the dusty corners of the shop and the even dustier recesses of her memory. Each step across the creaking floorboards seemed to dislodge another question, another possibility. The air around her felt thick with unspoken words and Ashley found herself struggling to breathe, to think clearly amidst the swirling eddies of revelation and doubt.

"What else don't I know about you?" she wondered aloud. "What other secrets have you hidden in this shop?"

Ashley's gaze swept across the cluttered space, seeing it with new eyes. Every antique, every dusty book, every faded photograph suddenly held the potential for revelation. She'd thought she was here to say goodbye to her father, but perhaps she was here to truly meet him for the first time.

The bell above the shop door jingled, startling Ashley from her reverie. For a moment, she froze, irrationally expecting to see her father walk in, ready to explain everything. But no, it was just the wind, the door not quite latched.

She moved to close it, pausing to look out at the quiet street. Stillwater hadn't changed much in the years she'd been gone. The same storefronts lined the sidewalks, the same trees shaded the square. But now, Ashley realized, she was seeing it all through a different lens.

"I wonder what other stories this town is hiding," she mused, her eyes lingering on the bookshop a few doors down. Miriam's bookshop.

Closing the door firmly and locking it, Ashley returned to the office. She gathered up the letters, handling them with a new reverence. These weren't just pieces of paper; they were fragments of a life she'd never known, a side of her father she'd never seen.

"Alright, Dad," she said, addressing the empty room. "You've got my attention. Let's see what else you've been keeping from me."

With renewed purpose, she began to systematically search the office. She pulled out drawers, rifled through file cabinets, and examined every nook and cranny. Each new discovery – a hidden compartment in the desk, a locked box tucked behind a painting – only fueled her determination.

As the afternoon wore on, Ashley found herself piecing together a narrative she'd never imagined. Receipts for dinners at romantic restaurants. Ticket stubs from concerts and plays. A small, velvet box containing a delicate silver locket – clearly meant as a gift.

"You had a whole life I knew nothing about," Ashley murmured, turning the locket over in her hands.

She sank back into the chair, exhausted. The emotional toll of the day's discoveries weighed heavily on her. She'd come here thinking she knew exactly who her father was – a difficult man, set in his ways - precise, incapable of change. But now . . .

"Why didn't I see it?" she asked herself. "I was so sure I had you figured out. But there was so much more to you than I ever knew."

The realization brought with it a mix of emotions – regret for the years lost, anger at being kept in the dark, and a strange, unexpected hope. Hope that perhaps, through these letters and mementos, she might finally come to understand the man her father truly was.

Ashley's gaze fell on a framed photograph on the desk, one she'd overlooked earlier. It showed her father and Miriam, their faces alight with laughter, standing in front of the bookshop. They looked . . . happy. Genuinely, unabashedly happy.

"I can't remember the last time I saw you smile like that," Ashley whispered, tracing her father's face in the photograph. "Maybe I never did."

The sound of footsteps on the sidewalk outside pulled Ashley from her contemplation. She glanced at her watch, surprised to see how late it had gotten. The shop had been closed all day, and she realized with a start that she hadn't eaten since breakfast.

As if on cue, her stomach growled. Ashley smiled ruefully, imagining what her father would say about her forgetting to eat. He'd always been insistent on regular meals, even when work was busy.

"Alright, Dad," she said, standing up and stretching. "I'll take a break. But don't think this means I'm done investigating."

She carefully gathered up the letters and other items she'd discovered, placing them in a box for safekeeping. There was still so much to go through, so many questions left unanswered. But for now, she needed food and time to process everything she'd learned.

As Ashley stepped out onto the quiet street, locking the shop door, she felt a shift in her perspective. Stillwater no longer seemed like a place she needed to escape from. Instead, it had become a mystery to be unraveled, a story waiting to be told.

"I'm going to figure this out," she promised herself, her steps purposeful as she headed towards the diner down the street. "I'm going to understand who you really were, Dad. And maybe . . . maybe I'll understand myself a little better too."

The air was crisp, carrying with it the scent of autumn. As Ashley walked, she found herself noticing details she'd overlooked before – the way the setting sun painted the old buildings in warm hues, the cheerful displays in shop windows, and the friendly nods from passersby.

For the first time since arriving in Stillwater, Ashley felt a spark of something she hadn't expected – curiosity. Not just about her father and Miriam, but about the town itself. What other stories were hidden behind these familiar facades? What secrets did the other residents hold?

As she pushed open the door to the diner, the bell jingling overhead, Ashley realized that her journey was just beginning. She'd come to Stillwater to close a chapter of her life, but instead, she found herself at the start of a new one.

"Well, Dad," she murmured, sliding into a booth and picking up a menu, "I guess I'm not done with this place just yet. Let's see where this story leads."

The diner was comforting in its ordinariness - the clink of plates, the murmur of other patrons, the hiss of the coffee machine. She slid into a booth near the window, the sun fading behind the distant hills, casting long shadows across the worn leather seats. She would have a quick dinner, a meal alone, followed by the solitude of the apartment above the shop, where she would sleep the kind of sleep only a long day could bring.

But sleep didn't come easy.

Ashley switched on the light beside her bed, the soft glow cutting through the shadows that seemed to cling to the corners of the room. She breathed out a quiet sigh, rubbing her eyes before propping herself up. Her fingers found their way to the phone, dialing the number that had long since become second nature. The apartment seemed emptier now, quieter, with a stillness that stretched out into the dark - suffocating and oddly comforting in its silence.

"Hello?" Laura's voice came through, warm and familiar, with just a hint of concern.

"Laura," Ashley exhaled, her chest loosening at the sound. "I couldn't sleep . . .I don't even know where to start."

"Ashley? What's going on? Are you alright?"

Ashley leaned back in her father's old chair, the creaking of the wood grounding her in the present. "I'm not sure," she murmured, staring at the familiar outlines of the room. "I've found . . . things. About my dad. About why my mom left. It's like I'm looking at my entire childhood through a funhouse mirror."

She could hear Laura shifting, probably sitting up straighter in their shared bed so far away. "Tell me," she said softly.

Ashley's words tumbled out, a torrent of discovery and confusion. She spoke of the letters, of Miriam, of the pressed flower that seemed to hold the key to decades of secrets.

"Oh, Ash," Laura murmured when she finished. "That's . . . a lot to process. How are you feeling?"

Ashley paused looking at the room around her. "Honestly? I feel like I'm five years old again, lost in a sea of adults who know more than they're telling me. But also . . . I don't know. There's a strange sort of relief in finally understanding why things were the way they were."

"Do you think you'll talk to your brother about this?"

Ashley sighed, pressing her forehead against the cool glass. " I have to, don't I? He has a right to know. But . . . he's so upset at me already for leaving. How do I tell him that everything he's been holding onto is built on lies?"

There was a moment of silence, filled only by the soft sound of their breathing. Then, in her soft, steady way, Laura spoke.

"With honesty and love, Ash. The same way you've always faced difficult things."

Ashley felt a smile tug at her lips despite everything. "What would I do without you?"

"Probably make impulsive decisions and forget to eat," Laura teased, drawing a chuckle from Ashley.

After a quiet beat, Laura's voice returned, softer now. "Are you sure, though? About how you're connecting everything? Are the dots pointing you to the right place?"

Ashley hesitated. The question pressed gently against her, but she knew her answer. "Yes," she said, her voice firm. "I'm sure. Absolutely."

"I'm here for you, my love. Always. I wish I could be there with you. Getting time off from work is difficult."

Ashley considered it, torn between the desire for Laura's comforting presence and the need to face this on her own. "It's okay," she said finally. "This is something I have to do on my own."

"Okay," Laura said, a soft sigh in her voice. "I love you, Ash. Remember, no matter what you find, it doesn't change who you are."

"Love you too."

As Ashley hung up, she felt steadier, more grounded. Everything around her was still full of secrets and memories, but with Laura's words echoing in her mind, she felt ready to face them.

6 The Whispers

Ashley stirred, the soft chorus of birdsong pulling her gently from sleep. It wasn't a sound she often noticed back in the city, where the rumble of garbage trucks and the staccato burst of honking horns intruded on even the earliest hours. Here, in Stillwater, the birds' melody seemed almost deliberate, as if they had gathered just outside her window to deliver this delicate morning gift. She stretched under the weight of the old quilt, her muscles uncoiling slowly, and let her gaze drift to the window.

The light poured in gently, golden and warm, slipping between the slats of the curtains like something alive. It spilled over the rooftops of the small town below, illuminating the familiar shapes she had long ago taken for granted. Smoke curled from the bakery's chimney at the corner, twisting lazily upward as if reluctant to leave its warm hearth. A man in a green jacket moved briskly toward the hardware store, a coffee cup balanced in one hand and a bag of tools slung over the other, his stride resolute, as if the day's work had already claimed him. Across the street, the florist emerged, her apron tied in a crisp bow at her back. She paused, squinting at the sky before flipping the sign on the door to *Open* with a practiced, almost ceremonial, gesture.

Ashley lingered at the window, her breath fogging the glass slightly as she leaned closer, absorbing it all. When she was younger, Stillwater had felt stifling, as though its quiet cadence sought to hold her in place when she wanted so desperately to leave. Now, there was a clarity to its simplicity, a steady hum of life that seemed to hold answers just out of reach, as if the town itself had been waiting for her to notice.

She finally turned away, her feet pressing into the smooth, cool wood of the floor as she crossed to the bathroom. The water from the shower sputtered and groaned before it steadied, and she stepped beneath the warm stream, letting it loosen the tightness in her neck and shoulders. Yet even as steam began to fill the small room, her mind drifted back to the letters she had found the night before.

The paper felt delicate in her hands, almost fragile, as though it might crumble with the slightest pressure. The words were written in a careful, flowing hand, the script curving gently across the page. Each phrase was tender, and in a way that took Ashley by surprise, deeply personal. *My love*, Miriam had written. *I am always here for you.* The letters held an intimacy that was both foreign and comforting, emotions her father had never allowed her to see. Promises and confessions spilled from the page, revealing a part of him she had never known existed.

And yet, the only thing Ashley knew for certain was that her mother had left. That singular truth stood stark and immutable. She had been ten when it happened, old enough to catch the edges of their arguments but too young to understand their full meaning. Her mother's departure had been swift and silent, a suitcase packed in the space of an afternoon, the car pulling out of the driveway without so much as a goodbye. The air in the house had felt hollow after that, her father's presence looming like a shadow that never fully touched her.

Now, she wondered if Miriam had been the reason. Had her father been in love with another woman all those years, hiding it beneath his stoic exterior? Ashley pressed her forehead against the cool tile of the shower wall, her wet hair clinging to her face. The questions churned in her mind, their sharp edges catching on something that felt like grief or anger or maybe both. Whatever had happened between her parents, it was tangled up in secrets that might never fully unravel.

When she stepped out of the shower, the steam still clinging to the air, she dried herself quickly, the rough towel a small comfort against the chill of the room. She pulled on a pair of jeans and a sweater, her thoughts lingering on the letters. They had left her with more questions than answers, a deep curiosity gnawing at her. She found herself wondering what kind of conversation could unfold with Miriam. Would she open up, or would she evade, leaving Ashley feeling more uncertain than she had before?

The thought of facing Miriam felt too overwhelming for the moment. Ashley slipped on her boots, the leather stiff against her heels, and grabbed her jacket. She paused for a moment and made a quiet decision. Today, she would start with something simple - a stack of pancakes at the diner, with syrup, just the way she had with her father on Saturday mornings. There was something about the familiarity of it that felt like a refuge she could hold onto, even if only for a little while.

The shop's bell gave a soft jingle when Ashley eased the door open and stepped onto the sidewalk. Outside, the air carried a sharper chill than she'd anticipated, brushing against her skin with an unwelcome insistence. She pulled her jacket closer, her fingers catching on the zipper's worn teeth. She closed the door behind her, locking away the world of Miriam's letters - though they still clung to her mind, settling like the rich aroma of roasted coffee drifting from the café across the street.

Ashley walked to the diner, her steps following the route she had taken so many times before, though her thoughts were elsewhere, tangled up with the letters and the name that had rooted itself firmly in her mind. Miriam. The sound of it rang through her, insistent and strange, like a question she couldn't answer.

The sidewalk stretched out ahead of her. Mothers pushed strollers, a man in a crisp suit checked his watch at the corner, and teenagers lingered in a cluster near the ice cream shop, their laughter cracking like fireworks. Ashley's eyes drifted up to the street signs - not because she needed them, but out of habit. She had grown up here. These streets were part of her, though they felt slightly off-kilter now, like like a song she couldn't quite place.

The bookstore came into view before she realized she'd been heading for it. It sat tucked between a florist and a small grocery store, its green awning slightly faded but still charming. The display in the front window was tidy, and carefully arranged: a mix of paperback novels, journals, and a sign advertising a local author event next week. *The Stillwater Reader.* The name was painted in curling gold letters across the glass, understated and elegant. It was exactly the kind of place she imagined someone like Miriam running.

Ashley slowed her steps, her gaze catching on the florist's window, letting her eyes drift over the clusters of blooms - peonies in full flush, roses curling at their edges, daisies bright and unassuming. She stood there briefly, giving herself over to the distraction of color and life before moving toward the bookstore. Despite herself, her eyes strayed to the glass, drawn by the glimpse it offered of its interior world.

Inside, the shop seemed to radiate a quiet warmth. Shelves rose high, filled with books that seemed to hold their own gentle glow beneath the amber light. Toward the back, a wooden counter sat under a modest heap of books, beside a small tray of bookmarks. The space appeared untouched by urgency, its calm broken by neither customers nor motion. Ashley's gaze traveled over the room, seeking something unnamed, but the stillness of the shop held firm, suspended in its own unhurried dimension.

Her eyes drifted upward, to the flat above the bookstore, where she knew Miriam lived. The windows were shrouded in darkness, the curtains tightly closed. Ashley thought of the woman behind them, the one whose letters had been written with such intimacy and care. She pictured her father stepping into the bookstore, moving through its narrow aisles, and ascending creaking stairs to the apartment. In her mind, he turned his head slightly, a fleeting motion, ensuring the space behind him was empty of prying eyes. The thought unsettled her, caught between the improbability of such a moment and the certainty that it had happened.

"You're new here. Can I help you?"

The voice startled her. Ashley turned quickly, her heart lurching in her chest. A man stood a few feet away, holding a broom and wearing a green apron that matched the awning. He must have come from the florist's shop.

"No," she said, too quickly. Her voice sounded tight, unnatural. "Just looking around."

The man nodded, his expression unreadable, and went back to sweeping the sidewalk. Ashley forced herself to keep walking, her cheeks burning as if she'd been caught doing something she shouldn't. The bookstore faded behind her, but the tension in her chest didn't ease. She hated how suspicious she felt, how unsure of everything, even her own reasons for standing there.

At the corner, she hesitated. To her left, another café spilled out onto the sidewalk, its tables crowded with people chatting over coffee and pastries. On her right, the street dipped gently downward toward the diner.

She took another step forward, and the bustle of the street began to fade, replaced by the steady sound of her own footsteps. The houses she passed seemed smaller, more spaced apart, their gardens growing wild, full of unruly flowers. A flood of memories surfaced - shortcuts from her teenage years, the back alleys and quiet side streets she'd taken to get to school or the library.

By the time she reached the diner, the sky had shifted, more clouds drifting bout. The neon sign buzzed faintly, its letters spelling out *Dottie's* in bright red. The windows were streaked with fingerprints, and the booths inside were nearly full. Ashley paused at the door, her hand hovering over the handle. Then with a smile, she opened the door.

Pancakes awaited.

The bell above the diner's door rang sharply, cutting through the soft murmur of conversation and the clatter of plates and silverware. Ashley paused just inside, her eyes scanning the room. The scent of sizzling bacon and freshly brewed coffee filled the air, an inviting comfort that should have settled her, but only heightened her unease. Every head in the diner turned toward her at once, as if she had walked into the middle of a play rather than a casual breakfast spot. The eyes of the strangers, all trained on her, made her feel exposed as if someone had pinned a sign to her back: *George's daughter, here to see what's left of him.*

She moved toward the nearest empty booth, her boots scuffing against the tiled floor. Many of the patrons were older, retirees by the look of their knit sweaters and leisurely conversations. A man in a trucker cap sipped coffee at the counter, while a mother wrangled a toddler into a high chair near the window.

Ashley slid into the booth, lowering herself onto the vinyl seat. The cushion sighed under her weight. From here, she had a good view of the room. Nobody she recognized. Nobody who looked like they might recognize her, either - not beyond the polite whispering that had begun as soon as she walked in. An elderly woman leaned close to her companion, her lips moving behind a lifted hand. Across the aisle, a man with thick glasses glanced at Ashley, then quickly averted his gaze when she caught him looking.

She picked up the laminated menu in front of her and held it like a shield, though she didn't need it. There wasn't much to decide. This was the kind of place where breakfast was a universal language - eggs, bacon, pancakes if you were feeling indulgent. She had barely scanned the first column when the waitress appeared beside her booth.

"Morning," the waitress said brightly, holding a small notepad. She was a middle-aged woman whose warmth radiated from her freckled face, framed by a messy blonde ponytail that hinted at a life filled with both laughter and chaos. Her uniform was a little rumpled, and her apron was smudged with what looked like syrup, but her smile was genuine. A small nametag pinned to her chest read *Dottie*. "Coffee to start?"

"Yes, please," Ashley replied. "Black."

Dottie nodded and jotted it down, then paused, her pen hovering over the page as she studied Ashley more closely. "You wouldn't happen to be the new owner of the antique shop, would you? George's daughter?"

Ashley lowered the menu. "I am."

"I thought so," Dottie said, her expression softening. "I can see the resemblance. George was a good man. Always kind. He loved his grilled cheese and tomato soup. I'm sorry he's gone."

"Thank you," Ashley said, her voice quieter than she intended. "It's been . . . a lot."

Dottie nodded in understanding. "I can imagine. First week in town must feel like you're walking into a whole new world, huh?"

"It does." Ashley forced a small smile. "I keep thinking I'll recognize someone. But I don't."

"Well, give it time," Dottie said. "People around here, they remember things. They'll remember you. What can I get you to eat?"

"Pancakes," Ashley said, "with a side of bacon."

Dottie scribbled on her pad, tearing off the top sheet and tucking it into her apron. "Coming right up."

Ashley watched her go, her ponytail swaying as she wove between tables. She folded her hands on the table, unsure where to look. The whispers had quieted, but the glances hadn't stopped. The man with the thick glasses was studying the back of his spoon as though it held the secrets of the universe, but Ashley had caught him stealing another look.

The coffee arrived first, steaming in a white ceramic cup. Ashley cradled it in her hands, the warmth spreading through her palms. She stared into the inky surface, her mind drifting to the letters she'd found in the shop. Miriam. The name seemed to just float out there in her mind. There was so much about her father that she'd never known about. What else had he hidden, and why?

The bell above the door jingled again, and Ashley's gaze shifted instinctively toward the sound. A woman had entered, and in that moment, everything in the diner seemed to stop, like the world had suddenly quieted in her presence. It was Miriam. Her silver hair cascaded over her shoulders, a soft, flowing reminder of time's passage, but rather than diminishing her, it seemed to elevate her, giving her a quiet grandeur. Her face was not untouched by age, but shaped by it - each line a mark of experience, each imperfection a testament to a life well lived. There was a kind of elegance in the way she carried herself, a poise that suggested she was a woman who not only belonged here but in every room she entered as if her arrival was not an event but a certainty, the inevitable unfolding of something long-awaited.

Ashley froze, her fingers tightening around her coffee cup. The warmth of it suddenly felt distant, out of reach. Miriam's eyes found hers, and there was a moment of recognition - subtle, almost imperceptible, yet it sent a tremor through Ashley, like some long-hidden part of her had been awakened. Miriam's gaze held no judgment, only a quiet knowing, and she moved toward Ashley's booth with the ease of someone who had never considered whether their presence would be noticed.

"May I join you?" Miriam's voice was soft, but there was an unmistakable strength in the way she spoke, a quiet confidence that matched her every movement.

Ashley blinked, momentarily thrown off balance by the simple question. She was nervous - her pulse quickening in a way that felt foreign and unbidden.

"I - uh, sure," Ashley stammered, gesturing to the seat across from her. It seemed the only thing she could do.

Miriam's lips curved into a smile that was more of an understanding than a greeting. "Well, good morning," she said.

The morning light filtered through the windows of the diner, casting soft, diffused shadows over the place. Miriam settled into the booth with the kind of grace that made her seem untouchable, like someone who knew exactly how life was supposed to be lived but was unwilling to share her secrets with those who couldn't quite keep up.

"What will it be, Miriam?" Dottie asked. "The usual?"

Miriam glanced up at Dottie, who was standing patiently nearby, her pen poised over the notepad, waiting for the order. Ashley's eyes lingered on Miriam, though she didn't speak. She studied her father's old friend - the woman who had been more than a friend to her father, once upon a time. A flicker of something she couldn't quite place stirred in her chest as she watched Miriam's hands, delicate and precise, resting gently on the table. Her gaze shifted briefly, falling to the bare spot on Miriam's left hand, where a wedding ring would've been. There was no small indentation, no subtle trace of something that had once been there.

Miriam looked up at Dottie and smiled. "Of course. Thank you, dear."

Dottie jotted on her pad. "You got it, hun."

They sat in silence for a long moment, the hum of muted conversation, and the clink of silverware against ceramic cups filling the space between them.

Ashley poked at the napkin in her lap, torn between the need to speak and the need to remain calm, even though her nerves were fraying at the edges.

Dottie soon returned with their orders, setting down the hot cups and plates, the aroma of strong tea swirling through the air. Miriam reached for her tea, taking a delicate sip, the cup held between her fingers as though it were something precious.

"Everything going well at the shop?" Miriam asked, her voice soft.

Ashley's response was polite and automatic. "Yes, everything's fine. Just . . . organizing things, going through some of the old stock." She took a deep breath before adding, "I found a few surprises."

Miriam raised an eyebrow, setting down her cup slowly. Her eyes, bright and sharp, searched Ashley's face, her gaze lingering for just a beat longer than was necessary.

"Surprises?" Miriam repeated. "What kind of surprises?"

Ashley nodded. "The letters," she said, the word dancing between them like something fragile, delicate yet dangerous. "The letters you wrote to my father."

There was a pause, a moment of silence in which Miriam's fingers tightened around her cup. Her eyes flickered toward Ashley's face, and then, almost imperceptibly, she looked away.

"The letters?" Miriam echoed, her voice quieter now, more uncertain. "He kept them?"

Ashley watched the flush of surprise on Miriam's face, the way her hand fluttered in the air before resting again on the edge of her saucer. She nodded again, this time more firmly. "Yes, he kept every one of them, it seems. They're all there."

Miriam blinked rapidly, her breath hitching slightly. She didn't speak for a moment, and when she did, it was with an edge of discomfort. "I never thought he would -" She broke off, shaking her head as if trying to make sense of something that had no real explanation. "I had no idea he'd kept them."

Ashley's eyes never left her, watching closely, searching for the cracks that might show her the truth. Miriam fidgeted in her seat, her fingers tapping restlessly against the side of her cup. Ashley leaned forward slightly, her voice lower now but steady.

"So, it's clear, isn't it?" Ashley said, the bite of her tone sharp in the air. "It was you. It was your affair with my father that caused my mother to leave him. That's why she just . . . disappeared one day."

Miriam stiffened, the color draining from her face. The air in the café seemed to still as if everything in the room held its breath, waiting for her response. She looked at Ashley, an expression a mix of disbelief and sadness.

"No," Miriam said, her voice barely rising above a whisper, as though the word had to be coaxed from the depths of her resolve. "No, that's not how it happened."

Ashley sat back in her chair, a skeptical look creeping into her features. "Then what did happen? Tell me. My mother left, and you —" She stopped herself, not wanting to go further, not wanting to voice the words she was feeling. But they were there, all the same, lodged in her throat.

Miriam hesitated, her eyes dropping to her lap, where her hands twisted together in a tight knot. She seemed to shrink under Ashley's gaze, though she did not look away. She swallowed hard before speaking again.

"Yes, I loved your father," Miriam said, her voice a tapestry of emotions, threads of regret interwoven with the steadfast warp of truth. "Yes, I loved him. It's not something I can or want to deny. But your mother's leaving wasn't because of me, or us."

Ashley's eyes, sharp as cut glass, reflected her growing disbelief. She had lived through years of her father's granite-like stoicism and breathed the heavy air at countless dinner tables where her mother's name hung unspoken like a ghost. And yet here sat Miriam, a constant presence in his life, now attempting to absolve herself of blame.

"Why is it that I can't bring myself to believe you?" Ashley's words fell between them, heavy as river stones.

Miriam leaned in, her voice dropping to a whisper as if sharing a secret with the very air around them. "There's something you need to know. Something your father has kept locked away all these years. Something he never told you."

Ashley raised an eyebrow, folding her arms across her chest. "What's that supposed to mean? What didn't he tell me?"

Miriam sighed deeply, her lips pressed together as if struggling to find the right words. She didn't seem to know how to explain, how to ease the frustration that had been mounting in Ashley's voice.

"Your father," Miriam began slowly, "he . . . he kept things from you, Ashley. From your brother. To protect you both."

Ashley stiffened, the words sparking a familiar, bitter anger. "What are you saying?" she asked, her voice rising slightly. "What could he possibly have kept from me? I don't know what you're trying to say, Miriam."

Miriam's fingers gripped the edge of the table as she stared at Ashley, her eyes full of a deep, almost painful sorrow. She closed her eyes for a moment, collecting herself, before speaking again, her voice almost a whisper.

"I need to show you something," Miriam said finally, her tone more resolute. "Something that will help you understand what happened. I think it's time you saw it."

Ashley's curiosity piqued, but she wasn't ready to let her guard down just yet. "What is it?"

Miriam hesitated before answering. "There's a place I need to take you. It's not far, just a short drive. Past the next town to the east. It will help explain everything."

Ashley felt a flicker of hesitation within herself, but something about Miriam's quiet insistence made her want to follow, to hear whatever this was. She wasn't sure she could trust

Miriam, but something about the desperation in her voice made Ashley wonder what other truths she might be missing.

"I'll drive," Ashley said, standing from the table. Miriam looked up at her, a small but grateful smile crossing her lips.

"Thank you," Miriam murmured, her voice barely above a whisper. She stood slowly as if the gravity of the moment had already begun to settle upon her shoulders, each step a careful negotiation with the heaviness that lay ahead.

Miriam reached for her purse, her fingers brushing the worn leather before pulling out a few bills and placing them on the table with a quiet finality. As they left the diner together, the cold air hit them with a sharpness that made Ashley pull her jacket tighter around her shoulders. Neither of them spoke as they walked, the silence hanging between them like a thick fog. It wasn't the comfortable silence of familiarity; it was a silence laden with unspoken things. And yet, beneath it, Ashley felt something new stir within her, something unfamiliar and unsettling - a reluctant pull, an opening of the door to a past she had never truly understood. A quiet willingness, almost imperceptible, to face what had been left unsaid for too long.

7 The Stones

The drive eastward was quiet at first, the kind of silence that Miriam and Ashley had come to expect between them. The sound of the engine was a constant presence, a soft, steady hum that seemed to fill the car without any effort. A cool breeze slipped in through the slightly open windows, soft and insistent, brushing their skin as it passed by. The landscape unfolded before them in rolling waves of gold and green, interrupted now and then by a farmhouse or an old barn, their outlines faint against the vastness of the land. Miriam sat stiffly in the passenger seat, her hands clasped in her lap, her eyes fixed on the horizon as if it might offer her a script for what she needed to say.

Ashley adjusted her grip on the leather steering wheel, her knuckles briefly whitening. "Are we going to Silver Birch?" she asked, her voice breaking through the quiet like a skipped stone across a still pond.

Miriam turned her head slightly, considering the question. "We'll pass through it," she said. "But we're going a bit farther. Just a couple more miles east."

Ashley nodded, her gaze fixed on the road ahead. She hesitated, then added, "I haven't been to Silver Birch in years. Not since -" She paused, glancing at Miriam before finishing, "Not since my mom left."

Miriam's eyes wandered toward the window, tracing the soft changes in the light outside. The landscape stretched out in muted tones, its presence barely touching the stillness between them.

"Glass reflects nothing and absorbs everything," she whispered.

Ashley turned, not quite sure if she had heard correctly. "What was that?"

"Miriam's gaze remained fixed on the view for a moment longer before she spoke again, her voice more deliberate now, as though she were building something with her words. "I said, it's a beautiful place. Silver Birch. It's beautiful. Your mother always spoke of it so fondly."

Ashley's lips curved into a faint smile, though it didn't quite reach her eyes. "It was where she was happiest, I think," she said. "We used to spend summers there - just me, my parents, and sometimes a few cousins. My grandparents lived close by. There were cottages by the lake, and in the mornings, we'd go fishing or swimming. My dad wasn't much for boats, but Mom loved them. She said she could spend all day out on the water if she didn't have to come back and cook."

Miriam gave a small, quiet laugh, her gaze softening. "She was right about that. She never did enjoy being tied to a kitchen."

Ashley glanced sideways at Miriam, trying to read her expression. "You knew her?"

"Of course, I did," Miriam replied, her tone neutral. She clasped her hands a little tighter and added, "I think we were alike in some ways, your mother and I."

The conversation tapered off once more, and the car moved steadily forward as they neared the outskirts of Silver Birch. The town appeared slowly like a memory surfacing after years of being forgotten. The familiar sights began to take shape - the general store with its faded sign, the row of cottages tucked beneath the sprawling trees, and finally, the glint of sunlight on the water - the lake at the heart of it all.

"I used to sit by the water for hours," Ashley said. The words drifted soft and unanchored, hovering between conversation and memory. Her voice had dropped, turned inward - the way voices do when they're no longer speaking to another person but tracing the contours of something private, something held close. "There was this little bench near the edge of the dock. Weathered wood, gray as a winter sky. I'd watch the boats come and go, their white hulls rocking against the water's quiet rhythm. My dad mentioned once it was my mother's favorite spot. After she left, we never returned."

Miriam didn't say anything at first, her gaze fixed on the lake as it slipped into view - a wide, glimmering expanse cradled by dark green hills. Her expression was distant, unreadable as if the sight stirred something too tangled to unravel in the space of a few passing moments. She remained quiet as the road curved gently through the heart of Silver Birch, where life seemed suspended in a perpetual summer. The cottages stood tucked under canopies of oak and birch, their porches adorned with flower pots and wind chimes that swayed faintly in the breeze. A small general store with a sun-faded sign leaned slightly against time, and a weathered dock jutted into the water where a lone fisherman cast his line.

As the town thinned and gave way to open fields bordered by clusters of towering trees, Miriam finally spoke. "Keep going," she said softly, her voice almost lost in the hum of the tires against the pavement. "It's just a couple of miles from here, on the left."

Ashley's grip on the steering wheel tightened for a moment. She glanced quickly at Miriam, but her face offered no clue about what was to come. A dozen unspoken questions moved through Ashley's mind, each one clawing for attention, but she kept them at bay. Instead, she let the silence hang between them, thick with things they hadn't yet found the courage to voice.

The road narrowed as it stretched onward, flanked by a wall of ancient trees whose branches wove together high above, forming a canopy that seemed almost deliberate, like the vaulted ceiling of a cathedral. Shafts of sunlight filtered through in fractured beams, dappling the pavement in shifting patterns that moved like whispers of wind through the leaves. The air grew cooler, the dense green of the woods pressing in closer as they drove, and Ashley couldn't shake the feeling that the road was drawing them toward something they couldn't turn away from, even if they tried.

"There," Miriam said, pointing toward a narrow road that veered off to the left. "Turn here."

Ashley slowed the car, squinting at the small, almost hidden path. It was unpaved, the gravel crunching under the tires as they made their way beneath the shadow of the trees. The air seemed even cooler here, the dense canopy blocking out much of the light.

The trees parted abruptly, revealing a clearing bathed in soft light, where rows of weathered headstones stood like sentinels. Their gray and white surfaces, etched with names and dates, rose starkly against the tender green of the well-kept grass. The cemetery was small, no more than a quiet pocket of land nestled close to the shimmering edge of the lake. Beyond the stones, the water stretched wide and still, catching glimmers of sunlight that danced across its surface. The scene had a serenity that bordered on the sacred, a kind of timelessness that settled uneasily on Ashley's shoulders.

Ashley eased the car to a stop and turned off the engine. For a moment, neither of them moved. The weight of the place seemed to seep into the car, filling the silence between them. Ashley glanced at Miriam, whose face was turned toward the clearing, her expression unreadable but intent, as though she were bracing herself for something unseen.

It was Miriam who broke the spell, her movements deliberate and careful. She opened the door, stepping out with a slow precision that made Ashley pause. Had she been here before? There was something deeply familiar in the way she moved, a quiet reverence in her every gesture, as though each step held its own significance.

Ashley followed, her own movements heavy and graceless compared to Miriam's quiet, deliberate steps. The gravel crunched beneath her boots, each footfall echoing in the profound stillness that wrapped around the cemetery like a shroud. The air carried the faintest trace of pine and lake water, mingled with the damp, earthy scent of moss-covered stones and freshly turned soil. A breeze rustled the high branches above them, casting shifting shadows over the worn paths. But even the sound of the wind felt muted here, as though it, too, respected the weight of the place. Ashley shoved her hands into her jacket pockets, her fingers curling tightly, unsure whether it was the cold or the unfamiliar silence that made her feel out of place. It was as though they'd stepped into someone else's memory, a moment that didn't belong to her.

"What is this place?" she asked, her voice barely louder than the whisper of the wind through the trees. The words seemed to vanish as soon as they left her mouth, swallowed by the quiet.

Miriam stood still for a moment, her eyes fixed on the row of headstones ahead. The stones seemed to blend with the earth, their edges blurred by moss and age, as though they had always belonged to the land rather than being placed there. She took a slow step forward, her fingers brushing lightly against the cedar tree's drooping branches. Each movement was measured, careful, as if she were absorbing something that Ashley couldn't see, something fragile and sacred. Finally, Miriam broke the silence, her voice carrying the quiet certainty of a truth that had been held back for far too long.

"It's where your mother is," she said, her words so soft that Ashley almost doubted she'd heard them correctly.

Ashley froze. The air seemed to tighten around her, and for a moment, the world itself seemed to stand still. "What?" The word came out sharper than she intended, cutting through the silence. Her hands slipped from her pockets, her arms hanging awkwardly at her sides. "What do you mean?"

Miriam turned to face her, her expression grave yet strangely calm, almost as if she'd rehearsed this moment in her mind a thousand times. "I knew your father had never told you," she said gently, her voice steady but tinged with sadness. She held Ashley's gaze for a long moment, her own eyes shadowed with something Ashley couldn't yet name - a mixture of sorrow, resignation, and something else, something closer to guilt.

Ashley's heart was pounding now, a strange mix of confusion and disbelief rising in her chest. "Told me what?" she demanded. "That she's here? That she's dead? What are you talking about?"

Miriam took a step closer, her eyes steady on Ashley's. "It's not my story to tell," she said softly. "But your father . . . he couldn't bring himself to do it. I think it's time. You deserve to know."

Ashley felt her knees weaken, her legs trembling beneath her. She turned away from Miriam, staring out at the rows of headstones as if the answers she sought might be written there. "I don't understand," she said, her voice breaking.

"She didn't leave you, Ashley," Miriam said softly, her voice almost a whisper. Her eyes were fixed on a point somewhere over Ashley's shoulder, as though she were looking into the past, seeing things Ashley could only imagine. "She never would've done that."

Ashley stared back, the world around her narrowing to Miriam's face and the unspoken truth hovering between them. Her throat tightened, and she struggled to find her voice. "Then what happened?" she asked, the words catching in her throat. "Why did she disappear like that?"

Miriam paused, her eyes lowering to the ground, her fingers entwining nervously. "She wasn't well," she said, her voice heavy, as though the words themselves had a substance that pulled her down, grounding her to the earth beneath them. "It was all so sudden, faster than anyone could make sense of. By the time anyone realized how serious it was . . . there wasn't much that could be done. She went back to her parents, back to Silver Birch, where they took her to different doctors, hoping one of them would have an answer. There were so many trips to Boston. All the while your father ran the shop and took care of you and your brother. He needed the money to pay for the doctor's bills. But your mother's parents helped out too."

Ashley felt a strange calmness envelop her, a momentary pause in the constant motion of her thoughts. She stood on the edge of something she couldn't fully grasp, caught between understanding and disbelief. "What . . . what happened to her?" she asked, her voice barely more than a breath. Speaking the question out loud felt like a delicate thing as if uttering it could shatter the fragile connection she still held to the past.

Miriam let out a long breath, her shoulders slumping under a weight she'd carried alone for too long. "The doctors could only say it was something in her brain, something unraveling from the inside. At first, it was little things, details slipping through the cracks, easy to dismiss. But then . . . it was as if she were dissolving, piece by piece. Your father said there were days when she couldn't find herself - didn't know where she was or even who she was. She'd look at him, her eyes blank, not a trace of recognition. He hid all this from you and your brother."

Ashley felt the sting of tears, her chest tightening. "So she . . . she was losing herself?"

Miriam nodded, and her expression softened with something close to sorrow. "It was like watching a light flicker out. She knew, too. She could feel herself drifting away, and it terrified her. She was afraid you'd see her that way, afraid you'd remember her as someone she barely recognized herself. She lost so much weight, so quickly, and could barely walk at the end. But she was here, at Silver Birch, a place she always thought of as so peaceful. Your father thought, at the end, that your mother felt, maybe she could hold on to what was left, as long as she was here."

Ashley's voice was brittle. "And my father?"

"Like I said. He worked the shop." Miriam's voice trembled, and she wrapped her arms around herself as if bracing against a chill. "He didn't want to believe what was happening. He kept thinking that she would come home one day and things would be normal, and it would all go away. He was angry, Ashley. Not at her, but at the whole situation. At the doctors, at himself, at life for taking her away piece by piece."

Ashley looked out at the lake beyond the cemetery, her hands clenched at her sides. All these years, she'd blamed her father for her mother's leaving, for abandoning them without a word. But now, the anger she'd held so tightly had nowhere to go but inward, until it twisted into something sharper. She turned back to Miriam, her face flushed.

"I didn't know," she said, her voice hard. "I had thought that he just pushed her away."

Miriam's face softened, her hand reaching out but stopping just short of touching Ashley's arm. "I know, dear," she said quietly. "He was hurting, too People deal with pain in all kinds of ways, some better than others. He couldn't bear to see her that way, and I think, in his own way, he wanted to protect you from it, too. He thought he was doing the right thing."

Ashley shook her head, feeling anger rising once again, not just at her father, but at the years of silence, at the secrets that had turned her memories into something hollow. "He let me hate him," she said, her voice breaking. "He let me believe she'd just given up on us." She felt the bite of resentment rise up, not at her mother, but at the man who had turned her memory into a ghostly silence, a story he never cared to tell.

Ashley felt as though the ground had shifted beneath her. The memories she had held onto for so long - the happy summers by the lake, the sudden absence of her mother - were suddenly reframed, their edges blurred and reshaped by the truth.

"Why didn't he tell me?" she asked, her voice trembling. "Why would he let me believe she just abandoned us?"

Miriam reached out, her hand resting lightly on Ashley's arm. "You were so young," she said. "He thought he was protecting you He didn't know how to explain it. He thought it would be easier for you to believe she was still out there somewhere."

Ashley pulled away, shaking her head. "Easier?" she said bitterly. "Do you have any idea what it's like to grow up thinking your mother didn't want you? To carry that around every day?"

Miriam's eyes glistened, but she didn't look away. Her composure seemed to teeter on the edge of collapse, her breath unsteady. "I'm sorry," she said, her voice breaking under the weight of the words. "I'm so sorry, Ashley. I wish I could've done more, and been there for you in a way that mattered. I told your father that you and your brother deserved to know. That it would be easier, kinder, to be honest. But he wouldn't listen. He said it wasn't your burden to carry." She paused, her throat working as if the next

words might choke her. "He didn't want you to know that she went
. . ."

Her voice faltered, the sentence left hanging in the air like a
fragile thread. She looked away, her gaze falling to the ground,
where the light filtered through the trees in fragmented, uneven
patterns.

Ashley's pulse quickened. There was something more,
something Miriam wasn't saying, and it pressed against her like an
unseen weight. "Went what?" she demanded, the sharpness of her
tone cutting through the thick, oppressive quiet. "What is it?"

Miriam turned back to her slowly, and Ashley saw the tears
that had gathered spill over, leaving glistening tracks on her cheeks.
Her mouth trembled before she spoke, the words emerging soft
and broken, yet piercing in their simplicity.

"Mad," she said, her voice a whisper that felt louder than a
scream. "Your mother went mad. It's the only way I know to
describe it, and I'm so sorry for saying it like that."

Ashley looked at Miriam, the word *mad* hanging in the air
between them like a dark cloud, dense and threatening. Her heart
pounded in her chest as she searched Miriam's face for some hint
of reassurance, some thread of hope that she hadn't understood
correctly. "Mad?" Ashley repeated, her voice small, a fragile echo
of the first.

Miriam blinked rapidly, as though trying to focus on
something beyond the rawness of the moment. She carefully wiped
her eyes with her fingertips, but the tears kept coming. "Yes,
Ashley," she said quietly, her words slow and deliberate, each one
seeming to cost her something. "Eventually, the diagnosis came
back - severe dementia. It wasn't just the forgetting. It was the way

she started to unravel. The confusion, the . . . the paranoia. She stopped recognizing the people who were closest to her. I think it terrified her, in the end. And she couldn't . . . couldn't . . . bring herself to admit it, not to your father, not to anyone. By the end, your grandparents couldn't control her, couldn't keep themselves safe. She became too much to handle. Violent even. They had no choice but to send her away. She spent her last days away. At a facility in Burlington."

"An asylum?" Ashley could barely form the word.

Miriam nodded as if that was all she could offer.

Ashley felt her chest tighten, a coldness taking root in her heart, a quiet, uninvited presence that grew with each passing moment. "She left, never coming back," Ashley said, the words strangled by disbelief. "She couldn't even . . . remember us?"

Miriam shook her head, her lips pressed together tightly as though holding back more than she could bear. "She couldn't remember herself, Ashley. And I think that's what broke her. Your father tried to protect you from all of it. I think he thought, if he just kept it hidden, it wouldn't affect you. But that didn't make the hurt go away. It was like watching someone you love disappear, bit by bit. It's a kind of grief you can't even explain."

Ashley turned away, her eyes scanning the lake in front of them as if the ripples on its surface could offer some sort of clarity, some understanding of what she was hearing. But the more she tried to comprehend it, the more the pieces of her mother's decline slipped out of reach. She had never been told any of this. And now it felt as though she had spent years carrying around a version of her mother that wasn't real. The version of a woman who had left, yes, but for reasons she never knew, or could even comprehend.

Ashley whispered, her voice shaking despite her best efforts to keep it steady. "All he had to do was tell me the truth?"

Miriam's eyes softened, and she took a step toward Ashley, her hand outstretched but pausing before it reached her arm. "He didn't think you could handle it. He couldn't handle it. He was only trying to shield you. But all this time, you've carried something, haven't you? Not knowing what really happened to her."

Ashley nodded, her eyes stinging now. She hadn't realized, hadn't understood until this moment, how much of her life had been spent searching for answers in the wrong places.

"I should've been there for her," Ashley said, the guilt creeping in, twisting inside her. "I should've done something."

Miriam's voice was gentle but firm when she spoke again. "You were just a child, Ashley. What could you have done?"

Ashley let out a soft, broken sound, the words escaping her before she could stop them. "Hugged her," she whispered. "I could've hugged her."

And suddenly, Ashley understood how much had gone unsaid - not just about her mother's illness, but about the silence that hung over the entire family. Her grandparents, too, never mentioned their daughter. It was as though her mother had become a chapter in a book they all agreed to ignore, a part of the past no one dared to revisit. The absence of words spoke louder than any confession ever could.

"She didn't have to leave," Ashley said, her voice soft, the words tumbling out like something she'd been holding inside for a long time. There was a kind of disbelief in her tone, as though she couldn't quite believe it herself. "She didn't have to leave."

Miriam's expression faltered for a moment, her gaze drifting away toward the horizon. "She left because she needed to know what was happening to her. It wasn't just the forgetfulness, Ashley. It was the fear. The fear of becoming someone she didn't recognize, someone who couldn't take care of you anymore. She thought that if she just left, you'd remember her the way she was. And maybe she was right in a way. Maybe it was easier for her to disappear, so you could carry the memory of her with you instead of watching her fade."

For Ashley, it felt unjust and unkind. The idea that her mother had thought she was doing them a favor by disappearing, by taking herself out of the picture.

"You think she did it for us?" Ashley said, her voice thick with emotion. "That she thought it was easier for us if she just . . . left? She didn't even give us a chance to say goodbye."

Miriam's gaze softened, and she took a deep breath. "I think she thought she was sparing you from the worst of it. But sometimes, when people are in pain, they don't know how to do the right thing. They just do the best they can, even if it doesn't seem right to anyone else. From what your father told me, you wouldn't have wanted to have seen her . . . not like that."

Ashley turned her gaze to the lake once more, the smooth surface reflecting the quiet inside her. The things Miriam had said pressed heavily against her, demanding that she reconcile the mother she had known with the one who had slipped away into the recesses of her own mind. She wasn't sure what to do with it, how to make sense of the truth she had just learned. It felt as though she had spent years holding onto a story that belonged to someone else, a version of her mother that never truly existed.

But Miriam had given her something - something small, something fragile, but real. A glimpse into the truth. And for the first time in a long while, Ashley wasn't sure she wanted to turn away from it.

Ashley turned back toward the cemetery, her gaze scanning the rows of headstones. "Where is she?" she asked, her voice steadier now, though still tinged with anger. "Where's my mother?"

Miriam gestured toward a cluster of stones near the far end of the clearing. "She's over there," she said. "Come on."

They walked side by side, the sound of their footsteps breaking the stillness, a gentle crunch of gravel underfoot. The air seemed to grow still with every step they took toward the headstone, the soft sounds of the world around them fading into the distance. Ashley felt a familiar ache that seemed to have been building, a sensation of loss that had been with her for so long, now rising to the surface. It felt like it had been waiting for this moment, for her to finally arrive here.

As they neared the marker, Ashley's gaze fell to the smooth stone, and her breath caught. Her mother's name was carved into it with delicate precision, the letters almost glowing against the gray surface, stark and final. The dates marking her mother's life were plain, almost unassuming. The span between them felt impossibly brief, a moment that passed too quickly. She had been so young, so full of possibility, yet her life had faded so suddenly.

Ashley knelt slowly, her knees pressing into the cool earth beneath her, her fingers trembling as they traced the carved letters of her mother's name. Veronica Keller. The name felt foreign to her hand, disconnected from the woman who had once been vibrant and full of stories, of laughter. A wave of grief washed over her, raw and uninvited, followed by a sharp sting of anger - anger at the years lost, at the memories left behind that she would never be able to reclaim. And then, without warning, there was relief. It was a strange feeling, unfamiliar and almost disorienting, a quiet sense of something lifting, leaving her chest lighter than it had been in a long time.

"I don't know what to say," she murmured. as though speaking too loudly would shatter the fragile stillness that had settled around them.

Miriam knelt beside her, her presence steady and comforting. Her hand, warm and strong, rested lightly on Ashley's shoulder, the touch quiet but full of understanding. "You don't have to say anything," she replied, her voice low and calm. "Just being here is enough."

And so Ashley stayed there, the world around her moving in a way that no longer felt urgent or demanding. The silence seemed to shift to something softer, more forgiving. It was as if time itself had paused to allow her this moment. The lake, gleaming in the distance, reflected the light of the afternoon sun, its surface rippling gently, as though the water too was offering its quiet solace. Ashley felt the cool breeze against her skin, carrying with it the scent of pine and earth, a quiet reminder of the world outside this moment. For the first time in years, she allowed herself to relax, to release the tension that had been with her for so long, to feel something close to peace. It was fragile, fleeting, but it was there, a delicate thread of calm that wound itself around her heart, unspooling slowly.

8 The Revelation

The gravel crunched under the tires as Ashley eased the car from the cemetery parking lot, each pebble a tiny percussion instrument in an orchestra of grief. She looked up at the sky. More clouds. She had thought it might rain and had almost hoped for it as if the sky's tears could wash away the raw ache that clung to her skin like damp wool. But the clouds held their restraint, gray and swollen with something unspoken, a promise unfulfilled.

Miriam sat motionless, her hands folded tightly in her lap, pale fingers interlaced like the roots of an ancient tree, anchoring her to a spot Ashley couldn't see. She stared out the window at a world she seemed to have no stake in, her gaze sliding over fences and fields as if they were mere projections on a screen, insubstantial and fleeting. The sound of the engine filled the space between them, soft and insistent, a metronome marking time in a symphony neither of them had chosen to play.

Ashley's thoughts churned, jagged, and unfinished, like shards of glass in a kaleidoscope, constantly shifting and rearranging themselves into patterns she couldn't quite grasp. They circled back, again and again, to the single word Miriam had uttered at the graveside.

Mad.

The word felt like an invader, carving out its own room in Ashley's mind, demanding space she didn't want to give. It echoed in the caverns of her memory, bouncing off the walls of her skull, growing louder with each reverberation until it threatened to drown out all other thoughts. She wanted to cup her hands over her ears, to shut it out, but she knew the sound was coming from within.

She wanted to say something, to puncture the oppressive silence that had settled over them, but the right words refused to come. They hovered just out of reach, wisps of smoke that dissipated whenever she tried to grasp them. She glanced at Miriam, whose profile was set in an expression of resignation, her eyes fixed on the landscape as if she could divine some secret meaning from the rolling hills and scattered trees. There was something fragile about her now, a brittleness that hadn't been there before. She seemed to fold into herself, shoulders hunched, chin tucked, as if bracing for another blow from an unseen assailant. Ashley wondered if this was how people looked when they finally understood that the world could take everything from them, piece by piece until there was nothing left but the hollow shell of who they used to be.

Ashley didn't know what finally made her speak - whether it was anger, curiosity, or simply the need to fill the void - but the words spilled out before she could stop them. "So, you and my dad - what were you to each other?"

Miriam stayed silent, her focus on the shifting scenery beyond the window. Her eyes moved over the landmarks she'd seen countless times, though her thoughts seemed to drift far beyond the passing view. Ashley's question had reached her - she'd heard every word - but instead of responding, she let the question unfurl in the space between them, absorbing it without rushing to answer. Her fingers curled slightly against her lap, the motion small yet noticeable, as though she were gripping something unseen.

After a moment, she exhaled, the sound faint but deliberate. She had made up her mind. "That's a complicated question," she said, her voice soft but steady, a quiet strength beneath it. "And I suppose it deserves an answer." She drew in a long breath, one that seemed to reach some deeply hidden corner of herself, coaxing the words into being.

Ashley turned her head, watching Miriam now instead of the passing trees. "I'm listening."

"It was years ago," Miriam began, her voice not rushed but cautious like she was laying each brick of a story with care. "Before your father met your mother. Before either of us really knew what it meant to lose someone."

Ashley's gaze turned back to the road.

"We met at a time when we were both searching for something," Miriam continued. "I had just lost my sister. Cancer. Though it doesn't matter much what it was. Loss has a way of flattening all the details until the specifics hardly seem to matter. Your father . . . he'd lost his brother. A car accident." She paused, looking down at her hands. "We met at a grief group in Burlington. I wasn't even supposed to be there - I was visiting a friend, and she practically dragged me along. Your dad was there alone. I think he'd just moved back to Vermont to help his parents."

Ashley could almost picture it: her father, younger but with that same quiet intensity he always carried, sitting in a circle with others, speaking in measured tones while the rest of the group nodded solemnly.

"At first, we were just two people trying to make sense of things that didn't make sense," Miriam said. "We talked, long conversations after the meetings. Coffee. Cigarettes. Sometimes late into the night. There was something easy about talking to him. Like he knew how heavy it all was and wasn't afraid to deal with it."

"And then?" Ashley prompted, her voice soft.

"And then it became more," Miriam said simply. She glanced at Ashley, her expression carefully neutral. "We started spending time together outside of the group. A movie here, dinner there. It wasn't rushed. You know, the kind of thing that burns too bright and then fades. It felt steady. Good. Like we were helping each other rebuild."

Ashley's stomach tightened. "Did you love him?"

Miriam smiled faintly, her eyes still on the road. "I did. And I believe he loved me too. In a way, we saved each other for a while. Or at least, we tried to."

"What happened?"

"The same thing that always happens with grief," Miriam said quietly. "It changed us. But your dad had a way of holding onto things - his memories, his pain, the people he'd lost. I thought I was helping him, but sometimes it felt like he wasn't ready to let go. And me . . . I was looking for something I could hold onto, something steady to help me move forward. We ended up needing different things. Eventually, we both knew we couldn't find them together."

Ashley felt an unfamiliar sorrow rise within her, untethered to a specific moment or memory, but persistent all the same.

"We remained friends, though," Miriam added. "It wasn't easy at first, but we managed. He opened the antique shop. And me? Well, I opened the bookstore. We remained good friends, and when he met your mother, I could see right away that she was the person he'd been waiting for. She had this lightness about her, this way of pulling him out of his head. He needed that. And I was happy for him."

"You stayed in touch," Ashley said.

"We did," Miriam admitted. "We had a history, and it mattered to both of us. When your mom got sick, he started calling me more. I think he felt like I was one of the few people who could really understand what he was going through. He didn't talk about himself much - he mostly wanted to talk about her, about you and your brother. How he told me he was going to keep it all together."

"Why didn't he ever tell me . . . about you, I mean?" Ashley asked.

Miriam sighed. "I don't know. Maybe he didn't think it was important."

Ashley let the words sink in, her mind spinning. She thought of her father as she'd always known him: steady, reserved, unshakable. And now here was this other version, one she'd never even imagined - a young man grieving, falling in love, piecing his life together bit by bit.

"Did you ever -" she hesitated, unsure how to phrase it. "Did you ever wish things had turned out differently? That you and he -"

"No," Miriam said firmly, cutting her off. "I won't lie to you, Ashley. There was a time when I thought maybe we'd find our way back to each other. But it didn't happen, and that's okay. Your dad was exactly where he was supposed to be. With your mom."

Ashley nodded slowly.

They drove on in silence for a while, the road stretching endlessly ahead of them. When Miriam spoke again, her voice was softer, almost wistful. "He was a good man, Ashley. A kind man. And he loved your mom more than anything. I hope you know that."

Ashley remained silent.

The car turned onto the familiar streets of Stillwater, the town wrapped in a quiet that felt heavier now than it had before. Ashley looked at Miriam. "Thank you," she said.

Miriam smiled, a faint curve of her lips that seemed to hold more than she could say. "You're welcome."

The car slowed as Ashley pulled up in front of Miriam's small bookstore, nestled between the florist and the small grocery store with faded green awning. The street was quiet, late afternoon light casting long shadows across the sidewalk. She turned to Miriam, the silence between them thick with unspoken history.

"Did he tell you?" Ashley's voice was soft, almost a whisper. "About how things ended between us?"

Miriam's hands rested motionless in her lap. She glanced out the window briefly, then returned to Ashley. "Yes," she said, her voice steady. "And I was sorry that happened."

The word "sorry" hung in the air, weighted with something more than sympathy. Ashley nodded, her fingers gripping the steering wheel. Nothing more needed to be added. No further explanation was required.

Miriam reached for the car door, hesitating for a breath. Her profile caught the light from the window, a composed outline that hinted at something held tightly within. The soft sound of the door unlocking broke the car's stillness. "I hope I was able to help, Ashley," she said before stepping outside.

Ashley watched her walk toward the bookstore. As she drove away, thoughts of her father returned, slipping quietly into her mind - the conversations they had shared, the ones left unfinished, and the quiet spaces where words never quite found their place.

Then Laura's question from the night before surfaced, curling at the edges of her mind like smoke finding its way into hidden spaces. Ashley had been sure she'd traced the lines correctly, that the path forward would reveal itself in familiar contours. Now, the realization came quietly: the connections had led her somewhere she hadn't expected to go.

Ashley pulled into the familiar gravel driveway behind the antique store, the tires crunching softly as the car came to a stop. She sat for a moment, her hands still gripping the steering wheel, as if holding on might keep the world from spinning out of control. With a deep breath, she stepped out of the car, the cool air alive with the scent of autumn leaves and faint woodsmoke drifting from unseen fires. The key to the back door was where it had always been, tucked behind a loose brick in the foundation. Ashley's fingers trembled slightly as she retrieved it, the metal cool against her skin.

The store was quiet, filled with the particular stillness of objects that had outlived their original owners. Dust motes danced in the slanting sunlight that filtered through the windows, illuminating the careful arrangements of china, silverware, and old books. Ashley moved through the space, her footsteps muffled by the faded oriental rug that ran the length of the main aisle.

She paused at the foot of the narrow staircase that led to the apartment above, her hand resting on the worn banister. How many times had she climbed these steps as a child, racing up to find a toy to play with, or finding her mother cooking on the stove? The wood creaked beneath her feet as she ascended, each step feeling heavier than the last.

Ashley turned the key to the apartment door and nudged it open. The air inside wrapped her in a mix of her mother's lavender perfume and, unexpectedly, the faint, smoky trace of her father's pipe tobacco. It caught her off guard, an aroma she hadn't noticed in years. She told herself it couldn't be real.

She walked across the small living room, her steps slowing near the kitchen, where the chipped countertop stood unchanged. Familiarity surrounded her, each detail in the apartment carrying a quiet echo of her parents' lives. Finally, she reached the bedroom at the back of the flat, her heart pulling her forward and tugging her back all at once.

The room was bathed in the warm glow of the setting sun, casting everything in a soft, dreamlike light. Her father's presence lingered here - in the neatly made bed with its patchwork quilt, in the reading glasses perched on the nightstand, in the row of family photos lined up on the dresser. Ashley's gaze lingered on a picture of her parents on their wedding day, their faces young and radiant with hope.

She sank onto the bed, the springs creaking softly beneath her weight. And then, as if a dam had broken, the tears came.

Ashley cried for her mother, mourning the cruel unraveling that dementia had brought, pulling her apart piece by piece until only a faint echo of who she had been was left. She imagined the fear and confusion her mother must have felt, trapped inside a mind that no longer listened. Memories of her mother flooded her mind. She could see her, dancing in the kitchen to old jazz records, her laughter ringing out as she spun Ashley in her arms. She could hear her voice - the kind that had the power to ease any ache with just a few words. She wept for the woman who had once filled their lives with warmth and music, the one who had known exactly how to heal skinned knees and broken hearts with nothing more than her steady love.

She cried for her father, too, imagining the grief that must have consumed him. How had he endured it, watching the love of his life fade away, helpless to do anything about it? She pictured him sitting in this very room, surrounded by memories of better days, struggling to find the words to tell his children that their world was about to change forever.

The sobs wracked her body, hot tears soaking into the quilt. She cried for the years of silence that had stretched between her and her father, for the words left unspoken, the comfort ungiven. How different things might have been if she had known about Miriam, about the depth of her father's experiences with loss? Would it have bridged the chasm that had opened between them, or would it have only widened it further?

She cried for all the things she couldn't change or fix. She had been so angry with her father, believing he had driven her mother away. But now, with Miriam's revelations, the story had shifted. She saw his actions differently - not as the cause of their unraveling but as an effort to spare them the sharp edges of his sorrow. Yet in that attempt, he had closed them off, leaving them to stumble through their own grief without him.

As the tears began to subside, Ashley rolled onto her back, staring up at the ceiling. The room had grown darker. She thought about the man her father had been before she knew him - the grieving brother, the young man falling in love with Miriam, the husband, and father trying to hold his family together in the face of devastating loss. How many layers of him had she never seen, never even thought to look for?

She sat up slowly, wiping her eyes with the back of her hand. On the nightstand sat another photograph of her parents, encased in an elegant gold frame. Her hand hovered above it for a moment, uncertain. Then, with quiet resolve, she picked it up, her fingers tracing the smooth edges of the frame. She studied her mother's face, sharp and clear in her memory, as if time had not touched it. And then, her gaze shifted to her father.

The anger and resentment that had once gripped her heart softened, making way for a quiet compassion. She saw, in her father's face, the burden he had borne - the burden of his own uncertainties, the faltering steps he had taken, and the profound love that had held firm even when everything around them seemed on the verge of unraveling.

Outside, the sky had turned deep indigo. Ashley stood from the bed and moved to the window. Below her, the town of Stillwater stretched out, its lights flickering on in windows as families began their evening routines. She thought of her own family - fractured and imperfect, yes - but still held together by the threads of something intangible, a history shared and a love that could not quite be broken.

Turning to leave the bedroom, Ashley caught sight of her reflection in the mirror above the dresser. Her eyes were red-rimmed, her cheeks streaked with tears, but beneath that, something else was there - a new understanding, a trace of forgiveness. She drew in a steady breath, feeling herself move away from the long shadow she had carried, stepping into a light she hadn't realized existed.

9 *The Photo*

Ashley brushed a strand of hair from her face as she leaned over the dusty cabinet tucked into the corner of the shop. The air carried a faint mix of lemon polish and the earthy scent of aged wood, grounding her in a space that seemed immune to the rush of passing years. The sunlight slanted through the window glass, casting a stillness over the room that felt untouched by the years. She had spent the better part of the day cataloging new arrivals: a porcelain tea set, a set of wrought-iron sconces, and a set of mismatched copper keys. The shop had always been a sanctuary of sorts for her, a place where the past felt present but manageable, like a story written in ink rather than sand.

She heard the bell above the door jingle but didn't look up.

"I'm not ready for customers," she called over her shoulder, her voice light but edged with fatigue.

"Then why did you have the door unlocked?"

Owen's voice held a familiarity that reached back to childhood. She turned and found him near the front of the store, hands in his pockets, his shoulders drawn inward.

"I swept the sidewalk," she said evenly, meeting his gaze for only a moment. "Forgot to lock up after."

"Still here, huh," he said, his glance wandering over the shop's cluttered shelves. There was something in his expression - a mix of curiosity and discomfort like he wasn't sure if he belonged in this place anymore.

"Where would I go?" she asked, brushing her hands down the thighs of her jeans, a gesture more about grounding herself than any real need. "This place doesn't sort itself out. Inventory needs to be verified." She exhaled slowly, letting the last of her words dissolve into the air before turning to face him again. "But I know you were taking care of Dad," she said quietly, the unspoken truth resting between them, solid and unmoving.

Owen stepped further into the shop, his boots clunking against the uneven wooden floorboards. His face was drawn, and there was a tension in his jaw that made him look older than his thirty-three years. Ashley had always thought of him as eternally youthful, but now she saw the lines creeping in at the edges of his eyes.

"Funny how that works," he said, his voice sharp. "The shop needs you now, but it didn't seem to need you when Dad was still alive."

Ashley gripped the edge of the cabinet as if it might steady her, the cool wood grounding her in a moment she didn't want to face. The shop felt smaller suddenly, the air heavier, as though the shelves of antiques and forgotten memories were pressing in around her. She was dreading this conversation with Owen, the one that had looped endlessly between them since her return, and now, after what Miriam had told her, it felt even more impossible.

"Owen," she said softly, trying to ease the sharp edges of his anger, but he cut her off before the word had even landed.

"No," he snapped, his voice rising like a tide she couldn't hold back. "We're going to talk about this. We're going to hash it all out. You left, Ashley. You just left. I stayed. I was the one who watched him fall apart, the one who kept this place running when he couldn't even get out of bed. And now - now it's yours? Just like that?"

His words struck her, raw and heavy, a reckoning she couldn't avoid.

"I didn't ask for this," she said, her voice steady but low. "You think I wanted to inherit this place? You think I wanted to come back to Stillwater?"

"Then why did you? You could've signed the place over to me."

Time seemed to stand still, like the old grandfather clock that stood in the corner, its hands motionless.

"I came back because maybe I thought I could do something good here. Make something out of the mess I left behind."

Owen sighed. "Yeah, a mess you didn't have to live through. Do you have any idea what it was like to watch him - He stopped, shaking his head as if he couldn't bear to finish the thought.

Ashley moved through the room with unhurried steps, stopping near enough to notice the faint redness around his eyes.

"You're right," she said softly. "I wasn't here. And I'll never be able to change that. But, Owen, there are things you don't know. Things Dad didn't tell either of us."

He frowned, his brow furrowing. "Like what?"

Ashley hesitated. The words felt like stones in her mouth, heavy and unwieldy.

"Miriam," the name fell from her lips.

Owen blinked, thrown off by the sudden shift. "What about Miriam? She used to come by and help out when Dad got sick? She's always been so wonderful."

Ashley hesitated, her eyes flickering down to her hands as though she could find something there to hold on to. "Miriam told me something," she said, her voice faltering. "Something about Mom."

Owen's body stiffened, his breath catching. "What about Mom?"

Ashley swallowed, her throat tightening. "Mom didn't leave us because she wanted to. She was sick. Really sick. There was something . . . a degenerative illness. By the time she left, she wasn't . . . she wasn't herself anymore. She needed care. Care that neither Dad nor our grandparents could give her. They tried, Owen. God, they tried." Her voice shook as she spoke, the words carrying the pain of all the years that had passed. "But it got worse. Much worse. They had to send her somewhere - somewhere they could help her, but . . ."

Owen's eyes narrowed, his jaw rigid with a tension that made his words come out sharp. "But what?"

"She didn't get better, Owen." Ashley's voice dropped to a whisper, the room seeming to close in around them. "She passed away. A few years later. In an asylum. Dad never told us. He thought it would hurt too much. He didn't want us to know."

Owen watched her, his expression giving nothing away. "Why would he do that?"

"He thought he was keeping us safe," Ashley said.

"Safe? He never talked about the past. Whenever I asked, he'd brush it off - It doesn't matter.' I thought Mom left because of something he did."

"I'm not saying he was right," Ashley said, her voice tightening. "I'm just telling you what Miriam told me."

"But why didn't she tell me? She was always there," he said.

"She was helping him keep his secret, I suppose," she said.

Neither of them spoke. The silence expanded, filling the room like something tangible, pressing in from all sides.

Owen's gaze shifted suddenly, locking onto something behind her. "What's that?"

Ashley turned, following his stare. On the counter, almost hidden among the clutter, was a small wooden box, its lid askew as if it had been waiting to be discovered. She remembered finding it earlier, buried beneath some backstock, but hadn't yet bothered to see what it contained.

"I'm not sure," she replied, her voice soft, tentative.

Without another word, Owen moved past her as he reached for the box and lifted the lid. Inside, a stack of old photographs lay scattered, their edges curled and worn with time. He plucked one from the top, studying it with an intensity that made Ashley pause. After a long silence, he handed the photo to her.

Ashley took the photo and felt a pang of recognition. It was a picture of the two of them as children, standing in front of the shop with their father. She must have been about fifteen, Owen seven. Their father stood behind them, one hand on each of their shoulders, a rare smile on his face.

"I don't even remember this," Owen said, his voice softer now.

Ashley studied the photo, her thumb tracing the edge. "I do," she said. "It was the day we painted the sign out front. Remember? Dad let us pick the colors."

Owen searched for the memory, reaching back through time's haze. "I don't remember. What color did I pick?"

"You picked blue," Ashley said, her smile small but certain, "and I picked green. It looked terrible, but Dad didn't mind. He said it had 'character.'"

The chuckle that followed was hesitant at first, then real— simple, unguarded. For a moment, the old anger, the years of silence and loss, seemed to lift, replaced by something easier to hold.

"I hate that he kept that from us," Owen said after a while, his voice quieter now.

"I know," Ashley replied, her voice carrying the same quiet ache. "So do I. But maybe he thought he was doing the best he could. He wasn't perfect, Owen. He was just . . . a man."

Owen didn't answer right away, his eyes still fixed on the photo, as though he might find something more there - something he hadn't seen before. "I miss him," he said finally, the words heavy and simple, as if saying them aloud somehow made them more real.

Ashley closed her eyes, briefly, as if to shield herself from the truth. "Me too," she whispered.

They stood in silence, the photo between them, suspended in the air like a bridge over the distance that had grown between them over the years.

"Do you know where Mom is buried?" Owen's voice was quiet, almost reverent, and there was a sadness in his eyes that Ashley couldn't ignore. "I'd like to visit her."

Ashley nodded, a tear slipping down her cheek. "Silver Birch," she said softly. "I can take you there. We can go together."

Owen held her gaze for a moment, and something softened in his expression. "I'd like that," he said.

Then a shadow passed over his face, a hesitation that altered the moment between them. "There's one thing I've never understood," he said, his voice steady, threaded with a quiet urgency that stayed between them.

Ashley braced herself, already knowing where this was headed. "What's that?"

"Why did you leave?"

She had known this question would come, had rehearsed her answer in empty rooms and quiet moments, but none of it prepared her for Owen's voice - low, careful, waiting.

"I was only ten," he said. "You were here, and then you weren't. Dad never gave me a straight answer, even when I asked, and I always wondered why."

She could hear the years in his words, the space between then and now stretched thin but never closed. There was no undoing it, no rewriting the silence she had left behind. Ashley drew in a breath, steadying herself.

"I should have told you," she said finally. "I should have explained." She met his eyes, steadying herself against the tide of emotions that threatened to rise. "No more secrets."

He nodded, a quiet acknowledgment.

"Let's go see Mom," she said, her voice steady again, offering a smile that felt like a bridge between them.

The car coasted along the winding country road, its tires finding traction on the gravel with quiet assurance. Ashley's hands rested lightly on the wheel, her eyes trained ahead, focused on the path that stretched before them. The late afternoon sun bathed the fields in a warm, golden light, casting long shadows that seemed to reach out, stretching over the land in a slow, almost mournful sweep. Owen sat beside her, unmoving, his posture rigid, as if he were guarding some invisible space between himself and everything else. The silence in the car felt dense, a presence in its own right, neither of them rushing to fill it.

For Ashley, the silence seemed to take on a life of its own. It hummed with the memory of their brief, fragile conversation in the shop—Owen's simple question, asking why she had left. She had promised him no more secrets, but the truth, the whole truth, was tangled in her mind, too complicated to unravel in a single moment. Yet, she knew she had to.

The car moved steadily down the road, carrying them toward Silver Birch Cemetery - the place where their mother had been laid to rest. Owen didn't remember her. Not truly. He was far too young. But he'd tried, hadn't he? He'd studied the photographs, the way her smile crinkled the corners of her eyes, the tilt of her head. He'd listened to his father's stories, told with a lightness that never quite masked the tremor in his voice. He'd tried to build her in his mind, piece by piece, like a fragile mosaic, but she remained elusive, a ghost just beyond his grasp.

The landscape outside the car felt both known and strange, as though it had been waiting for them in a half-forgotten dream. The trees were beginning to shift, their leaves blushing with the first delicate tints of autumn - pale golds and soft oranges that looked as if they had been painted by an artist's brush. The fields stretched out on either side of the road, unchanged and yet somehow different, like the world had been quietly rearranging itself without them noticing. It was the same road, the same familiar horizon, but something about the air felt sharper now as if everything around them had been quietly altered by the passage of time.

Owen shifted in his seat, glancing over at her, the light catching the sharp lines of his face. "I never asked you," he said quietly. "What was she like?"

Ashley didn't look at him. She didn't need to. Her mind had already wandered down that road.

"She was . . . soft," she began, her voice almost a whisper. "Not in the way that makes you think of weakness, but in the way that someone can be both strong and gentle at the same time. She smelled like lavender, and she always had this way of folding her hands together when she was thinking. She was the kind of person who could make everything feel like it was going to be okay, even when it wasn't."

She paused, a catch in her throat, the road stretching out before them, its expanse somehow pulling at the edges of her thoughts. Owen sat still beside her, his presence quiet but undeniable. The distance between them seemed to shrink with each mile, his silence filling the space with an unspoken understanding. She could almost feel his mind turning over the questions he had asked about their mother, the ones he hadn't yet voiced but that hung between them, waiting for answers.

"She had this garden out back," Ashley went on, her voice growing more sure with each word. "It wasn't anything grand = just a small patch, really. But that's where she grew the most beautiful roses. They weren't the flashy kind, the ones you'd find in a florist's shop, with their bright, gaudy petals. These were soft, pale pink, the kind of color you'd see when the sun's about to dip below the horizon. I remember watching her kneel in the dirt, showing me how to plant them, teaching me like it was a ritual. She never let me get too close once they started blooming, though. She said I wasn't ready, that I needed to learn patience. I didn't get it at the time, but I think I understand now." She stopped, her eyes lost in some far-off thought. "The roses are gone now. Dad pulled them up. He replaced them with grass like it was nothing like it never meant anything at all."

"She had this garden out back," Ashley continued, her voice growing steadier with each sentence. "It wasn't anything extravagant—just a small patch, really. But she grew the most beautiful roses there. Not the kind you'd find in a florist's shop, with their bright, attention-grabbing petals. These were soft, pale pink, the sort of shade you'd see right before the sun dips below the horizon. I remember watching her kneel in the dirt, teaching me how to plant them, showing me the motions like it was something sacred. She never let me get too close once they started blooming, though. She said I wasn't ready, that I needed to learn patience. I didn't understand it then, but I think I do now." She paused, her gaze distant, caught in a memory. "The roses are gone now. Dad pulled them up. He replaced them with grass, like it didn't matter - like it was nothing, like it had never meant anything at all."

Owen's eyes were fixed on the road ahead, and Ashley could tell he was listening, completely absorbed in her words.

"I think you were too young to remember that," Ashley said, more to herself than to Owen.

"I don't remember the roses," Owen said suddenly, his voice flat, distant. "So much I missed."

Ashley glanced over at him. There it was again - this strange mix of disconnection and longing. He couldn't have been more than five when their mother left, and it wasn't a memory she could have shared with him. Their mother's illness had come on fast, like a storm you can't predict. Miriam had told her that much.

"I know you want to know what happened to her," Ashley said. "What happened before she . . . before she left."

Owen's eyes flicked to hers, and for the first time in a long while, his expression softened. "Yes."

Ashley took a slow breath, her fingers tightening on the wheel. "Miriam told me that Mom wasn't . . . wasn't herself when she left. Not in the way you think. She was sick. Really sick. They didn't know at the time, but it was dementia, and it was terrible. It took everything from her."

"I guess I still don't understand why Dad didn't tell us?" Owen said. "I just don't get it."

Ashley shook her head, her eyes straight ahead, but her thoughts tumbling, swirling. "Maybe he didn't know what to say. Maybe he thought that if he did it would hurt us too much. So he didn't. But all that did was make it worse. We thought she chose to leave, and that's what made it hurt so much."

She heard Owen shift next to her. "That's not protecting us."

"I know," Ashley whispered, her voice catching in her throat. "I know. But that's what he did."

Owen leaned back into the seat, his arms crossed tightly over his chest. His jaw was set, his gaze fixed on the blur of passing trees, as though the landscape could offer answers neither of them were ready to say aloud.

When they reached the cemetery, the sun had drifted lower, its golden light threading through the trees and pooling in uneven patches across the rows of graves. Ashley pulled the car to a stop, the engine cutting off with a final shudder. The silence that followed was profound, the kind that seemed to wrap around the place itself, broken only by the faint rustle of leaves stirred by a soft breeze.

"Ready?" she asked, her voice barely more than a whisper.

Owen just opened the door. Ashley followed him out.

"It's this way," she said.

She led him around the handful of stones tucked among the trees. The grass was neatly trimmed, an occasional flower planted at the foot of a grave. They walked toward the back, where their mother was buried, where the shadows deeper.

Ashley stopped when she reached the grave, where the headstone rose unassuming from the earth, unadorned but resolute. Her mother's name, into the stone, seemed to catch the fading light, the letters distinct against the muted gray stone.

"I don't even remember her face," Owen said, his voice rough. "Not really. I have some blurry memories, but . . . that's all."

Ashley looked at him, a small ache filling her chest. "I know. You were so young. Just a kid. You wouldn't remember her like I do. I . . . I remember how she'd laugh when she was happy. How she'd put on that old blue dress when we went to the fair. I remember how she'd sit by the window at night and watch the stars, just staring out like she was looking for something."

Owen's gaze drifted, unfocused as if searching for something he might have dropped years ago and no longer knew how to find. The lines of time seemed to cross his face—both the past and the present mingling in a quiet turmoil just beneath his features. "Even if I could picture her clearly," he said, his voice soft, steady with restraint, "I'm not sure I'd want to hold on to those memories."

"Why do you say that?" Ashley asked.

Owen's fingers moved over the headstone with a deliberate slowness that suggested something deeper than mere hesitation. "Memories," he said, "they're like water. Memories are like water, not because they spill away so easily, but because they hold a depth we often forget. It's like the surface of a pond - calm, clear, a perfect reflection - but when we go beneath the surface, we stir things up - silt, lost buttons, the past we thought we had put behind us. It all comes back. We crave for the stillness to return, for that smooth surface, but the past stays with us. It tells us that even the most peaceful memories conceal a living world beneath. Things are always growing, decaying, shifting in ways we can't see. We may never fully understand what's beneath the surface, but we feel it - its presence, its pull. Sometimes it drags us under, leaving us gasping. But other times, we come up with something unexpected - a smooth stone, a piece of colored glass - something we didn't even realize we were looking for. And when we hold it to the light, we understand. The depths, the forgotten fragments, are part of us too. Maybe they always were."

Ashley stepped toward him, her movements unhurried, as if afraid to disturb the delicate quiet between them. Something unspoken lingered in his expression, a sadness so deep it seemed to settle into the folds of his posture, into the way his shoulders curved inward. She could feel it radiating from him, not in words or gestures, but in the stillness that surrounded him as if the world itself had paused to accommodate his grief.

"But there are some memories," he continued, "that aren't meant to be preserved. They're like photographs left too long in sunlight - faded, distorted. Holding them too tightly only makes them more brittle." His eyes, when they met Ashley's, were unexpectedly steady, a quiet intensity burning beneath their surface.

"Sometimes," he said, "forgetting is its own form of mercy."

The words lingered between them, fragile and charged as if spun from the finest glass, poised on the edge of breaking with the slightest touch.

"I know," Ashley said quietly. "Maybe not everything from the past is meant to be remembered."

They stood there, the silence stretching between them like a thread neither dared to cut. The late afternoon carried a quiet chill, the kind that seeped into the edges of things - grass that bent without a breeze, shadows that pooled in the grooves of the headstone. Owen placed his hand on the cool stone. His gaze was unfocused, and distant, searching for something long buried, a memory too elusive to call his own.

After what felt like an eternity, he spoke, his voice with a slight tremble. "Do you think she would've wanted me to know all this?"

Ashley watched him for a moment, her arms crossed against the evening's deepening cool. "I don't know," she said. "I think she would've wanted us to find some kind of peace. But I also think she'd have wanted you to know the truth."

They stood there for a while longer, the day stretching out in front of them. The sun was much closer to the horizon now. Soon it would be gone and the sky above the cemetery would turn to a deep, dusky blue.

Ashley turned to leave. "It's getting late. We should head back."

Owen nodded, and they walked back to the car. As they drove away from the cemetery, the road felt longer, the night settling in with its own kind of heaviness.

The silence between them stretched on until Ashley was finally ready to answer his question. She took a breath. "You asked me about why I left."

He looked over at her, his face weary. "I did. But I guess it doesn't matter now."

"No, it does," she insisted. "No more secrets. When I left . . . when I left Stillwater, I wasn't just running away from everything. There was something . . . something that happened."

Owen raised an eyebrow. "What?"

"I kissed a girl in high school," Ashley said, the words feeling strange on her tongue. "I knew what I was doing. I kissed her and she kissed me back. I didn't tell anyone. But some other kids must've seen it and told on us. Dad found out, and he got so angry. He couldn't understand. He yelled at me, and said it wasn't natural. And I yelled back and said some things I . . . well . . . things I now regret. He told me I wasn't welcome here anymore. So, I packed up and I left. I took the bus to New York City. I started over."

She kept her eyes on the road, not looking at Owen.

"He never told me any of this," Owen said softly. "Only said you two had an argument and you left."

"I know," Ashley replied.

10 The Decision

The road between Silver Birch and Stillwater had a peculiar way of stirring old memories, like the miles themselves knew the stories they had once held and were eager to share them with anyone paying attention. Owen sat beside her, silent, his arm resting against the car door. She looked at him briefly, wondering how much he truly understood about the decisions she had made.

She adjusted her grip on the wheel. "I've been thinking about Dad. About why I left." She paused, drawing in a deep breath that seemed to draw the air from the car around them. "I wasn't ready to talk about it before, but I think I need to now. It all began in my junior year of high school. I was sixteen."

Ashley told Owen about the unusual warmth of the day, a surprise for early spring. The school principal had called their father in for a meeting, something she hadn't been told about. When she came home, she could feel the tension in the air. Their father's anger hung between them, and she was certain he knew what had happened at school. It was in the way he turned his face away, the way the room held its breath when she walked in. There were no words at first, but everything was clear.

"I got a call today," he said, his voice measured but brittle. He didn't sit, just stood in the doorway to the living room where Ashley had been doing her homework. "The principal says you were caught kissing another girl behind the gym."

Ashley froze, her pencil hovering above her notebook. She tried to gauge whether this was anger, confusion, or something worse. "Dad -"

His voice cracked like a whip, cutting her off. "Is it true?"

She nodded, knowing there was no point in denying it. "Yes," she said, her voice trembling. "But it's not what you think."

"Oh, it's exactly what I think." His words were sharp, leaving no room for argument. "What were you thinking, Ashley? Do you know what people are going to say about this family? About me?"

She looked up at him, her heart pounding. "I wasn't thinking about what other people would say," she shot back, the tremor in her voice replaced by something stronger, something defiant. "I was just -"

"You were just what?" he interrupted again. "Throwing everything away? Ruining your future?"

"I'm not ruining anything," she said, standing now, her own anger rising to meet his. "I kissed someone. That's all. Why does it have to be this big, awful thing?"

"Because it is!" His voice filled the small room. "Because it's not normal, Ashley. It's not right."

She felt like the ground beneath her was crumbling, every word he said tearing away at something she'd only just discovered about herself. "You don't get to decide what's right for me," she said, her voice shaking with emotion. "You're not even trying to understand."

"I understand plenty," he said, his tone icy now. "You think the world is going to accept this? Do you think people won't judge you? You're my daughter, and I'm telling you, this isn't the life you're supposed to have."

Ashley stared at him, her vision blurring with tears she refused to let fall. "Maybe it's exactly the life I'm supposed to have."

They stood there not saying a word, his anger boiling. Finally, he turned away, shaking his head. "I don't even know who you are anymore," he scoffed, and then he was gone, leaving Ashley alone in the living room, her world forever changed.

Ashley could still hear her father's voice, sharp and unrelenting. Even now, years later, it seemed to ripple through her, a sound that had never fully settled. She swallowed hard, her throat tightening against the memory. Owen deserved to know, even if it meant unearthing something she'd spent so long trying to bury.

"That was the moment I knew I couldn't stay," she said, her voice catching before she steadied it. "Not in that house, not with him. I felt like I didn't belong there anymore."

She glanced at Owen, bracing herself. What would he say? Would he leap to their father's defense, or simply stay silent, detached, and indifferent?

"I didn't know he was like that," Owen said. "I mean, I guess I was too young to see it."

Ashley studied him for a moment, her little brother grown now, his face lined with traces of thoughtfulness that hadn't been there before. She let out a long breath, the kind that felt like shedding a layer of armor.

"He wasn't always like that," she said, her gaze drifting back to the road. The rolling hills in the distance blurred together, a backdrop for thoughts she rarely shared. "Things changed when he lost Mom. I think he loved us - maybe not in the way we wanted, but in the way he could. But there were things he just couldn't accept. And for me, that was too much to live with."

The car filled with the quiet rhythm of tires rolling over asphalt, a sound that seemed louder in the absence of conversation. For a moment, Ashley wondered if she'd gone too far, if she'd asked Owen to carry more than he was ready for. Then he spoke again, his voice careful, almost as if testing the air.

"I know he regretted it," Owen said, his eyes flicking toward her before darting back to the window.

Ashley's hands shifted slightly on the steering wheel. "You think so?" she asked after a pause, her voice thoughtful, distant. "He could be so stubborn. Once he made up his mind about something, it was like moving a mountain to change it. Miriam told me he often spoke about me. He told her that he believed in me and that he loved me. And I found things - birthday cards, letters, postcards he wrote to me but never sent. I think . . . I think he didn't know how to fix things."

"I don't remember much," he admitted. "But I do remember him yelling. I remember thinking if I just stayed small, stayed out of the way, maybe I wouldn't make it worse."

Ashley's felt a knot of guilt and grief tangling inside of her. The image of her brother as a child, trying to shrink himself into invisibility, hit her with a force she hadn't expected. "I'm sorry," she said, her voice thick. "There were times I wished I had taken you with me. I really did. But I didn't know how."

Owen looked at her then, his expression softening into something so vulnerable it reminded her of the boy he had been. "You were just a kid yourself," he said quietly.

His words settled over her gently, like a hand on her shoulder, easing a burden she hadn't realized she was still carrying. She nodded, blinking against the sting in her eyes. Outside, the sun was dipping lower, casting the hills in deep, burnished hues of gold and pink, a reminder that time was always moving forward, even when the past pulled at her.

"Leaving was the hardest thing I ever did," she said after a long silence. "But staying . . . staying would've been impossible. I think I would've lost myself if I'd stayed."

Owen reached across the console, his hand brushing hers for just a moment before retreating. It wasn't much, but it was enough.

"You did what you had to do," he said.

Ashley remembered the night she left. The house felt still, an unusual kind of stillness that seemed to press in from every corner. She waited for the light in the hallway to go out, for the soft click of her father's door to close behind him. The sound of his steady breathing assured her he was asleep. She packed quickly, stuffing clothes into a duffel bag and grabbing the small stash of cash she'd hidden away in a shoebox under her bed. It wasn't much - just the money from her allowance, earned by helping at the shop - but it would be enough for a bus ticket, a few meals, and maybe a few nights at a cheap hotel.

She paused in the doorway of her room, looking back at the life she was about to leave behind. The faded posters on the walls, the stack of books by her bed, the quilt her grandmother had made for her when she was little. It all felt like someone else's life now, like she'd already become a stranger to the girl who had lived here. She crept down the stairs and stepped out through the back door of the store, pausing to ensure it was locked before she closed it gently behind her.

The walk to Hudson Falls seemed endless beneath the wide, star-filled sky. The quiet of the night pressed in around her, and the road ahead seemed longer than it ever had before. When she reached the Greyhound station, it appeared almost abandoned, the dim glow of overhead fluorescent lights casting a sterile light across the empty space. With her duffel bag slung over one shoulder, she moved to the counter and purchased a ticket to New York City, the furthest place she could bring herself to consider. She sat down in a hard plastic chair by the window, watching the headlights of passing cars blur across the glass.

"I didn't have a plan," Ashley confided to Owen. "I just knew I couldn't stay. New York City felt vast enough that maybe I could lose myself there and start fresh."

Owen leaned back in his seat, absorbing her words. "Weren't you scared?" he asked.

"Terrified," Ashley admitted, her voice barely above a whisper. "But that fear was what kept me moving forward. If I'd paused to think about what I was doing for even a moment, I probably would've turned back."

The bus ride stretched on endlessly, filled with the low hum of the engine and the soft murmur of other passengers - a constant backdrop to her racing thoughts. By the time she stepped off the bus in New York City, dawn was breaking, casting a soft glow over the skyline that felt both exhilarating and alien.

The city pulsed with a restless rhythm of movement and noise, unlike the quiet predictability of Stillwater. Car horns blared, brakes hissed, and voices rose and fell like a symphony out of sync. She gripped the strap of her duffel bag, her fingers tightening as if the bag held not just her belongings but the last pieces of her identity. At seventeen, she was officially a runaway, and New York City was her escape route. Yet, standing there, the sheer enormity of it all bore down on her, and for a brief moment, she wondered if she'd made a terrible mistake.

The terminal smelled of diesel fuel and spilled coffee, mingled with something metallic she couldn't place. Ashley stood frozen, trying to decide where to go next. People moved around her in every direction, pulling suitcases, shouting at each other, or staring straight ahead as though nothing could break their stride. She had spent her life in a town where she knew the names of everyone, and now she was surrounded by strangers who didn't seem to notice or care that she existed. It was terrifying, but also strangely liberating. No one here knew her, and no one would be calling her father.

With no destination in mind, Ashley walked through the terminal and out onto the street. The city stretched out before her, glittering and grimy all at once. She saw a man hailing a cab with an elegance that seemed theatrical, a woman sitting cross-legged on the sidewalk selling knockoff purses, and a child holding tight to his mother's hand as they weaved through the crowd. The world was both bigger and smaller than she'd imagined, and she wasn't sure how to fit into it.

That first day, she walked and walked, and by the time the sun began to set, her feet ached and her stomach twisted with hunger. The few dollars in her pocket weren't enough for much, and she couldn't bring herself to spend them on something as fleeting as food. She'd have to find somewhere to sleep, and it wasn't going to be anywhere safe or comfortable. Her search led her to a pay-by-the-hour motel tucked into a row of aging storefronts. The neon sign above the door buzzed faintly, casting a flickering glow onto the cracked pavement below.

Inside, the clerk barely glanced up when she slid the cash across the counter. He handed her a key without a word, and she took it, her fingers brushing against the cold metal. The room was everything she had expected - dim, with a sagging bed in the center, the carpet stained in places, and the bathroom harboring the unmistakable scent of mildew. She stepped inside and locked the door behind her, sliding the deadbolt into place. The sound of it seemed to seal her in, marking the moment she was alone.

Ashley sat on the edge of the bed, staring at the peeling wallpaper. She wanted to cry but felt as though the tears were stuck somewhere deep inside her, refusing to come out. Instead, she lay down fully dressed, her duffel bag pressed to her chest like a lifeline. Fear and doubt crept in as the hours ticked by. What if she couldn't make it here? What if this was the best her life was ever going to be?

She closed her eyes and whispered a promise to herself, the words so quiet they barely filled the space between her and the ceiling. "You'll figure it out. You don't have a choice." And even though her voice trembled, she clung to the vow as tightly as she held her bag, willing herself to believe it.

"Thinking back on it, I don't know how I managed," she told Owen with a hint of pride. "I got a job as a waitress. The pay was terrible. But eventually, when I had enough money, I rented a small room in a shared apartment with three other girls I barely knew. It was cramped and chaotic, but it felt like an escape." She smiled softly at the thought. "I worked double shifts, juggling plates and coffee cups, saving every penny I could find. It wasn't easy, but there was something exhilarating about it. It felt like freedom.

"I applied to colleges once I'd saved up enough for the first semester. I took classes during the day and worked at night. It was exhausting, but I loved it. For the first time, I felt like I was building something for myself."

Ashley leaned back slightly, her gaze drifting to the window as if the miles rolling past outside mirrored the years she was recounting. "But there were nights when I thought I wouldn't make it," she said. "I'd come home after a double shift, my feet aching and my hands smelling of dish soap. I'd sit at that tiny desk crammed in the corner of my room, trying to keep my eyes open long enough to finish a paper or read a chapter. I wasn't always sure what I was chasing, but I knew I couldn't stop. And then, it was off to classes."

Owen was silent, absorbing her words, his eyes fixed on her. The look in his eyes was unmistakable - one of admiration, maybe something deeper, something that made her feel as if the moment stretched on between them. "I don't know if I could've done what you did," he said.

Ashley laughed, but it wasn't entirely out of humor. "It's called survival," she admitted. "The city was overwhelming, and I was just a kid trying to survive. I made mistakes - plenty of them. There were nights when I walked home alone after a late shift, clutching my pepper spray and praying I'd get there safely. And there were times when I wondered if Dad was right - if there was something wrong with me."

Her voice softened, almost imperceptibly. "But then, something would happen - a professor would praise my work, or I'd get a slightly bigger tip than usual, or I'd laugh with my roommates about something ridiculous. Those moments reminded me why I was doing it. They made me believe I could. Especially when I met Laura."

Owen leaned forward slightly, his voice tentative. "Girlfriend?"

Ashley's smiled, a lightness entering her expression that hadn't been there before. "I met her my second year of college," she told Owen. "She was sitting in the campus library, scribbling furiously in her notebook. I don't know what made me stop, but I did. I must've looked like a fool, standing there staring at her. But then she looked up and smiled, and that was it for me. She was magnetic, smart, kind, and a little sarcastic."

"She helped you?" Owen asked with a hint of hopefulness in his voice.

"More than she'll ever know," Ashley replied. "Laura reminded me that it wasn't just about survival - it was about living. And for the first time, I started to imagine a future that felt like mine."

Ashley paused, her hands resting lightly on the wheel as she glanced at Owen. "I don't regret leaving," she said. "It was the hardest thing I've ever done, the best decision I've ever made."

Owen nodded, his expression thoughtful. "You're brave, Ashley," he said simply.

"I don't know about brave," she replied, her voice just above a whisper. "Maybe just desperate. But sometimes, I think those two things aren't so different."

Ashley remembered her determination as she scoured every scholarship listing, her fingers flying over the keyboard late into the night. The glow of her laptop screen illuminated her face, casting shadows that danced across the walls of her cramped room. Each application felt like a lifeline thrown into an uncertain future, a chance to grasp something more than just survival.

When the letter arrived, its crisp envelope embossed with the university seal, it felt like a talisman in her trembling hands. She stood in the dingy hallway of her shared apartment, the peeling wallpaper and scuffed baseboards a reminder of how far she'd come and how far she still had to go. Her heart thundered in her chest as she tore open the envelope, afraid to hope yet unable to stop herself. The words swam before her eyes as she read them once, twice, three times, tears blurring her vision until the letter became a watery smear of possibility. The scholarship was hers - a full ride to finish her degree. In that moment, the years of double shifts that left her feet aching and her mind numb, the sleepless nights spent hunched over textbooks, all crystallized into something tangible, a hard-won trophy for her relentless pursuit of a better life.

Marketing became her passion, a field where her hard-won street smarts merged seamlessly with academic theory. She devoured case studies and consumer behavior models with a voracious hunger. In each lecture and textbook, she saw echoes of the city that had both challenged and shaped her - the subtle psychology of subway advertisements, the carefully crafted personas of street vendors, and the complex dance of supply and demand that played out in corner bodegas. Each class felt like a step closer to a future she was finally allowing herself to imagine, one where she wasn't just surviving, but thriving.

Laura's own scholarship news came just weeks later, her excited voice carrying through the phone as Ashley pressed it tightly to her ear as if she could pull Laura through the connection and into her arms. "I got it!" Laura exclaimed, her joy as infectious as her laugh. "And there's a position open at the campus library. It's perfect!" Ashley closed her eyes, savoring the moment, feeling the pieces of their shared dream falling into place like a long-awaited puzzle finally solved.

They moved in together, their tiny apartment a third-floor walk-up, barely large enough for a bed and a desk, with a kitchenette so small they had to take turns standing in it. But as they lugged boxes up the narrow staircase, giggling and breathless, it felt like a palace. Ashley paused in the doorway, watching as Laura hung a string of fairy lights along the window frame, her tongue caught between her teeth in concentration. The soft glow transformed the bare room, casting everything in a warm, hopeful light that seemed to push back the shadows of their past struggles.

"What do you think?" Laura asked, turning to Ashley with a smile that still made her heart skip, even after all this time.

Ashley crossed the room, wrapping her arms around Laura's waist, breathing in the familiar scent of her shampoo and the faint trace of library dust that always clung to her clothes. "I think," she said, resting her forehead against Laura's, "that this is the beginning of something amazing."

As they stood there, bathed in the gentle light of their new home, Ashley felt a sense of peace settle over her like a warm blanket. The road ahead was still uncertain, filled with challenges yet to come. For the first time since that night she had stepped off the bus - a scared seventeen-year-old with nothing more than a duffel bag and a pocketful of dreams - she felt an undeniable sense of belonging. It wasn't a sudden realization, but rather a quiet certainty that had been building over time, like layers of sediment settling until the ground beneath her was firm and sure.

Owen turned to her, his eyes a mirror of their father's, curious and tentative. The years of separation hung between them, a flimsy curtain slowly being drawn aside. "Are you still with Laura?" he asked, his voice barely above a whisper as if he feared the question might shatter the delicate rapport they'd built over the past few hours.

Ashley's smile carried the quiet ease of someone accustomed to happiness, not the fleeting kind but the sort that settles in over the years. It was a reflection of shared triumphs, of enduring the hard edges of life until they softened, and of finding peace in the unspoken. "Yes," she said simply, her gaze steady on the road, though her thoughts seemed elsewhere, tracing the contours of a well-tended past. "We're still together. She earned her degree in Library Science and works at the New York Public Library on Fifth Avenue. She loves books, always has."

She paused, a small chuckle escaping her lips. "Of course, we don't live in that one-room apartment anymore. We've got a place in Brooklyn now, with actual rooms and everything. Even a room with all of Laura's books. You should see it, Owen. It's got these big windows that let in the most amazing light, and there's a little balcony where we grow herbs and flowers. It's not much, but it's ours."

Owen's face softened. "That's . . . that's really great, Ashley," he said, his voice carrying a note of admiration that surprised them both. "I'm glad you found someone who makes you happy."

Ashley glanced at him, her smile widening into something brighter, more reminiscent of the girl she'd once been. For a moment, the years fell away, and they were just a brother and sister sharing a moment of connection. "Me too, Owen," she said, her voice thick with emotion. "Me too."

As they continued down the road, the quiet between them had shifted. It was no longer burdened with unspoken words but carried a sense of something new, something hopeful. The path ahead stretched out in front of them, bathed in the soft glow of possibility, like the delicate string of fairy lights they had once strung up in that small New York City apartment, years ago.

11 The Work

The sun dipped toward the horizon, casting orange and pink across the sky. Ashley drove past the "Welcome to Stillwater" sign, the town unfolding like a memory just out of reach. The streets held onto their old shapes, yet something about them felt distant, rearranged by time. She glanced at Owen, his gaze steady on the passing buildings, taking it all in without a word.

"Strange, isn't it," she said softly. "Coming back here after so long. Everything looks the same until you realize it isn't."

Owen nodded, his gaze still on the window. "Yeah," he replied. "Strange works."

They drove past the old high school, its brick facade a stark reminder of shared memories and diverging paths. Ashley's fingers tightened on the steering wheel as they approached the turn that would take them to the shop.

"Hey," Owen said suddenly, turning to face her. "You hungry? We could stop at the diner before heading home. If that's alright with you."

"The diner," she repeated, a small smile tugging at her lips. "Yeah. Good idea."

She made a left turn instead of a right, heading towards the center of town. The streets were quiet as most of the shops had started to close for the evening. As they rounded the corner, the neon sign of the diner came into view with its cheerful glow.

"Well, I'll be damned," Ashley muttered as she pulled over. "Is that Dottie? Still there?"

Owen smiled. "It is her place."

As they stepped out of the car, the smell of coffee and grilled onions wafted towards them, achingly familiar.

They paused at the entrance, both seemingly reluctant to be the first to push open the door. Finally, Ashley reached for the handle. The bell above the door chimed as they entered.

The few patrons that were there looked up as they entered, curiosity evident in their gazes. Ashley felt exposed suddenly, acutely aware of how much she had changed, feeling as if she almost belonged here – in Stillwater.

"Nice to see you again."

The voice cut through Ashley's thoughts, and she turned to see a Dottie approaching, a coffee pot in one hand and a look of delighted surprise on her face.

"You're always here," Ashley said.

Dottie laughed, the sound warm and familiar. "Where else would I be, honey? Someone's got to keep this place running." She turned to Owen, her smile widening. "And Owen. My goodness, look at you two."

Owen nodded, a small smile playing at the corners of his mouth. "Hey, Dottie."

"Well, don't just stand there," Dottie said, gesturing towards an empty booth. "Sit down, sit down. It's nice to see the Keller children together. I'll get you some menus and water."

They eased into the booth, the vinyl seat cool beneath them. Dottie was already there, setting down menus and two glasses of water, her eyes darting between them with barely concealed curiosity.

"So, how'd the day go?" Dottie asked.

"Eye-opening," Ashley replied.

She and Owen exchanged a glance with a smile.

"Well," she said, "that sounds like an interesting day. How about I get you two some coffee while you look over the menu?"

As Dottie bustled away, Ashley and Owen fell into silence, both pretending to study the laminated menus. Ashley's eyes skimmed over the familiar items - the Blue Plate Special, the Trucker's Breakfast, the Mile-High Apple Pie - but her mind was elsewhere, grappling with the reality of everything that had been said.

"So, what about us?" Owen asked, his voice barely above a whisper.

Before Ashley could respond, Dottie returned with their coffee. "Here you go," she said, setting down the cups. "You two ready to order?"

Ashley and Owen ordered - a burger for Owen and a chicken salad for Ashley. They handed back the menus.

As Dottie walked away, Ashley took a sip of her coffee, using the moment to gather her thoughts. She reached across the table, her hand finding his. "We learned a lot," she said, her voice quiet but firm. "About about Mom, about Dad. But mostly," she paused, squeezing his hand gently, "mostly, we learned that the past is just that. It's behind us, Owen. It doesn't define us. It can't touch us anymore." She wasn't sure if she believed it, not entirely. But it felt true, in this moment, sitting across from her brother in the warm, familiar glow of the diner, the smell of coffee and frying bacon filling the air. It felt like a place to start.

Owen smiled, a small, tentative thing, and gave a nod. He withdrew his hand, taking both hands now and wrapping them around his coffee mug. "You know, when you think about it, Dad never stopped hoping you'd come back," he said. "He kept your room exactly the same, you know."

Ashley felt tears prick at the corners of her eyes. "I know. I saw it when I got here," she murmured.

They lapsed into silence again, the hum of the diner's other patrons and the clatter of dishes from the kitchen filling the space between them. Ashley found herself studying Owen's face, noting the changes time had wrought. The round-cheeked boy she remembered had been replaced by a man with sharp cheekbones and a dusting of stubble.

"I'm sorry I left you to deal with everything on your own," she told him. "It wasn't fair."

Owen looked up. For a moment, Ashley thought he might brush off her apology, and retreat behind the wall of hurt and resentment.

"No," he agreed. "It wasn't fair. I didn't understand it back then. But . . . I get it now . . . why you did it."

"I want to make it right," she said. "I know I can't undo the past sixteen years, but I want to try to be a better sister. If . . . if you'll let me."

Owen was quiet for a long moment, his gaze fixed on his coffee cup. When he looked up, there was a vulnerability in his eyes that made him look suddenly young. "I'd like that," he said softly.

Just then, Dottie arrived with their food, setting the plates down with a flourish. "Here you go," she said. "Anything else I can get you two?"

Ashley and Owen shook their heads, murmuring their thanks. As Dottie walked away, Ashley picked up her fork, suddenly realizing how hungry she was.

They ate in silence for a while, the familiar tastes of diner food bringing back a flood of memories. Ashley felt her shoulders loosen, the stiffness that had gripped them since her arrival at Stillwater slowly unwinding.

"So," Owen said between bites of his burger, "tell me about New York City. What's it like?"

Ashley smiled. "It's . . . intense," she said. "Exciting and exhausting and overwhelming, all at once. There's always something happening, always somewhere to be or something to do."

"Sounds completely different from Stillwater," Owen commented, a hint of wistfulness in his voice.

Ashley nodded. "It is. But deep down, I think, I miss this," she gestured around the diner. "The quiet, the familiarity. In New York City, everything's always changing. Here, it's like time stands still."

Owen chuckled. "Trust me, it doesn't. Things change here too, just slower, I guess."

As they continued to eat, the conversation flowed. Owen told her about his job at the hardware store, about the house he'd bought on the outskirts of town, a modest structure that seemed to hold more promise than its weathered exterior suggested. There was something in the way he talked about these mundane details that revealed more about him than any direct confession: a careful man, methodical, who found comfort in structure and routine.

Ashley watched him, curiosity threading through her thoughts. She wondered whether his world stretched beyond the hardware store, beyond their father's quiet expectations. Before she could stop herself, the question left her mouth, a gentle probe into the geography of his personal life. "Got a girl?"

He shook his head accompanied by a rueful smile. "Between the hardware store and helping Dad, there was never the time."

The conversation shifted then, as conversations between siblings often do, with a natural, unspoken choreography. "Tell me about how you made it," Owen said, his eyes meeting hers with a mixture of curiosity and something deeper - a tentative hope for reconnection. "About your job and everything."

"You know," she began, her voice soft against the hum of the engine, "I never thought I'd make it in New York City. Not really. Even after I got into college, even after I started doing well in my classes, there was always this voice in the back of my head telling me I was just playing pretend."

Owen turned to look at her, his expression a bit of curiosity and something else - regret, perhaps, or a dawning understanding. "But you did make it," he said, his words more a statement than a question.

Ashley nodded, a small smile playing at the corners of her mouth. "I did. But it wasn't easy. God, it wasn't easy."

She thought back to her senior year of college, to the endless nights scouring job boards on campus for any opportunity that might give her a foothold in the industry. The rejections had piled up, each one a paper cut to her confidence, but she'd persevered.

"I must've applied to fifty different internships in my last year of college," she said, shaking her head at the memory. "Maybe more. I got so many rejections I could've wallpapered my dorm room with them. But then, finally, I got a bite."

The memory of that day was still vivid in her mind. She'd been sitting in the campus coffee shop, nursing a lukewarm latte and trying to muster the energy to start another cover letter, when the letter had come through. She'd almost missed it, buried as it was among a flood of other letters and ads. But it was an offer for an interview at a small but well-respected ad agency in the heart of Manhattan.

"It was this tiny boutique agency," Ashley explained, her eyes bright with the recollection. "They specialized in fashion and lifestyle brands. I remember walking into their office for the interview - it was this converted loft space, all exposed brick, and huge windows. I felt so out of place like everyone could see right through me to the small-town girl underneath."

Owen listened intently, his earlier hostility softening into genuine interest. "But they gave you the internship, right?"

Ashley laughed, a sound tinged with both pride and self-deprecation. "They did, though I'm still not entirely sure why. I think maybe they saw how hungry I was, how desperate I was to prove myself. The internship was grueling. I worked harder than I'd ever worked in my life, often staying at the office long after everyone else had gone home. I fetched coffee and made copies, sure, but I also threw myself into every task I was given, no matter how small or seemingly insignificant.

"I was determined to learn everything I could," she said, her voice taking on a fiercer tone. "I watched how the account managers talked to clients, how the creatives brainstormed ideas. I volunteered for every project, even if it meant working through the night. I think I survived on coffee and sheer determination that whole summer.

"My dedication didn't go unnoticed. By the end of the internship, I was allowed to contribute to a small campaign for an up-and-coming jewelry designer. It wasn't much - just a series of social media posts - but seeing my ideas come to life, seeing real people engage with something I'd help create, was so intoxicating.

"That was when I knew," Ashley said, her voice soft with the weight of the memory, "when I knew this was what I wanted to do with my life."

"Did you stay with that agency?" Owen asked.

Ashley shook her head. "No, they couldn't offer me a full-time position after graduation. But I got some great experience and went about building my portfolio, and they gave me something almost as valuable - a glowing recommendation and a list of contacts in the industry. I went about leveraging those contacts ruthlessly in the months following graduation, reaching out to everyone she could, attending industry events, and constantly refining my portfolio. It was a nerve-wracking time, filled with uncertainty and more than a few moments of doubt. But then, just as my savings were running dangerously low, I got the call."

"From who?" Owen asked.

"A big marketing firm," Ashley explained, her excitement at the memory bleeding into her voice. "They told me they had a junior position open in their creative department. The interview process was intense - multiple rounds, a practical test, the works. But I gave it everything I had. I stood in front of a panel of executives, my hands shaking slightly as I presented my ideas for a hypothetical campaign. I was terrified, but I channeled that fear into passion, letting my enthusiasm for the work shine through.

"When they offered me the job, I could hardly believe it," Ashley said, a hint of wonder still present in her voice even after all these years. "It felt like everything I'd worked for was finally paying off. The job was challenging from the start. I found myself surrounded by people who seemed to know so much more than I did, who moved through the world of marketing and advertising with an ease I envied. But I was determined not to let my insecurities hold her back.

"I asked questions constantly," she said, a rueful smile playing on her lips. "I'm sure I annoyed the hell out of some of my coworkers, but I didn't care. I was there to learn, to grow, to become the best I could be. My dedication paid off. Within a year, I was given more responsibility, and trusted with larger accounts and more complex campaigns. My ideas, once dismissed as too risky or unconventional, began to gain traction. I remember the first time one of my concepts was chosen for a major campaign. It was for this global fashion brand - you'd know the name if I said it. They were looking to rebrand, to appeal to a younger, more diverse audience.

"I threw myself into the project, spending countless hours researching trends, analyzing data, and brainstorming ideas. The concept I came up with was been bold, a departure from the brand's traditional image, but I believed in it fiercely. When I presented it to the client, I was terrified. "I kept thinking they were going to laugh me out of the room. But they loved it. They actually loved it. The campaign was a massive success, earning industry accolades and significantly boosting the brand's sales. It was my first real taste of success in the industry, and it was unbelievable. Seeing my work out there in the world - on billboards, in magazines, all over social media was surreal. I kept wanting to stop people on the street and say, 'Hey, I did that!'"

Owen chuckled. "I bet you did, too."

Ashley laughed. "I restrained myself. Mostly."

As they ate, Ashley continued to recount her rise through the ranks of the marketing world. She told Owen about the late nights and early mornings, the triumphs and the setbacks. She spoke of the mentors who had guided her, the colleagues who had become friends, and the competitors who had pushed her to be better.

"It wasn't all glamour and success," she told him, her voice taking on a more somber tone. "There were times when I doubted myself, when I wondered if I was cut out for this world. Times when I missed home so much it felt like a physical ache."

Owen's expression softened at this. "Why didn't you ever come back?" he asked gently.

Ashley was quiet for a moment. "I wanted to, sometimes," she said finally. "But I was afraid. Afraid that if I came back, even for a visit, I'd lose my momentum. That I'd get pulled back into the life I'd left behind."

She paused, her eyes fixed on his. "And I guess . . . I guess I was afraid of facing everyone. Of facing Dad."

Owen nodded, his eyes catching hers. "I get it," he said softly.

"You know, for all the stress and the long hours, I really do love what I do," she said steering the conversation to safer ground.

"There's something incredible about taking an idea, a concept, and turning it into something real. Something that can change how people think or feel."

She told Owen about some of her favorite projects over the years - the public health campaign that had helped increase vaccination rates in underserved communities, the ad series that had challenged gender stereotypes in children's toys, the rebranding effort that had saved a struggling local business.

"It's not always about selling products," she explained, her passion evident in every word. "Sometimes it's about changing perceptions, about making people see the world in a different way."

"I never really understood marketing," he admitted. "I always just thought of it as . . . I don't know, making ads. But it's more than that, isn't it?"

Ashley nodded, a warm smile spreading across her face. "It is. At its best, it's about communication, about connecting with people on a deeper level. It's about telling stories that resonate, that make people feel something."

She thought about the campaigns she was working on now, the ideas that were still taking shape in her mind. Even after all these years, the work still excited her, still challenged her in ways she never could have imagined when she first left Stillwater.

"I'm not saying it's always perfect," she said, her tone becoming more reflective. "There are aspects of the industry that I struggle with, ethical considerations that keep me up at night sometimes. But I believe in the power of communication, in the potential for marketing to be a force for good in the world."

Owen nodded, his expression thoughtful. "I can see why you love it," he said. "It suits you, you know? You're good at getting people to see things your way."

Ashley laughed, a bright, genuine sound that seemed to lighten the atmosphere in the car. "I'll take that as a compliment," she said, shooting him a playful glance.

Dottie approached with the check. "You two need anything else?" she asked, her eyes dancing between Ashley and Owen.

They shook their heads in unison, a synchronicity that surprised them both. Dottie gave a warm smile, the kind that comes from decades of watching people's stories unfold. "Good to see you both, together," she said.

Ashley reached for the check and placed a few bills down. The movement felt almost ceremonial.

A sense of lightness bloomed inside her, unexpected and delicate as a first spring flower. The weight she'd carried - sixteen years of silence, of separation, of unspoken pain - seemed to dissolve. Sharing her journey with Owen, watching understanding dawn in his eyes, feeling the first tentative threads of reconnection weave between them, had lifted something profound. The burden she'd grown so accustomed to that she'd forgotten its presence was now simply . . . gone.

"You know," Owen said as they left the diner, "I'm proud of you, Ashley. I am. What you've accomplished . . . it's pretty amazing."

Ashley felt a lump form in her throat, emotion threatening to overwhelm her. "Thank you," she managed, her voice thick. "That means more than you know."

"Do you want me to drive you home?" she asked.

"No," he replied, a smile breaking across his face. "It's a beautiful night. I think I'll walk."

Just as she was about to turn and walk to the car, he reached out, pulling her into a warm embrace. "We'll talk more," he promised, his voice low and earnest.

"I'd like that," she replied, her heart fluttering at the thought.

Ashley felt a sense of possibility she hadn't expected. The road that had led her away from Stillwater had been long and winding, filled with challenges and triumphs alike. But now, reconnecting with her brother, she realized that perhaps it had also led her back - not to the place she'd left, but to a new understanding, a chance to bridge the gap between her past and her present.

"Good night," Owen said softly.

Ashley nodded, taking a deep breath. "Good night," she said.

Watching him walk away realized it was time to start a new chapter - one that could perhaps bring together all the different parts of herself, bridging the gap between the girl who had left Stillwater and the woman who had returned.

With one last glance at Owen, she opened the car door and drove down the street toward the shop.

12 The Dreams

Ashley ascended the narrow wooden staircase, her fingertips gliding along the banister's softened surface. The wood held onto its history, shaped by the touch of countless hands - her family's, and those that came before them. She imagined the years pressed into its grain, a silent conversation between time and the objects it left behind.

The staircase creaked its familiar song, a melody of age and use that Ashley had long since memorized. She knew which steps to avoid to minimize noise, a habit born from late nights and early mornings when silence was a currency as valuable as the vintage treasures below. Tonight, however, stealth seemed an unnecessary luxury against the leaden weight of her fatigue.

At the top landing, she paused, her hand resting on the tarnished doorknob. The moment stretched, filled with the soft whisper of her breath and the muffled sounds of Stillwater settling into evening beyond the walls. Ashley closed her eyes briefly, gathering herself before opening the door.

She didn't bother with the light switch, letting the amber glow from the streetlamps seep into the room, painting it in soft sepia tones. The light filtered through the delicate weave of the gossamer curtains, casting shadows that stretched across the walls like something hesitant yet deliberate as if they were reaching for her with spectral fingers but unsure of their purpose.

The bed beckoned, an island of promised respite in a sea of antique furniture and faded memories. Ashley crossed the room and flopped onto the bed, her boots still on. As she sank into the mattress, the springs protested softly, as if sharing in her weariness. The cool air of the room kissed her skin. Her eyes closed, shutters against the world, and she felt herself begin to drift.

Sleep arrived quickly, pulling her under, a gentle wave that carried her into its embrace. As her awareness faded, Ashley's mind bloomed, unfurling like a flower touched by the cool night air. In this space between wakefulness and slumber, she wandered through cities of gleaming towers and crowded streets, so different from the quiet, familiar lanes of Stillwater. In this dreamlike state, she moved freely, without the weight of the expectations and unspoken obligations that defined her waking life.

As the night deepened, Ashley's breath slowed, the steady rise and fall of her chest a quiet counterpoint to the silence around her. She moved through memories - shards of moments long past, some vivid and others fading like old photographs, each one a thread in the fabric of her life. The images surfaced one by one, untethered yet familiar, tracing the contours of years she had long since left behind. They were not loud or demanding, but soft, gentle echoes of a time that had shaped her. Each one settled into her mind like a quiet visitor, leaving behind traces of who she had once been.

Ashley stood there, behind the gym, and watched Sarah, her heart thudding in her chest. Sarah was nervous, Ashley could tell. The way she fidgeted with the hem of her t-shirt, the way her eyes flickered back and forth like she wasn't sure whether to look at Ashley or the ground.

"I don't know, Ash," Sarah said, her voice tight, but the corners of her mouth lifted just a little. "I'm not sure we should do this."

"You're just saying that," Ashley said, almost teasing, "but you don't look like you mean it."

Sarah shrugged, but there was a nervous energy to the gesture. "I don't know," she repeated, glancing sideways. "This isn't . . . this isn't what we're supposed to do, right?"

Ashley took a step closer, her pulse racing. "Why not?" she asked. "Is it so wrong?"

Sarah's gaze dropped to the ground like she was trying to figure something out, or maybe she just didn't know how to answer. When she looked back up, her lips parted for a second like she was going to say something, but she didn't.

"Don't think. Just . . . do it," Ashley said, her voice steady in a way that surprised even her. It was the kind of confidence that only comes when you've already made up your mind. Her hand moved almost instinctively to Sarah's shoulder, resting there for a brief moment, feeling the warmth of her skin through the soft fabric of her shirt.

Sarah didn't pull away. She blinked, a quick, startled motion, and her chest rose with a long, shaky breath. The air between them thickened, heavy with what neither of them could yet say. Sarah's lips parted, but before she could speak, Ashley leaned in, her breath mingling with Sarah's in the space that felt too small for words.

Their lips met, tentative at first as if they were both testing the waters, unsure of how to navigate this new territory. But then, slowly, it deepened, a quiet urgency taking over. Ashley tasted the sweetness of Sarah's cherry lip gloss, felt the smoothness of her lips. For a fleeting moment, it was just them, caught in the simplicity of it. Her heart pounded in her chest, even as her hands trembled. She didn't think about the consequences, didn't question the way it felt like the world had shifted beneath them. She simply let it be, knowing that some moments - some feelings - are just meant to happen.

When they pulled away, Sarah giggled softly, nervously. "Well, that was . . . unexpected."

Ashley's stomach fluttered, but she forced herself to smile, even though she felt a little dizzy. She didn't know what was happening - didn't know what it meant. But in that second, she felt like she was finally touching something real.

"Yeah," Ashley said, feeling like the air between them had changed, had opened up into something new and full of possibility. "So . . . what now?"

Sarah tugged at the hem of her shirt, looking at the ground again, but this time, it wasn't with hesitation. She looked . . . unsure. There was something in her eyes that Ashley couldn't quite read, and it made her heart beat faster.

"Yeah," Sarah finally said, voice a little softer. "What now?"

Ashley didn't have an answer. There was so much she wanted to say, so much she couldn't put into words.

"I don't know," Ashley admitted. She could feel the nervousness in her voice. She wanted to say everything she was feeling right now - about how scared she was, how much she wanted this but didn't know what it meant for them - but the words wouldn't come.

It didn't matter. The moment was already slipping away. The sound of the marching band playing that damn fight song blared in the background. It felt like the world outside them was starting to come back into focus. The wind stirred the leaves in the trees nearby, and Ashley could smell the faint scent of the honeysuckle that climbed over the nearby fence.

For a moment, nothing mattered except Sarah's face - her eyes still wide, still waiting for something Ashley didn't know how to give. And then, just like that, the question that had been hanging in the air, unanswered, seemed to vanish.

"I don't know either," Sarah said softly, taking a step back.

Sarah's hand trembled slightly as she brushed a strand of hair from her face, and for the first time, Ashley saw the vulnerability in her eyes. That was new, something she hadn't expected, something she didn't know how to handle. She wanted to reach out, pull Sarah back to her, and make everything better, make everything clear. But she didn't.

Instead, they stood there, quiet for a moment, not really looking at each other, not really knowing what to say. Finally, Sarah spoke, her voice barely a whisper. "We should probably go back."

Ashley nodded. "Yeah. We should."

They both turned, stepping away from each other as if the moment had never happened, as if it was just a fleeting thing. But it wasn't. Not really.

As they entered the school again, something unspoken passed between them, an invisible thread that neither could touch but both could feel. The memory lingered with Ashley, an echo that stayed long after the dream had slipped away. A quiet ache settled in her chest.

What if she had said something different? What if she had acted differently? What if things had unfolded in another way?

But it was too late now, wasn't it? And all she could do was keep walking forward, leaving that moment behind.

The library was a sanctuary of whispers and worn pages, a place where time seemed to slow and the outside world faded away. As Ashley stepped through the heavy oak doors, she was enveloped by the familiar scent of aging paper, a comforting mustiness that spoke of countless stories waiting to be discovered. But there was something else in the air, too - a delicate floral note that danced just at the edge of perception. It reminded Ashley of her grandmother's garden in Silver Birch, of lazy summer afternoons spent among nodding roses and humming bees.

She wondered, not for the first time, if Mrs. Hanson, the librarian, dabbed rosewater behind her ears each morning before coming to work. The thought made Ashley smile as she made her way through the stacks, her fingers trailing lightly over book spines, feeling the raised letters and embossed designs beneath her fingertips.

The carpet muffled her footsteps as she rounded a corner and found herself in the classics section. Without really thinking about it, she plucked a worn copy of *Mrs. Dalloway* from the shelf. The book fell open easily in her hands as if welcoming an old friend. Ashley sank to the floor, crossing her legs beneath her, and began to read.

She was lost in Woolf's intricate prose, so absorbed that the presence of the girl standing above her went unnoticed until a shadow fell across the page. Ashley looked up, her heart skipping a beat when their eyes met.

The girl leaned against the shelves with an ease that made Ashley feel instantly aware of her own stiffness. Her dark hair was swept back into a messy bun, yet it looked like something effortlessly pulled together. The soft green sweater she wore highlighted the gold flecks in her hazel eyes, making them almost shimmer. Ashley shifted in her seat, suddenly conscious of the faded jeans and oversized sweatshirt that had become her uniform.

"Hey," Ashley murmured, her voice soft to avoid disturbing the library's quiet.

The girl's lips curved upward into a smile. "Hey yourself," she replied, her voice low, a sound almost lost in the silence. She idly traced the spines of the books beside her, but her eyes stayed locked on Ashley's, unblinking.

"Ashley," she said, offering her name as a gentle introduction.

The girl smiled, a bit warmer this time. "I'm Laura."

Ashley felt a warmth creeping up her neck. She gestured with the book in her hands. "Just doing some light reading," she said, aiming for nonchalance but hearing the slight tremor in her own voice.

Laura's smile widened. "Woolf? That's your idea of light reading?"

Ashley shrugged, feeling a mix of embarrassment and pride. "I like a challenge."

"Mmm," Laura hummed, her eyes sparkling with amusement. "It's quite the challenge indeed. Maybe, though, you might be in the mood for something a little less . . . cerebral."

The way Laura said 'cerebral' made Ashley's skin prickle. There was a depth to her voice, a hidden meaning that Ashley both feared and longed to unravel.

"Like what?" Ashley teased, partly to deflect her own racing thoughts and partly because it was true. Laura's fingers continued their dance across the book spines, but her eyes hadn't left Ashley's face since she'd arrived.

"Like something more interesting than Woolf," Laura replied, a smile playing on her lips. The words dangled in the air between them, charged with possibility.

For a moment, neither of them moved. Ashley could hear her own breath, steady and measured, and the rustling of pages as someone turned them in a nearby aisle. The murmur of the air conditioning filled the space, but it all faded into the background until only the space between them remained, vast and infinite.

Then Laura shifted, crouching down so that her face was suddenly level with Ashley's. This close, Ashley noticed the faint freckles scattered across Laura's nose and the sweet, almost citrusy scent that clung to her hair.

Time seemed to stretch and slow, like honey dripping from a spoon. Ashley felt as if she were standing on the edge of a cliff, her toes curled over the precipice, her heart pounding with both fear and exhilaration. She knew, with a certainty that both thrilled and terrified her, what was about to happen.

Laura reached out, her movements deliberate and unhurried, her fingers brushing against Ashley's cheek, tucking a stray strand of hair behind her ear. The touch was feather-light, but it sent sparks skittering across Ashley's skin.

And then Laura leaned, closing the last few inches between them. Ashley's eyes fluttered closed just as Laura's lips met hers.

Laura's lips were soft, the faint taste of cherry chapstick lingering. The world around them disappeared, just the two of them, steady and certain in a way Ashley had never felt before. Laura's hand found her cheek, cradling it with a tenderness that made Ashley's chest tighten. It wasn't possessive, but protective, as if she was holding something fragile.

Ashley's own hands moved instinctively, slipping around Laura's waist, feeling the warm texture of her sweater beneath her fingers. She could feel the steady beat of Laura's heart, matching her own, and for a moment, it was as though the space between them had dissolved entirely.

The kiss deepened, and Ashley felt as if she were falling and flying all at once. Her heart surged with an emotion she couldn't name - something bigger than happiness, more profound than desire. It was as if a missing piece of herself had suddenly slotted into place, completing a picture she hadn't even known was incomplete.

When they finally pulled apart, Ashley's breath came in short, quick gasps. She opened her eyes to find Laura watching her, a soft smile playing on her lips. There was a vulnerability in Laura's gaze that Ashley had never seen before - an openness that made her heart ache with tenderness.

Laura didn't say a word, and Ashley realized she didn't need to. Everything that needed to be said had been communicated in that kiss, in the gentle way Laura's thumb now stroked her cheek, and in the way their bodies leaned towards each other as if drawn by some invisible force.

Laura sat next to Ashley, foreheads touching, sharing the same breath. The world around them slowly came back into focus - the soft rustle of pages, the distant murmur of voices, the familiar smell of books. Yet something had changed, deep and irrevocable, like the ground beneath them subtly shifting, realigning in ways they couldn't fully comprehend.

Ashley knew that when they left this quiet corner of the library, things would be different. There would be conversations to have, explanations to give and a new path to navigate. But for now, there was just this: the warmth of Laura's hand in hers, the lingering taste of cherry on her lips, and the knowledge that whatever came next, they would face it together.

As if reading her thoughts, Laura squeezed her hand gently. "Ready?" she whispered, her eyes full of promise and possibility.

Ashley nodded, her heart full, an unfamiliar warmth flooding her. "Ready for what?" she replied, her voice catching the smallest edge of uncertainty.

Together, they stood, leaving *Mrs. Dalloway* behind, and stepped into a world of their own making, where the future had yet to be written.

Ashley woke with a start, her chest rising and falling as the remnants of the dreams slipped away like water through her fingers. She stared at the ceiling for a moment, her mind still half-caught in the haze of memory and longing. The room was brighter now, daylight pressing against the curtains.

With a groan, she swung her legs over the side of the bed and stood. Her body felt heavy, but the sharp edges of fatigue had softened. She shuffled to the bathroom, turned on the shower, and let the hot water cascade over her. Steam filled the small room, and she leaned against the tiled wall, letting her thoughts drift back to the previous night. Spending time with her brother again after so many years had been . . . a lot. The shared understanding between them, the truth of what had happened to their mother, had drawn them together in a way she hadn't thought possible. And their father - well, there was still so much to untangle there. Regret, she thought, was a powerful thing, but she wasn't sure if it was enough.

Dressing quickly in jeans and a soft sweater, she moved to the kitchen and made a pot of coffee. The scent filled the apartment, warm and grounding, and she poured herself a cup before heading downstairs to the shop.

The antique shop was quiet in the mornings, and Ashley liked it that way. The front windows framed a view of Stillwater's main street, where the town was just beginning to wake. She sipped her coffee, watching as a couple of shop owners swept their stoops, and a woman in a blue coat walking her dog. The simplicity of it all felt like a balm, a reminder that life carried on even when hers felt so tangled.

As she stood there, a thought came to her, unexpected and light, like a bird landing on her windowsill. It filled her chest with something close to hope, and before she could overthink it, she turned and made her way to the back office.

The old phone sat on an old oak desk, its cord coiled like a snake. She set her coffee down, picked up the receiver, and dialed a number she knew by heart. The line buzzed twice before a voice answered.

"Hello?"

Ashley felt her breath catch for a moment before she spoke. "Laura, it's me. We have to talk."

13 The Search

Ashley stepped out of the antique shop. The streets of Stillwater stirred to life with their predictable rhythms - shopkeepers arranging wares, the distant scrape of a broom, a mother tugging her child's hand as he crouched to inspect a penny on the sidewalk. The town was as it always had been, its choreography unchanged by her absence, but today it felt like a background hum, muffled and irrelevant. She moved through it without seeing, without engaging, her thoughts elsewhere. Today wasn't about this town or its quiet persistence. Today was about him.

She slid into the driver's seat of her car, the leather stiff and unyielding in the cold, and gripped the wheel with fingers tingling from the chill. For a moment, she sat motionless, her breath fogging the windshield while the heater groaned and stuttered, trying to warm the cabin. The decision to visit her father's grave felt abrupt like a sudden ripple in her otherwise carefully ordered days. Yet the pull had been there all along - subtle, insistent, shaping her steps without her consent. It reminded her of the creek on the town's outskirts, where she'd spent endless childhood hours tossing stones and tracing patterns in the water - never roaring, but always moving, always wearing its own path into the earth.

The narrow streets of Stillwater slowly surrendered to the emptiness beyond, the modest sprawl of town dissolving into open road. As she drove, the sound of her tires against the pavement carried an unnatural clarity, a steady beat to her hesitation. She knew the way, though not by heart - it was the kind of memory that lay buried until summoned, unearthing itself with every curve and dip. When the cemetery appeared, it did so quietly, almost apologetically. A rusted iron gate leaned slightly to one side, its hinges streaked with orange. A wooden sign, long bleached by sun and rain, bore the faintest shadow of letters. The single oak tree near the entrance stood steadfast but weatherworn, its bare branches rattling faintly in the wind.

She pulled beneath its canopy, dry leaves scattering with each step. Drawing her coat close against the sharp air, she hesitated, her gaze lifting toward the branches, searching for something - an answer, an invitation. Her fingers brushed the iron gate, tracing its coarse ridges. It felt solid enough, but it trembled faintly under her touch, a whisper of resistance. This was a place she had kept at the edges of her mind, her avoidance both deliberate and reflexive. She thought about having to stand here, stiff and detached as if observing the scene through a pane of glass: a casket descending, the soil falling like muted thunder. It had been easy to avoid such moments, to let them belong to someone else's sorrow, to file it away under grief yet to be claimed.

She pushed the gate open. The sound of the hinges, a slow metallic groan, startled her - not for its volume, but for the way it carved through the hush, slicing cleanly through the stillness that had pressed in around her. It felt like an intrusion, a reminder that she was not simply drifting through an untouched space but stepping into something that carried history, something that had held others before her.

The cemetery was rather small, just rows of weathered headstones scattered without much order. She moved slowly, her boots scuffing the gravel path as she scanned the names. The wind rustled the brittle leaves clinging to the branches, and for a moment, she thought about turning back. She could leave. No one would know she'd come here. Her father certainly wouldn't know. Or would he?

She continued searching for him. It reminded her of when she was a child, trailing behind with her small feet landing lightly, hesitant, in the places where they weren't always welcome. Even later, when she was old enough to stock shelves or sweep the wooden floor of his store, he always seemed just out of reach - close enough to see but walled off by an invisible barrier that she never learned how to cross. He spoke in gestures and silences, his focus elsewhere, leaving her to decipher the gaps. Now, here she was, chasing him again, even in death, the pattern stubborn as ever.

Finally, she saw it. The headstone stood unassuming, simple, and unadorned, much like the man himself. Just his name, *George Keller*, carved with precision, the barest markers of his time here on earth - dates that seemed as if his life had been reduced to a fleeting punctuation. She knelt, brushing away the leaves that had gathered at its base, her fingers clumsy and numb from the cold, feeling the weight of everything she hadn't said pressing against her chest. It was just like him to be here without fanfare, she thought, waiting in silence for someone to notice.

"Hi, Dad," she began softly, the words awkward and unfamiliar as if they belonged to someone else. She hadn't known what to expect - perhaps the strange comfort of feeling his presence, or the miraculous emergence of the right words, perfectly formed and waiting for her to speak them. Instead, there was only the cold press of her knees against the earth and the low, steady sound of the creek winding its way just beyond the cemetery's edge. The absence of answers seemed to echo her own uncertainty.

She took a slow, deep breath, her fingers twisting together in her lap as if searching for something to anchor her. "I almost didn't come," she said, her voice uneven but determined. "I kept thinking about it - turning it over in my mind - and every time, I told myself I wasn't ready, or that it wouldn't matter if I did." Her breath caught briefly snagged on some unseen thread, but she pressed forward, the words steadying themselves as they spilled free. "But I think it does matter. At least . . . it matters to me. I've been searching long enough." She paused, eyes resting on the creek, the sound of the water like a quiet witness to the truths she had never managed to say.

Her attention shifted back to his name, the rough edges of the engraving casting faint shadows in the gray light of the overcast sky. "You know. I've learned some things about you. Things I didn't know. I guess, in your own way, you tried to make things right. That you were sorry for how it all turned out. That matters more than I ever thought it would."

She paused, her breath catching as the lump in her throat swelled, making it harder to continue. "I wish you'd said that to me," her voice breaking. "I wish I'd let you. Maybe if I hadn't been so angry . . . maybe if I'd been less like you, we could've talked about it. Maybe we could've understood each other instead of getting lost in the silence."

The breeze picked up, scattering the leaves around her in small spirals. She closed her eyes for a moment, letting the wind carry away the sharp edges of her thoughts. "I blamed you for a lot," her voice steadier now. "For Mom leaving, for how things fell apart after she was gone. I told myself you should've held it together, for us. For me. But now . . . I don't know. I don't know if I would've done any better in your place."

The words felt strange to say aloud, but as they drifted in the quiet space between her and the stone, they didn't feel wrong. They didn't carry hesitation or regret, and for the first time in a long while, they didn't feel like a transgression or an unbearable burden. They were simply honest and true.

"I've been trying to understand things," she continued. "Trying to make sense of it all. Owen and I talked, and we're trying, too. He misses you, you know. He even told me so. None of us are good at that sort of thing."

She looked up at the sky, the light fading as the gray deepened. "I don't know what I expected to find here," she said in a whisper. "But I think . . . I think I just needed to tell you that I'm sorry. For all of it. You deserved so much better than what I was able to give. And I hope, somehow, you can forgive me."

The quiet that followed was not an absence but something full, layered with all that remained unspoken. Years gathered around her, pressing close, their presence both aching and familiar. Memories surfaced - pieces of a childhood, glimpses of a life that had slipped beyond reach. Regret wove itself through something gentler, harder to name - perhaps even a sense of release. She stayed, hands resting against the cold earth, breath measured, until the chill worked its way inward, threading through her bones with a persistence that refused to be ignored.

When she stood, she felt surprisingly lighter. The cemetery, which had once seemed like a place to avoid, now felt like a place she could return to - a place where the distance between them had finally narrowed, where something like reconciliation had quietly taken root. Perhaps she had come to terms with things, or maybe it was just the beginning. Either way, it was a start.

"Goodbye, Dad," her voice more certain than it had ever been. She paused, a moment stretching between them, and added with an almost reluctant smile, "I'll be back. I've got someone to introduce you to. Someone special."

Her fingers brushed the stone once more, not in finality, but in connection, a gesture that felt more like an invitation than a goodbye.

She turned away, the burden of her past and the quiet of the cemetery still pressing down, but lighter now, as if her next steps were already unfolding. As she passed through the gate, the world beyond felt brighter, more open as if the creek's steady current had carved something deeper inside her - something soft, something new, and perhaps something like hope.

Ashley parked in front of the shop, the gravel crunching beneath the tires until the engine sputtered and stopped. She sat quietly for a moment, her gaze fixed on the faded brick of the building's back wall. The morning's visit to the cemetery stayed with her, an unease that refused to leave. Her father's grave was simple, just as he would've wanted. "No need for fuss," he always told her. She'd stood there for a long time, replaying the moments between them - the arguments, the silences, the things they'd left unsaid.

Back at the shop, she was determined to bury herself in work. It was quiet inside, the kind of silence that came from decades of objects absorbing stories. Furniture polished smooth by years of hands, glass cases reflecting what sunlight filtered through the front windows, shelves lined with trinkets whose purposes were long forgotten.

She grabbed the clipboard holding the inventory list she'd printed from the computer. It was nearly done - a catalog of her father's life's work. She ran her fingers down the list, her handwriting neat and deliberate. Only a few items left to mark off.

She moved through the store with purpose, taking stock of the glass oil lamps on the second shelf, the brass candlesticks near the window, and the small collection of porcelain figurines that had always seemed out of place in her father's otherwise rugged collection.

By the time she finished, the sunlight streaming through the windows had shifted, casting longer shadows across the floor. She glanced at the clock on the wall and realized it was nearing lunchtime.

Ashley put on her jacket, locked up the shop, and stepped out onto the street. The wind carried the faint smell of fresh bread, guiding her toward the heart of Stillwater. She walked down the street and stopped in front of "The Stillwater Reader."

The bookstore was a cozy oasis tucked between the florist and the small grocery store. Its windows were filled with carefully arranged stacks of books, their spines promising adventures, wisdom, and escape. Ashley pushed open the door, and the familiar chime of the bell overhead welcomed her.

Inside, the air was warm and faintly sweet, as if the books themselves exhaled stories. Shelves towered around her, filled with paperbacks and hardcovers, their edges softened by countless fingers.

She wandered toward the classics, letting her fingers trail along the spines. Faulkner, Fitzgerald, Steinbeck. Her hand paused over Hemingway. She pulled a worn copy of *A Moveable Feast* from the shelf and flipped through the yellowed pages. The scent of old paper rose to meet her, tugging at a memory she couldn't quite place.

"You like Hemingway?"

Ashley turned and saw Miriam standing just a few feet away. Her gray hair was gathered in a loose bun, and she wore a cardigan with wooden buttons. Glasses rested on the bridge of her nose, and her arms were crossed, a broad smile spreading across her face.

"I don't know if 'like' is the right word," Ashley said, holding up the book. "But there's something about his writing, the way he captures a moment, that stays with you."

Miriam nodded. "He had a way of stripping everything down to its essence. No frills, just the truth." She stepped closer, glancing at the book in Ashley's hands. "That one's a favorite of mine. There's something so vivid about the way he writes about Paris, the people he knew."

Ashley smiled. "It makes you feel like you're there, sitting in some smoky café, listening to him argue with Gertrude Stein."

Miriam laughed softly. "Exactly." She looked at Ashley more closely then. "It's good to see you again. How's everything going at the shop?"

Ashley glanced down at the book, her fingers brushing its frayed edges. "I think I've got a handle on the inventory. But it feels strange, though, being there without him."

"It will for a while," Miriam said gently. "But it's good you're there. He poured so much of himself into that place. It's part of him, you know?"

Ashley nodded, her throat tightening. She slipped the book back onto the shelf and met Miriam's gaze. "Would you have lunch with me? At Dottie's? I could use some company."

Miriam's smile widened. "I'd love to. Let me grab my bag."

Ashley watched Miriam disappear behind the counter, a quiet sense of gratitude sweeping over her. Miriam had been a constant in her father's life, an unspoken part of their world, and by extension, she'd become a part of Ashley's too. There was something reassuring in her presence, a steadying force, a reminder of things that had endured even when so much else had shifted.

When Miriam returned, they stepped out into the brisk afternoon together, the sound of the bookstore's bell fading behind them.

"Dottie's it is," Miriam said locking the door. "And maybe, if we're lucky, she'll still have some of her famous apple pie."

Ashley smiled. They made their way down the street, the rhythms of Stillwater moving gently around them.

The door to *Dottie's* swung open with a cheerful jingle, a patron stepping out and holding it for Miriam and Ashley, their smiles as warm as the diner's inviting glow. Hearing the chime ring out, Dottie glanced up from her task, wiping her hands on a well-worn apron and flashing them a smile, one that had embraced countless faces over the years. The air was rich with the aroma of freshly brewed coffee and the buttery warmth of biscuits, and somewhere in the background, a whisper of cinnamon promised comfort and nostalgia.

"Miriam," Dottie said with a smile, her attention shifting to Ashley. "And Ashley. It's good to see you both."

Ashley returned the smile and gave a small nod. Miriam moved closer, her voice low in gratitude as she embraced Dottie briefly. The diner was quiet, with only a few familiar faces scattered across the room, each person absorbed in their food or the rustle of a newspaper.

"Your usual?" Dottie asked, her voice like a melody that had played between them for years. Miriam slid into the booth, its worn vinyl surface warm under her, the afternoon light spilling through the window and catching the edges of its age.

Miriam nodded. "Yes, please."

Dottie turned her attention to Ashley. "And for you, Ashley dear?"

Ashley quickly looked away from Dottie's quiet, knowing look. There was something in her voice - soft but sharp - that hinted at more than just a meal on her mind.

The menus were already on the table. Ashley took a quick glance. "Just coffee and a salad," she replied

"Coming right up," Dottie said.

As Dottie's footsteps faded into the soft clatter of the kitchen, Ashley asked, "What's your usual?"

Miriam's lips curved into a soft smile, her eyes crinkling at the corners. "Oh, it's nothing fancy," she said, her fingers absently tracing the worn edge of the table. "For lunch - just a bowl of

Dottie's chicken and dumplings. Been ordering it since I was about your age."

Ashley's eyes widened slightly, before quickly looking away, her eyes settling on the window where the townfolk walked by.

Miriam watched her for a moment, seeing not just the young woman before her, but echoes of herself at that age - all sharp edges and carefully guarded vulnerabilities. She resisted the urge to reach across the table, to bridge the gap that seemed both inches and miles wide.

Instead, she continued softly, "My mother used to make it, you know. Not quite as good as Dottie's, mind you, but close enough that the first time I tasted it here, I nearly cried." She paused, letting the words settle. "Funny how a simple bowl of soup can hold so much."

The light streaming through the window softened a bit as a cloud drifted by – softening the frayed menus, the worn edges of the table, and even Miriam's face.

Dottie walked over, setting a cup of tea and a coffee on the table. "Food'll be right up soon."

Ashley and Miriam smiled, each saying, "Thank you."

"I wanted to thank you," Ashley began, her voice quieter than she intended. "For telling me about my mother. For being honest."

Miriam nodded but said nothing, letting the words come as they would.

"I . . . I believed something that wasn't true," Ashley continued, her hands wrapping around the warm cup of coffee. "When I found out how close you and my father were, I thought my mother left because of an affair you two were having."

Miriam winced, just slightly, and Ashley noticed.

"And I'm sorry," Ashley continued. "I'm sorry for ever thinking that about you. It wasn't fair. It wasn't right." Her fingers twisted the paper napkin in her lap.

Miriam's face seemed to unfurl in understanding, her eyes holding a depth of compassion that transcended judgment. Her hands remained perfectly still, folded with a precise elegance. "You don't need to apologize, Ashley," her voice was a gentle current that carried no reproach, no anger. "You were just trying to make sense of something difficult to understand. Your mother leaving . . . it was . . . well, it was complicated for everyone."

Ashley nodded, swallowing hard. She traced the rim of her coffee cup with a fingertip. "You were there for my father when he needed someone," she said. "I didn't thank you for that before, but I'm thanking you now."

Miriam looked down at the table, her lips pressed into a thin line, the corners tugging downward with remembered sorrow. She took a deep breath. "He was a good man, Ashley," she said at last. "No one deserves to be alone at the end." Her hand moved across the table, gently resting over Ashley's.

Ashley met Miriam's gaze for a long moment before withdrawing her hand, her fingers shaking ever so slightly. She reached for her coffee, and took a sip, letting the warmth and bitterness of the drink settle in her chest, steadying her, and bringing her back to the present.

"I told Owen everything," she said. "About Mom. About Dad." She paused, her eyes fixed on a chip in the tabletop, tracing its jagged edge with her gaze. "We actually went to Mom's gravesite."

Miriam looked at her, something like relief passing over her features. "I'm glad to hear that. Closure is a powerful thing."

Ashley nodded. The word 'Closure' felt inadequate, an imperfect description of the complex emotions she had navigated. "Standing at my mother's gravesite, surrounded by headstones and the shifting grass, with Owen there beside me - his presence grounding me - it was more than I expected."

For a moment, they sat in silence, interrupted only by the clatter of plates and Dottie's familiar hum as she worked behind the counter. Before long, Dottie emerged from behind the counter, her arms laden with plates of home-cooked goodness. She placed their lunches before them with a flourish, her eyes sparkling with pride as she announced each dish like a cherished secret.

"Speaking of Owen," Ashley said, her voice filled with warmth, "He did a great job at the shop, helping Dad. The inventory looks perfect."

Miriam's smile was gentle, a quiet acknowledgment of the complicated threads that bind families together. "That's good to hear," she replied. "Your dad always said Owen had an eye for detail."

"He does," Ashley agreed.

Miriam raised an eyebrow. "What about it?" she asked, her tone curious but guarded.

Ashley hesitated, her words caught in her throat like a bookmark stuck between pages. "You mentioned it's been hard to keep up with. I was just wondering if - well, I don't know how to say it." She trailed off, her eyes darting to Dottie behind the corner.

Miriam's voice was soft, yet insistent, urging her forward. "Just say it, dear."

Ashley drew in a deep breath, trying to gather courage. "Have you ever thought about selling it?" she finally asked.

Miriam blinked, clearly caught off guard. "Selling it?"

"Yes," Ashley said, her voice gaining confidence like a tentative reader finding their rhythm. "I mean . . . when we met you mentioned that it was a lot of work for you. I was thinking maybe it's something you've considered . . . selling the bookstore, that is." She looked at Miriam searching for a reaction, any reaction.

Miriam leaned back, her hands resting on her lap. "I won't lie," she said, her voice clear. "Well, the thought has crossed my mind. But I wouldn't sell it to just anyone. It's more than a business - it's part of Stillwater, a repository of dreams and stories. Whoever takes it on would have to love books and love this town."

Ashley's eyes were bright with understanding. "Of course. That makes perfect sense."

Miriam's gaze sharpened as she studied Ashley. "Why do you ask?"

"Well . . . " Ashley hesitated. She took another deep breath, then plunged ahead. "Because I'd like to buy it."

Miriam's mouth parted slightly as if she hadn't quite heard correctly, as if the very idea was so unexpected it needed a moment to settle into reality.

"You?" Miriam finally said. "Ashley, darling, you've got the antique shop to think about. How on earth would you manage both?"

"I wouldn't," Ashley said quickly, leaning forward. "I'd give the antique shop to Owen. After everything he's done - he deserves it. And truth be told, he's always had a better eye for it than I ever did."

"Running a bookstore isn't like arranging knick-knacks or polishing old silver. It's not something you just wake up one day and decide to do. What do you know about running a bookstore, Ashley?"

Ashley bit her lip, then smiled, a secret joy lighting up her face. "Nothing," she gleefully admitted. "But my friend Laura knows a lot about books."

Miriam tilted her head, curiosity overtaking skepticism. "Who's Laura?"

"She's my partner," Ashley replied, a blush creeping up her neck. "We live together in Brooklyn. She's got a degree in Library Science and works at the New York Public Library on Fifth Avenue. She loves books - more than anyone I've ever met. If we sold our place in the city, we'd have enough to buy the bookstore. And . . . well . . . we've talked about moving somewhere quieter anyway. I think Stillwater would be perfect."

Miriam stared at her, her expression unreadable, as if Ashley had spoken in a language she didn't fully understand.

"I know it's a lot to think about," Ashley added quickly. "And I don't expect an answer right away. But I thought . . . well, it couldn't hurt to ask. Sometimes the craziest ideas are the ones that change our lives, right?"

Before Miriam could respond, Dottie reappeared with two large slices of apple pie. The plates clinked softly against the worn tabletop. "On the house," she said with a wink that crinkled the corners of her eyes. "My-oh-my, you two look like you're solving all the world's problems over here, and world-saving requires pie."

Miriam smiled at her, then looked back at Ashley. "Thank you, Dottie. Didn't know if you had any slices left. We'll let you know how we make out with the world's problems." It was a promise, Ashley realized, not just to Dottie but to themselves.

Once Dottie had returned to the counter, Miriam picked up her fork and took a thoughtful bite of pie. The crust crumbled delicately, its buttery layers melting on her tongue, mingling with the tart sweetness of cherries. She chewed slowly, savoring the familiar comfort of Dottie's baking.

"I'd need time to think about it," she said. "You understand."

"Of course," Ashley said quickly.

"And I'd want to meet Laura," Miriam added. "If she's going to be part of this, I'd like to get to know her."

"Absolutely," Ashley agreed, her relief evident in the slight relaxation of her shoulders and the brightening of her eyes.

Miriam smiled and gently placed her fork down on the plate. "You've given me a lot to think about," she said, her voice carrying the kind of calm weight that made it seem like she was working through something much larger than the conversation at hand. "There's this cottage outside of Silver Birch," she continued, her eyes moving toward the window as if she could already see it there, standing in the distance. "I've been thinking about it for a while now."

She paused, her gaze lingering on the distant view, and for a moment, there was a quiet pause between them. "Maybe it's time," she added, her words gentle but firm as if the thought had come to her all at once, finally. She shifted in her chair, then turned back, a soft smile playing at the corners of her mouth. "It's small, of course. Just the right size for someone looking for peace. A little garden in the front, you know, nothing grand, but enough. And a fireplace for the winter."

Her voice softened further, carrying the weight of a dream she had held for so long. "I could sit there, reading, maybe a cup of tea now and then. No rushing, no demands, just . . . quiet."

Ashley grinned, a spark of excitement lighting up her chest. "Sounds wonderful." She could almost see Miriam in her mind, surrounded by books and the soft rustling of pine needles in the breeze.

The conversation flowed easily as they ate their pie, moving to lighter topics - childhood memories, shared stories of the town, even a little gossip about Dottie's rumored new beau. But despite the pleasant chatter, Ashley found her thoughts continually drifting back to the future that was unfolding before them.

For the first time in weeks, she felt something that had been missing: the sense that she wasn't just looking back, trying to make sense of the past, but forward, toward something new.

14 The Arrival

The bus wheezed as it pulled into the small station at Emberton, a single-story brick building with a faded sign that swayed gently in the wind. Autumn had fully taken hold in the hills surrounding the town, casting the landscape in gold and rust. Laura stepped onto the cracked pavement, holding her bag close. The sharp air brushed her cheeks, crisp and bracing. She adjusted her scarf, drawing in a breath laced with damp leaves.

She had never been to Stillwater. Her only impressions of it were Ashley's descriptions. Only after Ashley's recent call - insistent yet affectionate - Laura had agreed to visit.

"Come see it for yourself. You'll understand what I'm talking about," Ashley had said.

Laura glanced around the station. A group of older men sat on a nearby bench, their flannel shirts forming a patchwork of browns and reds, speaking in low, measured tones. A young mother, her toddler tugging at her coat, hurried toward the bus driver to claim a suitcase. But Ashley had not yet arrived.

The sound of an approaching engine drew Laura's attention just before a faded blue car came to a stop. It rattled once, threatening to stall, then settled into an uneven idle. Through the smudged windshield, she caught sight of Ashley leaning out of the driver's side window, auburn hair catching the late afternoon light. Ashley waved, her enthusiasm unguarded, an openness Laura had always found endearing. She hesitated for just a second, then hoisted her bag onto her shoulder and stepped toward the car.

Ashley was already out of the driver's seat, slamming the door with her usual unceremonious flair.

"There you are!" Ashley called out.

Laura smiled, stepping toward Ashley until they stood close enough to share the same breath. For a moment, they simply looked at each other, the space between them charged with something quiet yet certain. Then Ashley lifted her hands, framing Laura's face with a gentle touch, and their lips brushed together in a kiss - brief, unhurried, carrying with it a sweetness that sent a shiver through Laura's chest.

When they parted, a quiet understanding passed between them before they both turned their heads, scanning the space around them. The only movement came from the older men at the bench a short distance away, their backs turned, their conversation filling the air with the kind of careless volume that suggested they had seen nothing at all.

"Safe and sound," Ashley murmured under her breath.

Laura let out a quiet laugh, relief mingling with amusement. "It was risky though. I thought the bus was gonna fall apart a couple of times," she said.

Ashley's grin widened, her fingers brushing against Laura's before curling around them. "I noticed a few parts scattered alongside the road on my way here."

They both started giggling, the sound spilling out in uneven bursts, too sudden to hold back.

"Come on," Ashley said, squeezing Laura's hand once before letting it go. "Let's get going. Before I do something really scandalous, like kiss you again."

Laura laughed and followed as Ashley tossed her bag into the back of the car.

Ashley grinned. "You know, it's not every day I get to play chauffeur for someone from the big city. Good thing, too, or else you'd be hitching a ride with them." She gestured toward the bench, where the men were still talking, oblivious to the world around them.

"Oh my! No thank you," Laura giggled.

"We should go," Ashley said. "It's a bit of a drive and it's getting dark. I think you'll love the view."

Laura tucked herself into the seat, pulling her coat tighter as the chill air seeped through the vehicle's rattling frame.

"So, this is Stillwater country," Laura said, glancing out the window as they pulled onto the main road. The countryside stretched wide and endless, rolling hills painted with bare trees and the occasional barn leaning tiredly against the horizon.

"Actually it's Emberton country," Ashley corrected with a smile. "Stillwater's about an hour east. Fewer people, more trees, and a diner that'll change your life."

"Dottie's?" Laura asked, recalling one of Ashley's many stories.

Ashley shot her a grin. "You know it. Best apple pie in three counties, maybe more."

They settled into an easy rhythm as the car rumbled along the winding road. Ashley kept one hand on the wheel, the other gesturing animatedly as she pointed out landmarks - a creek she used to fish in as a kid, an abandoned schoolhouse she swore was haunted, the stretch of road where her dad had taught her to drive.

"You talk about this place like it's paradise," Laura said, her voice teasing.

Ashley shrugged. "It's not paradise. But it's . . . it's home . . . it feels like it's home."

Laura turned studying Ashley as the light shifted with the movement of the car. Ashley had changed since she'd last seen her, which wasn't that long ago. She seemed different, a steadiness to her now, a groundedness that hadn't been there before.

"And the bookstore. Does it feel like home, too?" Laura asked.

Ashley's grin returned, brighter this time. "Yes. You'll see. Miriam's been getting the store. I think she's excited to meet you."

Laura hesitated. "She's really okay with this? Selling it, I mean."

Ashley nodded. "I think so. She said she'd only sell it to someone who loves books and this town. And you, Laura, are exactly that person."

Laura smiled, though a faint doubt remained. She wasn't sure she loved Stillwater yet. But Ashley believed she would, and for now, that was enough.

By the time they reached Stillwater, the sun had dipped low, casting shadows over the quiet streets. The town was smaller than Laura had imagined - a single main road lined with brick buildings, their windows glowing warmly against the growing chill. She noted the hardware store where Owen worked, a bakery, and a barber shop with a red-and-white pole spinning lazily outside. There was Dotties, Miriam's bookstore, and the antique shop. It looked like something out of a storybook.

Ashley pulled the car in front of the antique shop. "This is it," she said, cutting the engine.

Laura stepped out of the car, her boots crunching softly on a carpet of fallen leaves. The crisp autumn air enveloped her, carrying the faint scent of earth, mingled with a whisper of something older and harder to name - as if history itself had soaked into the streets of Stillwater. She shivered slightly, not from the cold but from the unfamiliar quiet that seemed to blanket the town.

As she stood there, taking in the scene, Laura felt a sense of timelessness wash over her. This small town, with its weathered storefronts and unhurried pace, seemed to exist in a world apart from the frenetic energy of the city she'd left behind. The quiet wasn't just an absence of noise, but a presence in itself - a soft, enveloping silence that spoke of secrets long-held and stories waiting to be told.

Ashley came around to her side, grabbing Laura's bag from the back. "I'll show you the flat upstairs. It's not much, but like I said, it's home."

The shop door creaked open with the reluctant groan of decades-old hinges, a sound that seemed to carry the weight of countless stories. Laura stepped inside, and immediately the shop wrapped around her like an old, slightly musty embrace. The air was thick with the complex perfume of antiques - a blend of weathered mahogany, leather-bound books, and that indefinable scent of time itself. Inside, the shop was a labyrinth of curiosities: shelves crammed with books, mismatched furniture, tarnished silverware, and forgotten trinkets. The dim light from a few overhead bulbs gave the space a cozy if slightly eerie, atmosphere.

"It's a bit of a mess," Ashley said, setting Laura's bag down near an ornate dresser. "But it's my mess, at least for now."

Laura wandered toward a bookshelf, her fingers gliding over the spines of old volumes. "It's beautiful," she murmured. "Like stepping into a remembered moment."

Ashley tilted her head, watching Laura with a soft smile. "That's exactly how I felt the first time I saw it. Like it already knew me."

They climbed the narrow wooden staircase at the back of the shop. The flat upstairs was small to Laura, but inviting: a cozy living room with a sagging couch, a kitchen that looked like it hadn't been updated since the fifties, and small bedrooms just visible down a narrow hall. A vase of dried flowers sat on the windowsill, their faded petals catching the last light of the day.

"Well, this is it," Ashley said, setting Laura's bag down by the couch. "I told you it wasn't much."

Laura turned to her. "It's perfect."

Ashley lifted a hand, light and deliberate, brushing a stray strand from Laura's face. The space between them brimmed with quiet energy, a silence that carried everything neither had spoken.

"I missed you," Laura whispered.

Ashley's response emerged like a low, resonant chord: "I missed you, too."

Their lips brushed together, not in haste, but with the careful grace of two souls finding their way back. The kiss carried the softness of a familiar melody, unforced, unwritten, yet wholly known. When they parted, Ashley's hand sought Laura's, fingers weaving together in a silent vow.

The bedroom was a sanctuary of muted tones and intimate textures. The hand-stitched quilt bore the marks of patient craftsmanship, its patterns telling stories of care and time. A small lamp cast an amber glow that softened edges and transformed shadows into something tender and protective.

Their undressing carried a quiet reverence - not driven by urgency, but by the simple act of allowing themselves to be seen. Each gesture was slow, a wordless recognition of the space they shared. The quilt folded around them, soft and worn, Ashley's arm encircling Laura in a way that spoke of protection rather than possession.

Stillness gathered between them, not empty but filled with something unspoken, something known. Their breaths moved in a shared cadence, interrupted only by the distant hush of a passing car, a reminder that beyond this moment, the world continued on.

Laura's fingers traced idle patterns on Ashley's skin, mapping territories of connection. "This town is quieter than I expected," she murmured with a soft laugh.

"Stillwater grows on you," Ashley responded. "It's the kind of quiet that settles into your bones. Gentle. Persistent."

When Laura looked up, her eyes held a question, open and uncertain. "Do you think I'll belong here? Do you think we will?"

Ashley's smile carried both reassurance and promise. "You will, and so will we."

They drifted into sleep, enfolded in each other and the quiet of a night that enclosed them, whole and undisturbed.

The morning light traced delicate shapes across the quilt. Laura stirred first, her eyes opening to the unfamiliar room. Disorientation came and went in a breath, fading when she felt Ashley's warmth beside her. The pieces of the moment arranged themselves, forming something that felt both unexpected and entirely right.

Ashley's arm rested over her waist, her breath a quiet presence against Laura's neck. Laura remained still, absorbing the closeness, the way it felt like returning to something she had always known. She ran her fingers along Ashley's arm, drawn to the softness, the quiet certainty of touch.

"Mmm," Ashley murmured, nuzzling closer. "What time is it?"

Laura glanced at the old alarm clock on the nightstand. "Just after seven."

Ashley opened her eyes, a slow smile spreading across her face. "Good morning," she said, her voice still husky with sleep.

"Good morning," Laura replied, turning to face her. The intimacy of the moment washed over her, and she felt a flutter in her chest.

Ashley leaned in, pressing a soft kiss to Laura's lips. "How did you sleep?"

"Better than I have in months," Laura admitted. "Though I'm not sure if it's the quiet or the company."

Ashley chuckled. "Probably a bit of both." She stretched, her movements languid. "Want to shower before we head out?"

Laura nodded. "Sounds perfect."

The bathroom was small, barely big enough for two. Still, they moved around each other with an ease that came from years of familiarity. Ashley turned on the shower, letting the water warm while Laura brushed her teeth.

"It might take a minute," Ashley said, her voice apologetic. "The pipes are old."

Laura smiled, her words muffled by the toothbrush. "That's okay."

When they stepped into the shower, the rush of water filled the small bathroom, a sound both calming and intimate. The warmth of it softened the sharpness of the space, making everything feel a little less defined. Steam swirled up, blurring the light overhead, and the world beyond the bathroom seemed farther away, quieter. Ashley reached for the shampoo, her fingers brushing against the cool plastic, but Laura's hand covered hers, steady and familiar.

"Let me," Laura said, her voice soft with a quiet insistence.

Ashley turned, her damp hair falling in soft waves over her shoulders as she gave herself over to the moment. Laura's hands moved gently through the strands, working the shampoo in with care. The fruity scent of the lather filled the air, and Laura's touch was unhurried and tender.

Ashley closed her eyes, a soft breath escaping her, the tension she hadn't known she was holding dissolving beneath Laura's hands.

"You have magic hands," Ashley cooed.

"I missed this," Laura replied, rinsing the soap from Ashley's hair, watching it disappear down the drain in delicate spirals.

Ashley turned to face her, droplets clinging to her skin like a scattering of tiny jewels. Her eyes met Laura's, clear and unguarded. "I love you," she said simply.

For a moment, neither of them spoke. Laura reached for the soap, her hands moving over Ashley's shoulders and arms, following the lines of her body. Ashley mirrored the gesture, her fingers tracing soft paths over Laura's back, rediscovering contours that felt both known and unfamiliar.

When the water began to cool, they stepped out, their laughter filling the quiet as they fumbled for towels. The mirror was clouded, the room holding onto the heat of the shower. Ashley wrapped Laura in a towel, her arms pulling her close, drawing warmth between them.

"Stillwater's waiting," Ashley said.

Laura leaned in, her lips brushing against Ashley's ear. "Let it wait," she whispered.

The world beyond their room faded to a soft hum, the distant sounds of Stillwater's evening settling like a gentle blanket around them. Ashley reclined against the rumpled sheets, her fingertips tracing idle patterns along the landscape of Laura's back. Their bodies moved in concert, a dance both intimately known and thrillingly unfamiliar, as if they were explorers mapping terrain that had always been there, waiting to be discovered.

Laura's mouth found the hollow of Ashley's neck, and lingered there, warm and insistent. Ashley closed her eyes, giving herself over to the sensation. In this suspended moment, the burden of family secrets and small-town mysteries lifted, replaced by a lightness that spread through her limbs. The tangle of emotions that had knotted inside her since arriving in Stillwater began to loosen, unraveling beneath Laura's touch.

For now, there was only this: the soft press of skin against skin, the quiet catch of breath, and the feeling of being wholly present, wholly known. Ashley let the moment wash over her, a brief respite from the complexities that awaited beyond their door.

When the room fell silent except for the beating of their hearts, Laura shifted to rest her head against Ashley's chest. Ashley ran her fingers through Laura's hair, damp from the shower and curling at the edges. "Are you ready?" she asked, the words more invitation than question.

Laura's eyes met Ashley's. "I think I've always been ready," she said, her smile small but certain.

Ashley kissed her forehead, pulling her closer. "Good," she said.

They dressed quietly, Laura pulling on a soft sweater and jeans, Ashley opting for a flannel shirt and worn denim. As Ashley braided her damp hair, Laura wandered into the kitchen, drawn by the promise of caffeine. She was starting to feel anxious about the day.

"Coffee's in the cabinet above the sink," Ashley called out.

Laura found it and set about making a pot of coffee. The familiar ritual calmed her nerves somewhat, giving her hands something to do. As the coffee began to percolate, filling the small apartment with its rich aroma, Ashley joined her in the kitchen.

"Smells good," she said, wrapping her arms around Laura from behind.

Laura leaned back into the embrace. "I hope Miriam likes me," she said quietly, the unease in her voice unmistakable.

Ashley pressed a kiss to Laura's cheek. "She'll love you. Just be yourself."

"What if myself isn't enough?" Laura asked, turning in Ashley's arms.

Ashley cupped Laura's face in her hands. "Laura, you are more than enough. You're kind, you're smart, you're funny. Miriam will see that."

Laura nodded, trying to believe it. "Okay."

They sipped their coffee, Laura's gaze drifting toward the window where the town below slowly stirred to life. Stillwater was awakening - shopkeepers pulling open their doors, the first few cars making their way down Main Street, and a scattering of early risers heading toward the diner for breakfast or the nearby café for coffee and pastries.

As they went to leave, Laura hesitated by the door. "Are you sure it's okay? Us, I mean. In a small town like this?"

Ashley took Laura's hand, squeezing it gently. "It's more than okay. It's wonderful."

They made their way down the narrow wooden stairs, the steps creaking under their feet. The antique shop was quiet, the treasures within still slumbering under a thin layer of dust. Ashley locked up behind them, and they stepped out onto the sidewalk.

The morning air carried the essence of autumn—a delicate blend of fallen leaves and distant memories. Hints of cinnamon and dried maple lingered, soft as whispers. Laura took a deep breath, feeling the cool breath of the season fill her lungs with its quiet promise of change. Ashley's hand found hers, their fingers intertwining with the same effortless grace they had perfected over years of loving, their connection as natural and inevitable as the changing of seasons.

As they walked towards Miriam's bookstore, Laura couldn't help but notice the curious glances from passersby. She felt exposed and vulnerable under their scrutiny.

"Ashley," she whispered, "maybe we shouldn't hold hands. It might be too much for such a small town."

Ashley's grip tightened slightly. "Laura, look at me."

Laura met Ashley's gaze and found strength in the warmth she saw there.

"I don't care what anyone else thinks," Ashley said firmly. "Love is more powerful than hate. And what we have . . . it's love . . . pure and simple."

Laura felt something loosen in her chest - a knot of anxiety unraveling as she squeezed Ashley's hand tighter.

"You're right," she said.

They continued down the street hand-in-hand. Laura let go of her usual pace, letting herself take in the charm of Stillwater. The storefronts were quaint, like something from another time. Many of them seemed untouched by the years. Flower boxes hung from windows, the late-blooming flowers offering bursts of color against the backdrop of an autumn landscape that appeared almost too perfect to exist.

As they neared Miriam's bookstore, Laura's unease resurfaced, though it was softened by a growing sense of anticipation. This was more than just a visit - it was the beginning of something new, a chance to build a connection with someone who held great significance for Ashley.

The storefront was inviting; large windows displayed carefully arranged books alongside comfortable reading nooks visible inside - a place where stories came alive beyond their pages.

Ashley paused at the door turning towards Laura. "Ready?"

Laura took a deep breath and nodded. "Ready."

As Ashley pushed open the door, the bell chimed softly above them, a gentle herald announcing their arrival.

Laura was entranced. The scent of books, leather, and possibility embraced her. Shelves stretched from floor to ceiling, their wooden frames worn smooth by countless hands seeking literary treasures. Stacks of novels teetered precariously on side tables, their spines a rainbow of faded colors and gilded lettering. In one corner, a pair of overstuffed armchairs invited patrons to lose themselves in the pages of a newly discovered story.

And there, behind an old wooden counter that had surely witnessed decades of literary exchanges, stood Miriam. Her silver hair gleamed in the soft light, catching the golden hues of the setting sun. As she caught sight of Laura, a warm smile spread across her face, etching deeper the lines that spoke of a life well-lived and stories yet untold. In that moment, Laura felt as though she had stepped not just into a bookstore, but into a chapter of her own unfolding narrative.

"You must be Laura! I've been so looking forward to meeting you," Miriam said, her voice rich and welcoming.

Laura felt the firm warmth of Ashley's hand around hers as they moved forward, the door closing gently behind them with a soft chime. The sound resonated, not simply marking their arrival but offering something more - a quiet invitation, a promise of what lay ahead. Stillwater unfolded before them, a town steeped in its own secrets, where love seemed to thrive in the cracks of its timeworn streets and the faint echo of history filled the air, waiting for someone to give it voice. Together, hand in hand, they walked on, hearts open to the stories they might discover, to the life they might build, to whatever awaited them beyond this moment.

15 The Bookstore

The interior of the store unfolded like a secret, inviting exploration and promising discovery. A fireplace glowed in the far corner, light shifting across a small reading nook. Two mismatched chairs, one upholstered in faded velvet and the other worn leather, framed a table stacked with half-read books and a teapot stained by years of use. Beneath it all lay a threadbare rug, its once-bright colors muted with time, holding the space together like an unspoken promise of comfort.

"This is amazing," Laura said, her voice hushed, as if she might disturb the quiet reverence of the room.

Miriam's eyes crinkled with amusement. "It's something, isn't it? Thirty years of my life are in these walls. Every book, every shelf, every quiet corner carries a piece of me. Letting it go . . ." She trailed off, her smile shifting, touched with something softer. "Well, it won't be easy. But Ashley assures me you're the right person."

Laura turned to Ashley, who leaned against the counter, arms crossed, a small, knowing grin forming. "I'd honor what you've built here," Laura said, meaning every word.

Miriam gave a small nod, her silver hair reflecting the firelight. "That's all anyone can ask."

She turned toward the counter, hands moving with familiarity through the motions of preparing coffee. The scent drifted through the room as she selected two cups from an uneven collection, filled them, and carried them over to the nook. Laura and Ashley sank into their chairs, the warmth from the fire reaching their legs while Miriam placed the cups before them, steam curling into the air.

Miriam leaned back in her chair. It creaked. She cradled her cup of tea, letting her gaze wander over to the fire for a moment before speaking.

"Stillwater," she said, "is a place where people hold onto things - old habits, old grudges, and, occasionally, old friends. We've got our fair share of eccentrics. Take Edgar McDowell over at the hardware store. He's convinced there's a secret tunnel under Main Street, left over from Prohibition. Spends his Sundays digging around his basement trying to find it."

Ashley laughed softly, shaking her head. "Owen says he'll tell you that story every time you walk in."

"Has he ever found anything?" Laura asked intrigued.

"Oh, just splinters and the occasional bruise," Miriam said with a laugh. "But he's harmless. Then there's Eleanor Kimball - she runs the bakery. Makes the best apple turnovers you'll ever taste. But don't ask her for a discount. She'll go on about the rising cost of butter until you're sorry you ever brought it up."

"That sounds like her," Ashley said, smiling. "I made that mistake once when I was a kid. She gave me the longest speech on inflation I've ever heard. Must've been an economist in another life."

"Didn't stop you from eating the turnover, though," Miriam teased.

"Sure didn't," Ashley said.

Laura listened, picturing the people, the moments. "It sounds like everyone here has a story."

"Oh, they do," Miriam said. "Like Willow Garner, who knits those little scarves she sells at the market. Lost her husband fifty years ago, but she still makes him one every winter. Says he'd be cold without it."

"Does she still wear her purple hat?" Ashley asked, leaning forward.

"Every single day," Miriam confirmed, shaking her head with a quiet fondness. "It's worn through in spots, but you'd think it was a crown."

Laura's gaze drifted to the fire, letting these glimpses of Stillwater settle in her mind, the way lives crossed and held onto each other here. "It sounds like a place where everyone's lives are so . . . intertwined."

Miriam's expression turned thoughtful. "That's one way to put it. They'll drive you mad sometimes with their nosiness or their stubbornness, but when it matters, they're there. When your roof leaks, they show up with tarps. When you're down and not feeling well, they bring you soup. It's maddening and beautiful all at once."

"It sounds like home," Laura said glancing at Ashley.

Miriam met her gaze, her smile small but full of meaning. "Can I ask you something, Laura?"

"Anything," Laura replied. "Anything at all."

"Who is your favorite author?"

Laura hesitated for only a moment, surprised by the question. It wasn't that she didn't have an answer, but something about Miriam's curiosity made her pause. She lifted her cup, took a sip, and set it back down before speaking.

"I'd have to say, Ernest Hemingway," she replied, her voice carrying a quiet reverence.

Miriam raised an eyebrow. "Hemingway, huh? I can see that. He has that straightforwardness, doesn't he? No frills. Which of his novels do you like best?"

Laura didn't even have to think before responding. "*A Canary for One.*"

There was a beat of silence before Miriam's expression flickered - just a trace of surprise that she quickly masked. Ashley, too, froze, her fingers instinctively curling around the edge of her own cup.

The room seemed to hold its breath for a moment.

Miriam's expression shifted, her gaze resting on Ashley for a moment before returning to Laura. "*A Canary for One,*" she said. "You have an eye for something remarkable."

Laura nodded, though she wasn't sure why it mattered so much. "I think it's the way Hemingway captures such small, intimate moments. The way the character's world slowly unravels under the weight of simple decisions. There's something so haunting about it."

Ashley felt a chill wash over her, the memory surfacing with an almost physical clarity. She had found the book on her father's desk, opening it to page 143, just as the letter from Miriam had instructed. The details returned to her without effort - the creak of the leather binding, the scent of paper long undisturbed, the hush of pages moving beneath her fingertips. And then, waiting there, a pressed yellow flower. Its petals had lost their brilliance and faded to the color of parchment, a quiet trace of what once had been.

Miriam's voice pulled her from the depths of her thoughts. "I had a first edition of that story," she told Laura, eyes distant now, her words slow. "I gave it to Ashley's father."

Ashley blinked, her pulse quickening.

"Ashley's father was . . . very fond of Hemingway," Miriam added.

"Why?" Ashley asked before she could stop herself. "What was it about the book?"

Miriam's lips parted, then closed again as she seemed to choose her words carefully. "Your father and I . . . you know, we shared many things. Whenever he would visit me in the store, and if I was busy he would sit and read through it. So, I decided to give it to him. I never asked him why he liked it so much."

Ashley's breath caught in her chest. "A yellow flower pressed in its pages."

Miriam nodded with a smile. "His favorite color."

The room, with its soft shadows and firelight, suddenly felt heavier, as if the air itself was laden with secrets and old regrets.

"I suppose I gave him the book because I thought it might help him see himself clearly again. It was a gesture of sorts, a way of reaching out to the man I knew before everything - before he disappeared into his work, his family, his own complicated life."

She looked at Ashley, her gaze full of something that almost resembled sadness, but also a kind of understanding. "His life became difficult and he changed. Just like we all do. But I think whenever he looked at the book he remembered the person he used to be."

Laura shifted uncomfortably. She wasn't sure if she was intruding, but she knew that these were the kinds of moments that shaped people, that bound them together, for better or worse.

Miriam cleared her throat. "But enough about that. I didn't mean to bring up old memories. You must have your own thoughts on *A Canary for One*, Laura. What draws you to it?"

Laura smiled faintly, shifting her focus away from the past that hung between Miriam and Ashley's father. "I think it's the way the story reveals the fragility of human connection," Laura said softly. "The way two people - one broken and one uncertain - try to find meaning in each other, even when the world around them seems so bleak. Maybe that's how we get through things."

Miriam smiled. "I think you might be right."

She settled into her chair, her hands folded in her lap. "So," she said after a moment, "what about you, Laura? How did you end up in this line of work? What made you love books so much?"

Laura was caught a bit off guard and thought about the question. She had never quite been asked it in such an open way before. Not by anyone who wasn't already part of her past, part of her routine.

"I graduated with a degree in library sciences," Laura's voice was steady, a hint of pride coloring her words. "From the same college where I met Ashley." She glanced at Ashley, offering a small smile, though it felt a little forced. "And after that, I went straight into work with the New York City public library system. Been there for over ten years now."

Laura's fingers trailed along the spine of a nearby book. "You know, it's more than just a job for me. Books . . . they're like old friends, each one holding a piece of someone's soul. When I walk into the library each morning, it's like stepping into a grand conversation that's been going on for centuries." Her eyes lit up, a warmth spreading across her features. "There's this quote I love, by Jorge Luis Borges: 'I have always imagined that Paradise will be a kind of library.' And in a way, that's what it feels like to me. A paradise where stories live and breathe, where ideas take flight."

She turned to Ashley with a smile full of shared memories. "Remember how we used to spend hours in the university library? You'd be buried in your business texts, and I'd be lost in some obscure poetry collection. It was like we were explorers, charting new territories with every page we turned."

Ashley nodded, her own expression softening at the recollection. "You always did have a way of making even the dustiest old book sound like an adventure waiting to happen."

Laura laughed softly. "That's because every book is an adventure. A chance to see the world through someone else's eyes, to live a thousand lives in the span of a few hundred pages. It's magic, pure and simple. And I get to be a guardian of that magic every single day."

Miriam leaned back slightly in her chair. It creaked again. This time a bit louder. "So, you work in one of those big libraries in the city?"

Laura tucked a strand of hair behind her ear. "The main branch, with the lions out front."

Miriam chuckled. "I saw them once, years ago. Regal beasts. You ever stop to wonder what they'd say if they could talk?"

Laura smiled. "Probably something wise. Or maybe they'd complain about the pigeons."

Miriam chuckled again. "I like that. But tell me, what made you want to work there? A library in the middle of all that noise and hurry - seems a strange fit for a place like New York."

Laura's gaze drifted to the rows of books neatly stacked on Miriam's shelves. "I've always loved books. Not just for what's in them, but for what they do. They're like keys - to other lives, to other worlds. When I was a kid, my library felt like the only place that made sense. It was quiet, organized, and safe. The librarian there - Mrs. Lathrop - she made it feel like a place where I belonged."

"A good librarian can do that," Miriam said. "A good bookshop owner too, though people don't always see it that way."

Laura tilted her head, intrigued. "Do you think it's different? I mean - what you do here in the store and what I do at the library – is it different?"

"Sure. But not as much as you'd think." Miriam gestured to the rows of books behind her. "Every one of these has a story, just like the people who walk through that door. My job is to help them find the one they need. Or sometimes, the one they didn't know they needed. Isn't that what you do?"

Laura considered this. "I suppose so. But in the library, it feels bigger, more . . . impersonal sometimes. We get hundreds of people a day. It's hard to make those connections."

Miriam leaned forward. "And yet, you try. Otherwise, you wouldn't be sitting here, talking about Mrs. Lathrop. You wouldn't still be doing it."

Laura let out a quiet laugh. "Fair enough." She hesitated. "I guess I love the idea that someone can come in feeling lost, unsure of what they're looking for, and leave with something that might change them. It's not always a book - it could be a conversation or just a quiet moment in a busy day - but it's something."

Miriam sipped her tea. "That's what it's all about, isn't it? Giving people a little bit of something good. Even if it's small."

Laura glanced around the shop, at the way the light slanted through the windows, bathing the shop in gold. "This place feels like that. Like you've created a sanctuary."

Miriam gave a wistful smile. "Maybe. But sanctuaries only work if someone's willing to tend to them. You do that every day in your library, even in the middle of that crazy city."

She felt an unexpected sense of validation. "You make it sound noble."

"It is," Miriam said simply. "And don't let anyone tell you otherwise."

Laura thought about her library, about the endless faces she saw each day, the hurried questions, the rare moments when someone lingered long enough to share a story.

"I suppose we're not so different, after all," she said finally.

Miriam grinned. "Told you. Sounds like your job gives your life meaning."

"It does," Laura agreed. "It's a lot of quiet work. There's beauty in it, but there's also distance. It's not always easy to get close to those you help."

"Can't be easy for you. But that won't be a problem you'd have here," Miriam said. "Tell me, why do you think you could handle a place like Stillwater - a town where every life is threaded through with the ones that came before?"

Laura hesitated, caught off guard. "I . . . I think . . . I think it's because this town, this bookstore - it has a presence a big city's library never could. The stories here aren't confined to shelves or cataloged in silence. They breathe in the spaces between people, waiting to be noticed."

Miriam tilted her head, considering Laura's answer. "You're not wrong," she said. "Stillwater has a way of making you confront what you've tried to hide. It doesn't let you keep your distance for long."

"I think that's exactly what I'm looking for," Laura said, her voice quiet. "To confront something. Something beyond the neatly shelved rows of library books - beyond the city I've spent my life in."

Ashley shifted in her seat, catching Miriam's gaze, but neither of them spoke. Laura felt as though they were both waiting for something, but she wasn't sure what.

Miriam cleared her throat. "You know, Laura," her tone light but thoughtful, "I've seen people come and go from this town. They think they can handle it, that they can handle the smallness, the intimacy. But Stillwater . . . it has a way of pulling you back, of teaching you exactly who you are. Are you sure you're ready for that?"

Laura met Miriam's gaze steadily. "I'm not sure," she said. "But maybe that's the point."

Miriam nodded, her smile deepening, though there was still something unreadable in her expression. "I should tell you something about this bookstore," she said. "It doesn't make much money. Never has, never will. Not in this town. People come in, pick up a book here and there, but that's about it." She glanced over at the shelves as if the books themselves might be listening. "It's the kind of place that survives because it has to, not because it's profitable."

Laura didn't seem put off. She leaned forward slightly, her eyes steady on Miriam. "I kind of knew that," she said. "But I think it can be more than that. I've been thinking of things I could do . . ."

Miriam raised an eyebrow, intrigued. "Things, huh?" her tone not entirely dismissive but laced with doubt. "What kind of plans? After all, this is a sleepy little town."

Laura's lips curved into a faint smile, and she glanced at Ashley. "No disrespect, Miriam, but I think Stillwater can be more than just a sleepy town with a few bookshelves and old buildings. My dream is to have this bookstore be an important part of Vermont." Her voice carried a quiet conviction, a firmness that made Miriam pause.

"And how do you propose to do that?" Miriam asked, genuinely curious now. "How are you going to breathe life into this place?"

Laura, without missing a beat, replied with a glance at Ashley. "Well," she said, "I happen to know a very good marketing person."

Miriam followed Laura's gaze and looked directly at Ashley, who smiled.

"We have a few ideas," Ashley said, her voice light but with an edge of excitement. "We were thinking we could bring authors to Stillwater during the summer and fall festivals. Maybe have readings, book signings, events that get people excited about the bookstore."

"Authors?" Miriam repeated, her tone softer now. "To Stillwater?"

"Why not?" Ashley replied. "Stillwater's quiet charm could be the perfect backdrop for a weekend event. We could tie it into the festivals. It could draw people in, from here and beyond. Imagine - authors reading their works, mingling with the locals and visitors, sharing stories."

Miriam was quiet for a moment, the wheels turning in her head. "I'm not saying it's a bad idea," she said, "but Stillwater's not exactly a tourist hot spot."

"Maybe, we can change that," Laura replied. "It won't happen overnight, but we can start small. Get people talking. Bring a few authors, create a buzz, and build from there."

"You really think you can make that happen?" Miriam asked her.

Laura smiled, radiating a quiet assurance. "I do. I trust Ashley. And I trust myself to figure out the rest as it comes."

Ashley spoke up. "We've already thought through a few ways to market it. Nothing too elaborate at first. Just enough to spark curiosity, to start conversations." She glanced at Miriam, hoping to catch some trace of approval in her expression.

Miriam took a sip of her tea, her gaze fixed on them over the rim of her cup. The pause stretched, heavy, until finally, she set the cup down.

"Well," she said, drawing the word out as though testing its fit, "you certainly have my attention. I'm not saying it'll work, but if anyone can pull it off, it's probably the two of you." She let her gaze linger, then added, "I guess I'll just have to wait and see."

Laura straightened, meeting Miriam's steady eyes without flinching. "You won't be disappointed," she said simply.

For a moment, Miriam seemed to weigh Laura's confidence. Then she gave a small nod, conceding the point. "Alright then. Here's hoping you're ready for what you're stepping into. It's a lot to manage, but I think you'll do just fine."

Ashley shifted, her fingers tapping against the arm of her chair. Laura recognized it as her quiet way of working through nerves.

Miriam's attention moved to her with a small smile. "Stillwater has a way of settling into people. Some days, you'll want to pack up and go, leave it all behind. But then there'll be days when it feels like the only place in the world that truly sees you. That's what this town does - it keeps hold of you, whether you ask it to or not."

Ashley's fingers stilled. "I've run once before," she said quietly. "But I won't do that again. It's strange - you don't truly appreciate a place until it's no longer yours."

Laura studied Ashley for a beat, then turned her attention back to Miriam. "It sounds like you're saying the town doesn't just let you in - it claims you."

Miriam stood to make another cup of tea. "Oh, it claims you alright. You'll see soon enough."

They remained there for hours while the bookstore filled with a quiet warmth, the scent of paper and old wood deepening the sense of enclosure. Miriam wove stories of the store's early days, recalling the peculiar souls who had wandered through Stillwater and the unexpected bonds that had formed within its walls. Her voice carried the ease of someone who had told these tales many times, each telling adding something new to what came before. Laura listened, drawn in completely, her own questions giving way to the steady flow of Miriam's words, the rise and fall shaping something familiar, something that felt like home.

When it was time to leave, Ashley hesitated at the door, glancing back toward the shelves, the rows of spines standing like sentries in the dim light. Laura pressed her palm against the smooth wood of the counter, reluctant to break the spell. Outside, the evening had deepened, shadows stretching long across the sidewalk. The town's quiet felt heavier now, filled with something unspoken.

The door swung shut behind them, the bell's chime dissolving into the hush of the street. Laura exhaled, shoving her hands into her pockets. She turned to Ashley. "She's remarkable," Laura whispered.

Ashley smiled, a small, private thing. "She is."

She let her gaze drift down the road, past the low buildings and their golden-lit windows, past the trees that lined the square. Something about the place pressed against her, quiet but insistent, like a story she had once known by heart but had forgotten until now.

The evening sky unfurled above them, stars scattered in sharp relief against the deepening blue. Laura tilted her head back, drawn to their brightness, to the way they spilled across the expanse without hesitation. The constellations carried the quiet suggestion of something both ancient and immediate, their glow steady in the hush of the night.

"It's beautiful," she said. "You don't see stars like this in the city. There's too much light, too much noise. But here. It's perfect."

Ashley tucked her hands into her coat pockets. "It's home."

Laura glanced at her, their shoulders brushing as they walked. "It's our home," she said.

She turned to Ashley, their hands brushing as they fell into step together, and for the first time in what felt like forever, Laura let herself believe that maybe, just maybe, this little town - with its creaky shelves, firelit corners, and quiet oddities - could be a place she could claim as her own.

16 The Move

Spring in New York City brought a shift in the air, a quiet transformation that softened the edges of winter. The usual bite of exhaust faded, tempered by the warmth of street vendors grilling hot dogs and pretzels, by the scent of butter and sugar drifting from bakery doors. In the parks, tulips pressed through damp soil, trees uncurled fresh leaves, their surfaces catching the pale sunlight. Windows stood open, drawing in air touched with lilacs and the warmth of baked bread, and neighbors sat on stoops, their voices carrying through the evening, the city stretching itself into the longer days.

Ashley and Laura moved through their house, the once-familiar space transforming into a landscape of stacked boxes. Laura stood in the center, surrounded by the evidence of their lives, towers of belongings waiting for departure. The labels scrawled in thick black marker - Kitchen, Clothes, Books 1, Books 2, Books 3 - charted their history in uneven lines. Ashley's handwriting stretched across the last box, her loops and flourishes barely concealing her amusement at Laura's inability to part with even a single paperback.

Outside, the city droned and pulsed, a constant push and pull of movement she had once found intoxicating. Now it grated. The shouts of a street vendor cut through the noise, sharp with impatience. A car horn held its note too long, sending a jolt through her shoulders.

"You look like you're about to cry, or throw something," Ashley said as she stepped through the door, carrying two coffees.

Her smile was wide, her hair caught in the late-morning light. She looked completely at ease as if leaving a city was no more complicated than stepping off a subway.

Laura turned toward her, accepting the coffee with both hands like it was some sort of lifeline. "I'm not sure I know how to live anywhere else," she admitted. "I've been here so long."

Ashley laughed softly and set her own coffee down on the nearest box. "Stillwater is . . . slower. You'll actually get a chance to breathe for once."

"I don't think I remember how to breathe."

"Good thing I'm an excellent teacher," Ashley giggled slightly. "Lesson one: Stillwater has no subways, no cabs, and zero bodegas that'll sell you a banana at midnight. You're going to learn to plan meals like an adult."

Laura groaned sarcastically, rolling her eyes as she took a long sip of coffee. "You're not exactly selling me on it, you know."

Ashley smirked. "I'll remind you of that when you're sitting on the bench in front of the store with a book, listening to nothing but the wind. Speaking of books, did you really pack all of them? Ten boxes, Laura. Ten."

"Twelve and a half, actually," Laura corrected. "And don't start. They're important."

Ashley reached for a stray marker and began doodling on the side of one box, adding a pair of googly eyes to the 'O' in *Books*. "Important? Or just heavy? Those poor movers . . ."

Before Laura could respond, there was a sharp knock at the door. The movers had arrived, a pair of weary-looking men in uniforms that seemed too clean for their trade. In no time, they began hefting the boxes out of the house, each thud of boots resonated, amplifying the reality of change that just sat there like an uninvited guest.

As the house emptied, it seemed to stretch, its spaces widening in a way Laura had never noticed before. Without the weight of furniture and shelves, it became a collection of rooms, each one holding the echo of a life that had passed through. The walls once layered with stories, now stood bare, indifferent to the leaving. She ran her fingers along a windowsill, the rough grit beneath them a reminder of what remained, no matter how often she had wiped it away.

"Do you think I'll miss it?" she asked.

Ashley smoothed the final moving blanket. "Probably. But not in the way you think. You'll miss the idea of it. The version of yourself that lived here. But you've already grown past that."

The silence bloomed between them, rich with an unspoken understanding. "When did you become so profoundly knowing?" Laura's said acknowledging the quiet transformation.

"About the time I decided to uproot your life and drag you along for the ride," Ashley teased, handing Laura her coat.

The last box was loaded, and the house stood bare. The movers waited, their truck double-parked drawing the ire of passing drivers. Laura lingered in the doorway, looking back at the house one final time. It felt wrong to leave without a proper goodbye.

"Ready?" Ashley shouted from the car.

Laura hesitated and with a deep breath. "Goodbye, house. I'll never forget you." She closed the door firmly behind her.

The city receded in the rearview mirror, skyscrapers giving way to bridges, then to rows of suburban houses that seemed too orderly to be real. Soon, the Hudson River gleamed in the distance, its surface reflecting a dull silver under the afternoon light. Laura watched it all slip away from the passenger seat, her coffee untouched in the cupholder.

Ashley's fingers curled around the steering wheel, her left hand guiding the car along the winding road. Her right hand lay relaxed on her denim-clad thigh, thumb absently tracing the worn fabric. The radio crackled softly, punctuating the air with snippets of familiar melodies, interspersed with the gentle hiss of interference.

"Do you remember when you first moved here?" Ashley asked.

Laura's gaze drifted to the passing landscape, a kaleidoscope of urban sprawl and pockets of green. A ghost of a smile played at the corners of her mouth. "I don't like to think about that," she admitted. "But once I found my footing, this city felt . . . limitless."

"And now?"

"Now I feel like it wasn't limitless, but instead tiring," Laura admitted. "It's as if the city's wrung me dry, and I don't have anything left to give it. Stillwater showed me that."

Ashley glanced at her. "That's why we're doing this. Stillwater's about being. Trust me, you'll see."

"You sound like you're writing an ad for the Vermont tourism board," Laura said.

Ashley laughed. "Maybe I should. I'd probably make a fortune."

Laura's eyes drifted back to the window, pulled by the shifting view beyond the glass. The landscape had altered again, revealing a pastoral stretch that reached into something deep within her. Slopes curved along the horizon, their green expanse interrupted by farmhouses and barns that carried the marks of years gone by. The worn wood and peeling paint held stories of generations past.

The miles stretched out before them, and the conversation ebbed and flowed, a river of words flowing between them, touching on the profound and the mundane with equal reverence. They dissected the nuances of their favorite films, unearthed long-buried childhood aspirations, and marveled at the peculiar charm of small-town eccentricities. Ashley had a tale or a joke to balance it all, her laughter filling the car like sunlight through a cloudy sky.

As the first roadside markers for Stillwater materialized, Laura felt a strange mix of emotions bubbling up within her. This was it - the moment that marked the threshold of a new beginning, a pristine chapter waiting to be inscribed. Yet, for the first time in her life, she found herself hesitating at the edge of the blank page, unsure how to craft the opening line of this uncharted narrative.

Ashley slowed the car as they passed the town's welcome sign, its paint chipped but still cheerful. "Almost there," she said.

"Almost there," Laura repeated.

Entering Stillwater, a mural stretched across the side of a brick building, bright blues, and greens depicting a farmer and a river running through a field of wildflowers. Nearby, the bakery displayed a chalkboard sign boasting *Fresh Apple Turnovers Today!* in looping script. Laura's gaze shifted to a man walking briskly down the sidewalk with a sheep on a leash. She opened her mouth to say something, thought better of it, and then couldn't resist.

"Funny isn't it," she chuckled. "This is a real place."

Ashley grinned but kept her eyes on the road. "It's real enough. Everyone will know your name and your coffee order by next week."

They rolled to a stop in front of the bookstore. Laura looked up at the sign, *The Stillwater Reader*, and felt a strange flutter in her chest, like the quiet insistence of something long forgotten coming back to life.

As they climbed out of the car, Miriam appeared from the front door. Her hair was a gray cloud barely tamed into a bun, and she moved with a briskness that belied her years.

"Ah, there you are," she said, extending a hand to Laura. "I'm so happy you're here." Her voice was warm.

"Thank you," Laura said, shaking Miriam's hand.

Ashley stepped forward, her arms encircling Miriam in an embrace that spoke of shared history. "Yes. Thank you," she breathed, her gratitude ringing like the last notes of a beloved song.

"Come on, let's get you both settled. I moved out last week. Don't mind the stairs in the back - they're older than I am, but they haven't given out yet." Miriam said.

Inside, the bookstore's familiar scent of paper and wood polish was a comforting aroma that Laura thought she might never get tired of. The staircase out back was narrow and creaky, leading them to a heavy wooden door that Miriam easily unlocked.

"Here we are," Miriam said, stepping aside to let them in. "It's not the Ritz, but it's got charm. And quirks. I think you'll love it."

Laura stepped inside and took in the space. The apartment was smaller than she had imagined, but cozy in a way that felt immediate and welcoming. Rays of golden afternoon light poured through two lofty windows, their panes like portals to the outside world, illuminating the bare walls and vacant corners. Along one wall, built-in bookshelves stood tall, their barren shelves yearning for the weight of stories and memories. The wood grain, bathed in the soft glow, seemed to whisper promises of cozy evenings and literary adventures to come. Laura's gaze lingered on the shelves, imagining them filled with all her cherished volumes.

Ashley was already inspecting the kitchen, which was tucked into one corner of the main room. "A single burner stove and a sink the size of a cereal bowl," she laughed. "This'll be . . . interesting."

"Didn't I say charm?" Miriam handed Ashley a set of keys. "If you need anything, just let me know. I'm so glad you two are here." She smiled, then added, "It's a good place to start over."

Ashley caught the pause in her expression, the way her eyes held something unspoken before she turned and disappeared down the stairs.

The afternoon passed in a blur of unpacking and small discoveries. In one corner of the apartment, Laura found a stack of old postcards tied together with a ribbon. Most were blank, but one bore a message: *Stillwater is lovely in the fall. Wish you were here.* She turned it over in her hand, wondering who it had been meant for.

Ashley was wedged between open boxes in the kitchenette, pulling out mismatched utensils when Laura joined her in the tiny kitchenette.

"Think we'll fit everything in here?" Ashley asked, holding up a colander that seemed comically large in the cramped space.

Laura leaned against the counter. "We might have to get creative. Or eat a lot of takeout."

"Takeout?" Ashley laughed, setting the colander aside. "There's no takeout here in Stillwater."

"Of course there is," Ashley said. "I'm sure Dottie will fix you a plate to go."

They worked quietly for a while, passing objects back and forth, making guesses about the things Miriam had left behind - a chipped teacup, a set of silverware missing all but one fork. When the unpacking reached a natural pause, Ashley went to the windows and pulled them open, letting in the cool air.

They both stood at the windows that overlooked the town, the main street bordered by shops and so many large, colorful, flower pots. Laura leaned forward, letting the cool evening air brush against her skin.

"It's so quiet," she said. "I don't remember the last time I heard quiet like this."

Ashley stepped behind her, her arms looping around Laura's waist. "It's different, isn't it? Like the whole place is holding its breath."

Laura tilted her head. To her, it wasn't holding anything - it was waiting, offering a town full of stories, secrets she hadn't yet earned the right to hear.

"Do you think this will work?" she asked suddenly.

Ashley's chin rested lightly on her shoulder. "What part?"

"This. Us. Here." Laura gestured vaguely toward the square, the bookstore, and the apartment behind them. "Starting over."

Ashley reached for her hand, threading their fingers together. "It's worth trying. And if it doesn't, we'll figure something else out."

Laura let the answer settle between them, her gaze drifting over the square, watching as the last rays of sunlight painted the buildings in warm hues.

"I think you're right," she said, squeezing Ashley's hand. "It's worth trying."

They stood there as the town settled in for the night, voices growing softer, lights winking out one by one.

Ashley sighed. "We should get to bed."

Laura turned toward her, tilting her head with a small smile. "You think the town will still be here in the morning?"

Ashley laughed, tugging her toward the bedroom. "Guess we'll find out."

Morning entered the apartment slowly, filling the room with a honeyed light that stretched across the wooden floor. Laura stirred beneath the quilt, half-dreaming of bells ringing in the distance, their chimes dissolving into the scent of bread baking somewhere close. The air smelled different here - clean, unhurried - unlike the thick, restless city air she had grown used to. She blinked awake, turning onto her side, and saw Ashley standing at the window, barefoot, holding a cup of coffee with both hands. The sun edged around her, outlining the folds of her sweatshirt, the loose waves of her hair.

"You're up early," Laura said, her voice still thick with sleep.

Ashley turned, smiling. "There's nothing like mornings here. The way the world feels like it's waking up with you."

Laura groaned, stretching as she pushed the quilt aside. "Look at you, waxing poetic. You're already a walking travel brochure. Next, you'll be making jam and entering it in the county fair." She smirked, but secretly, she agreed.

Ashley laughed low and warmly. "Come see for yourself," she said. "It's worth it."

Laura shuffled over, still in her oversized T-shirt, and stood beside Ashley. Below them, the town was waking at its own unhurried pace. Eleanor Kimball, apron tied neatly at her waist, propped open the bakery door, and the scent of cinnamon and sugar lifted into the street. Edgar McDowell, bundled in his gray wool cap, stood in front of the hardware store, sweeping away stray leaves from the night before. A pair of cars idled near Dottie's, their drivers chatting through rolled-down windows. Beyond the rooftops, the hills stretched upward, their edges still caught in a lace of morning mist.

Laura let out a long breath. "It's wonderful."

"Wonderful?" Ashley turned to her, amused. "Try perfect." She extended the cup, their fingers touching briefly, a warmth separate from the coffee.

Laura took a sip letting the steam curl against her lips. "Okay," she said, swallowing. "You win."

The first day of work at the bookstore officially began with a knock on the door. Laura was kneeling on the floor behind the counter, organizing boxes of unsorted books, while Ashley was wiping down the shelves with a damp cloth. They exchanged a glance.

"Expecting someone?" Laura asked.

"Nope," Ashley replied, heading for the door.

When she opened it, there stood Miriam with a large smile and a basket looped over her arm. "Good morning, girls," she said, stepping inside before Ashley could invite her. "Thought I'd bring you a little welcome gift."

Laura emerged from behind the counter, brushing her hands on her jeans. "Miriam, you didn't have to - "

"Nonsense," Miriam interrupted, setting the basket on the counter with a flourish. "Stillwater always welcomes its own."

The basket was brimming with treasures: a jar of raspberry jam, a small tub of applesauce, a baguette from the café, and a neatly folded, hand-knitted scarf in shades of blue and gray. Beneath these was a printed map of the town, annotated in Miriam's beautiful handwriting.

"This," Miriam said, holding up the scarf, "was made by Willow Garner, of course. Her knitting's improving, I think. And this jam," she tapped the jar, "is from the Haverford farm. Best you'll ever taste."

Ashley grinned. "We'll be set for breakfast, at least."

Miriam laughed. "You'll be set for more than that. And look, here comes someone else to welcome you." She stepped back to the open doorway and called out, "Jacob! Come say hello!"

A boy of about ten, with a mop of dark curls and a pair of sneakers that looked too big for his feet, trotted over from across the square. He had a book clutched to his chest and an eager gleam in his eyes.

"This is Jacob," Miriam announced as he stepped inside. "Smart as a whip. He'll visit you each day, and he's obsessed with the stars. Jacob, this is Laura and Ashley. They're new here, living above the bookstore."

Jacob's eyes widened. "Like you did?"

Miriam chuckled. "Yes, Jacob. They own the bookstore now."

"Cool." He held up his book. "Do you guys have a telescope?"

Ashley smiled. "No. Why?"

Jacob beamed. "Because tonight there's going to be a meteor shower. We can watch it together and I can show you all the constellations! I know all their names."

Miriam patted his shoulder. "Jacob's practically the town astronomer. If you let him, he'll talk your ears off about space."

Jacob's enthusiasm was contagious, and Laura found herself smiling. "We'd love that, Jacob. We can watch it together. Come by tonight."

"Really?" His grin widened. "Okay, I will! I'll bring my telescope!"

Miriam gave his shoulder a gentle push. "Run along now. You've got chores to do before you can stay up stargazing."

The boy dashed off, his oversized sneakers slapping against the sidewalk. Miriam turned back to Laura and Ashley. "Well, I'll leave you to it. Oh, and that map in the basket — you'll see the bookstore is circled with a note *Under New Ownership*. Now, everyone will know the change."

Ashley saw Miriam out, thanking her again for the basket, and when the door closed, the shop was quiet once more.

"We've got a lot to do," Ashley said, making sure the sign on the door was flipped to *Closed*.

Laura stood in the center of the bookstore, hands on her hips, measuring the mess. Stacks of books slumped against the walls, some threatening to tip with the next breath of air, while unopened boxes crowded the floor like forgotten luggage.

"So much to do," she said. "Where do we even start?"

Ashley picked up a dusty copy of *Pride and Prejudice* and turned it over in her hands. "With the classics, obviously."

Laura sighed. "I'm serious."

"So am I." Ashley slid the book into place on an empty shelf and stepped back with a nod. "See? One book down, a million to go."

Laura shook her head but couldn't suppress a smile. "Fine. You take fiction, and I'll tackle nonfiction."

They fell into a steady back-and-forth, hands moving from box to shelf, dust rising and resettling in the air. Now and then, one of them would unearth a book worth a pause—a forgotten childhood favorite, a long-out-of-print edition, a volume with an inscription so personal it made them both wonder about the person who had once held it close.

"Look at this." Ashley lifted a leather-bound book, the gold lettering almost rubbed away. "First edition. Probably worth something."

Laura glanced over. "If it doesn't crumble in your hands first."

Their conversation came in bursts, threaded between stretches of quiet concentration. The light outside stretched long across the floor, shifting from the pale brightness of morning to the golden slant of late afternoon. By the time they paused to take in their progress, the shelves had begun to take order, the floor no longer an obstacle course of half-packed boxes.

Ashley dropped into a worn armchair by the window, brushing the dust from her jeans. "We deserve a break."

Laura lowered herself into the opposite chair with a sigh. "And maybe some of that jam."

Ashley laughed. "Now you're speaking my language."

They sat quietly, watching the town beyond the glass. A couple strolled past, pausing to admire the window display. Mrs. Kimball from the bakery locked her door for the night, balancing a paper bag against her hip. Across the street, someone switched on the string lights over the café patio, their glow warming the dusk.

Ashley let her head rest against the chair, exhaling slowly. This place was beginning to feel like something she had always known, something she had been meant to return to. The shop, the town, the way the sky dimmed into a deep indigo while voices drifted in from the street - it wasn't just familiar. It was hers.

The day had stretched long, filled with the rustle of pages and the quiet satisfaction of progress. Laura and Ashley stood side by side, surveying their work one last time with a mixture of pride and exhaustion. The shelves now held neat rows of books, their spines a colorful tapestry against the aged wood.

"I think we've earned our keep today," Ashley said, brushing a strand of hair from her forehead.

Laura nodded, her eyes tracing the familiar titles. "It's starting to feel like our own."

"Starting to?" Ashley raised an eyebrow. "I'd say we're well on our way to – "

A sharp rap on the window cut her off. They turned to see Jacob's face pressed against the glass, his breath fogging the pane. He held a telescope, the stand awkwardly tucked beneath one arm, the metal glinting in the fading light.

Ashley unlocked the door, the lock giving way with a soft snap. "Jacob, I thought you had forgotten us."

The boy burst in, gripping his telescope. "I didn't forget!" His voice tripped over itself in excitement. "The meteor shower! We have to go now!"

Laura glanced at her watch. "Oh, Jacob, but it's getting late. We were just about to -"

"You promised." His expression faltered, energy pulling inward, his fingers shifting on the telescope's body. "You said we'd watch it together."

Ashley and Laura exchanged a glance, an entire conversation passing between them without a word. Ashley lifted a shoulder in concession. "Well. We did."

Jacob's face lit up once more. "Great! I know the best place. Let's go!"

They trailed behind him, securing the bookstore before stepping onto the quiet street. The cool air wrapped around them, crisp with the scent of springtime. Jacob took the lead, his oversized sneakers clapping against the sidewalk, arms wrapped around his equipment like a prized possession.

"Where exactly are we going?" Laura asked, her breath visible in the cool night air.

"You'll see," Jacob called back, not slowing, his movements brimming with purpose.

They climbed the slope beyond the last row of houses, the town unfurling beneath them. Lights from Stillwater scattered across the valley, mirroring the emerging constellations overhead. At the hilltop, Jacob stopped, setting up his telescope with the swift certainty of someone who had done this many times before.

"This," he declared, stepping back, "is the best spot in all of Stillwater to see the stars."

Ashley and Laura stood silent, taking in the view. The sky stretched endlessly above them, a canvas of deep blue dotted with pinpricks of light.

"It's beautiful," Ashley breathed.

Jacob beamed. "Wait till you see it through the telescope. Look!" He pointed excitedly. "There's the first one!"

A streak of light cut across the sky, gone in an instant. Then another, and another.

"Make a wish," Laura murmured.

Ashley turned to her. "What would you wish for?"

Laura considered for a moment. "Nothing," she said finally. "I think I have everything I need right here."

Jacob's voice broke through their moment. "Come on, I want to show you Cassiopeia!"

They took turns peering through the telescope, Jacob's enthusiasm infectious as he rattled off facts about each constellation.

"And that one there," he said, adjusting the telescope slightly, "that's Cygnus, it's cross-shaped. But if you really look at it, it looks like a swan in flight, with a long neck, short tail, and wide wings. Do you see it?"

Laura nodded, her eye pressed to the eyepiece. "I see it. It's amazing, Jacob."

As the night wore on, the meteor shower intensified. Streaks of light crisscrossed the sky, each one eliciting a gasp of wonder.

"You know," Ashley said, her voice soft, "I used to think the stars were lonely. But look at them. They're not alone at all. They're part of something bigger, something beautiful."

Laura felt a warmth spread through her, one that had nothing to do with the chill in the air. She reached out, taking Ashley's hand in hers.

Jacob's voice cut through their silence. "Oh! Did you see that big one?"

They laughed, turning back to the sky. The night unfolded around them, threaded with wonder and the quiet happiness of something new taking shape. When the last streaks of light faded, Jacob packed up his telescope, his eyes drooping with sleep but still bright with leftover excitement.

"That was great," he said, fighting back a yawn. "We'll do it again."

Ashley brushed a hand over his hair. "Anytime, Jacob. You're always welcome at the bookstore."

They walked Jacob home, the streets of Stillwater hushed, houses lined up in quiet watchfulness. On the way back, the shop's light glowing ahead, Laura felt something shift inside her - calm, certain, whole.

"You know," she said. "I think we made the right choice."

Ashley squeezed her hand. "I think so too."

They climbed the stairs to their apartment above the bookstore, the events of the day settling around them like a comfortable blanket. As they got ready for bed, Laura caught Ashley's eye in the mirror.

"What do you think tomorrow will bring?" she asked.

Ashley smiled, that same soft smile that never failed to make Laura's heart skip a beat. "I don't know," she replied. "But I can't wait to find out."

They lay together, sleep pulling them under while the last streaks of light faded from the sky. Laura turned toward Ashley, listening to the quiet, the steady rise and fall of her breath. For the first time in years, tomorrow didn't feel like something to brace against. This town, small and unassuming, had become something more. With Ashley beside her and the night stretching wide above them, she felt anchored, a part of something that made sense.

17 The Summer Festival

Many seasons passed and then came a summer day when the air in Stillwater felt soft against the skin, carrying the scent of pine trees and the fainter, sweeter perfume of something just on the verge of blooming, a promise whispered on the breeze. It was the kind of day that felt infinite, where each moment lingered as if reluctant to move on. The sunlight filtered through the elms that lined the streets, casting delicate shadows that danced like living things across the road. The town had come alive with the Stillwater Summer Fest, a celebration that seemed to breathe in rhythm with the town itself More than an event, it was a collection of the small things that made Stillwater what it was - pies with golden latticed crusts, hand-knitted scarves displayed with care, families strolling through the streets, moving at a pace that suggested there was nowhere more important to be.

But this year, there was something new, something almost intangible that hummed beneath the surface. Miriam felt it, though she couldn't yet put it into words. It was as if Stillwater, for all its quaint traditions, was beginning to stretch its limbs, to embrace possibilities she'd once thought improbable.

She wasn't one for festivals. The noise, the crowds, the constant movement - it had always felt like an intrusion. But today, for reasons she couldn't quite articulate, her steps felt lighter. It was as if she were walking through the years themselves, not just the streets, her memories and the present moment overlapping in a strangely comforting way.

As she moved down Main Street, The festival unfurled like a living canvas, each detail etched with a delicate precision. The children's laughter floated above the grass, a weightless melody that seemed to hover just beyond the edges of memory. Scents wove themselves together - barbecue's smoky warmth embracing the sweet whisper of fresh-baked pastries, creating an atmosphere both familiar and ephemeral. Vendors' voices rose and fell, a rhythmic chorus of commerce and connection, their bright canopies billowing like soft flags of possibility.

She passed the antique store and caught Owen's eye. He was preparing for the day, straightening a display in the window. He lifted a hand in greeting, a brief, familiar exchange before turning back to his work. Further down the street, Willow Garner sat in her usual spot, her purple hat standing out amid the morning's muted colors. She was surrounded by her neatly arranged knitting, her hands moving with steady ease. When she looked up, her smile arrived suddenly, like sunlight breaking through cloud cover.

And then, the bookstore.

She passed the antique store and caught Owen's eye. He was preparing for the day, straightening a display in the window. He lifted a hand in greeting, a brief, familiar exchange before turning back to his work. Further down the street, Willow Garner sat in her usual spot, her purple hat standing out amid the morning's muted colors. She was surrounded by her neatly arranged knitting, her hands moving with steady ease. When she looked up, her smile arrived suddenly, like sunlight breaking through cloud cover.

And then, the bookstore.

Miriam stopped at the curb, looking toward the building that had once been the center of everything. The wooden sign above the door, painted years ago with a playful tower of books, still swayed with the breeze. Near the entrance, a board displayed the names of upcoming authors, their scheduled readings carefully noted in chalk. The bookstore had been hers for so long, a place where the world made sense. Now, it belonged to Ashley and Laura. A new version of itself, familiar but no longer shaped by her hands.

She could see the faintest reflection of herself in the glass door, the outline of her figure softened by the bright displays behind it. The thought struck her that it wasn't just a store anymore. It was something bigger, something that had grown beyond her. Laura and Ashley had made it that way.

The distant strains of a fiddler's lively tune carried through the air. She shifted her stance, the ache in her knees a familiar reminder of her age, and let her eyes wander. Across the way, near the bakery stand, she spotted them: Ashley and Laura.

They walked hand in hand, their heads bent close together as they shared a private laugh. Ashley's free hand gestured animatedly, and Laura tilted her head to listen, her smile soft but steady. The sight of them, so at ease with each other and the world around them, tugged at something deep inside Miriam. It wasn't jealousy, not exactly. It was more like nostalgia, a wistful ache for a time when she too had felt so unburdened.

Ashley noticed her first. She lifted her hand in a wave, her smile breaking wide and genuine. "Miriam!" she called, her voice carrying easily over the din of the festival.

Laura looked up then, her face lighting up as she followed Ashley's gaze. They crossed the street toward her, weaving through the crowd with a kind of unhurried grace that only came from familiarity.

"How's the day treating you?" Ashley asked.

Miriam paused, her hesitation a fleeting shadow before a smile bloomed across her face. It was a small thing, born of instinct rather than deliberation, but genuine nonetheless. "I'm just taking in the sights," she replied. "You two seem to be enjoying yourselves."

Ashley's laughter rippled through the air, light and contagious. "We certainly are. But tell me, did Willow Garner catch your eye?"

Miriam leaned in, conspiratorial. "How could you miss her with that ragged purple hat sitting atop her head."

Their shared laughter rose and mingled within the symphony of festival sounds.

"It's perfect, isn't it?" Laura said, her eyes bright as she glanced around.

Miriam nodded slowly, her gaze returning to the bookstore. "I don't think I've ever seen Stillwater quite like this. It's different, that's for sure. But it's good. Better, even."

Ashley grinned, giving Laura's hand a playful squeeze. "We're just following your lead, Miriam," she said. "You built the foundation. We're just adding a little flair."

Miriam felt a sudden lump in her throat, the weight of Ashley's words settling over her like a warm blanket. She had always thought of the bookstore as hers, as something static and unchanging. But maybe that had been the problem. It wasn't meant to stay the same. It was meant to grow, to evolve.

"I'm glad you're here," she said quietly. "Both of you."

For a moment, the three of them stood there, a small island of stillness in the middle of the bustling street.

Eventually, Ashley and Laura moved on, heading back toward the bookstore, where a group had already gathered for the next reading. Miriam stayed where she was, watching them disappear into the crowd. She felt a rush of emotion she couldn't quite name - pride, yes, that was it, but something else too - a kind of yearning.

The past had always been her anchor, her refuge. But now, for the first time, she found herself looking toward the future with something like hope.

By evening, the streets of Stillwater glowed under lanterns hung from post to post, their soft sway nudged by a passing breeze. The warm illumination fell across cobblestones worn smooth by decades of footsteps, casting shifting patterns that danced with the shadows of the festivalgoers still milling about. Children darted between stands, their laughter a melody rising above the hum of conversation and the soft strains of music played by a local trio in the gazebo.

The bookstore had carried a current of motion and sound throughout the day. Its narrow aisles, once quiet refuges, filled with the shuffle of feet and the low murmur of voices, occasionally broken by bursts of applause from the back, where authors shared their work. Even Miriam, who had spent much of her life shielding herself from the energy of crowds, found herself drawn into the liveliness. She remained by the counter longer than intended, catching pieces of conversations, letting herself be drawn into a discussion with a poet from Burlington on the lasting power of Emily Dickinson.

She wasn't accustomed to this - moving through disorder without strain. Yet, with each passing hour, she felt less inclined to push against it, more open to being carried along. When the day neared its conclusion, a quiet unrest stirred in her. She hadn't expected to wish for more time.

When the night finally arrived, and the crowd began to disperse, Miriam stepped outside. The streets exhaled the last remnants of the day's noise, a hush settling over the city like a held breath after too much conversation. She stood at the edge of the bookstore's threshold, arms crossed loosely, and took in the scene. Across the way, she spotted Ashley and Laura. The two of them were near the bakery's darkened storefront, their hands clasped, heads bent close as they shared a laugh that was audible even from where Miriam stood.

She watched them with a quiet pride, the kind that swells not born of personal triumph but from seeing joy take root in others - a joy she had, in some small way, helped nurture. It wasn't a pride she'd known often in her life, but here it was, undeniable and warm.

She thought of everything that had brought them here: the weight of loss, the untangling of old griefs, the rediscovery of connections long frayed. She thought of Ashley's father, and how he would've loved this night, this version of Stillwater where light and laughter had filled the cracks he had once left behind.

As Ashley leaned in to kiss Laura's cheek, Miriam found herself smiling. She hadn't been certain, not at first, about their plans for the bookstore or their return to Stillwater. But now, watching them, she knew. They belonged here, as much as she ever had. Perhaps more.

The thought drifted lightly through her mind, like a gentle breeze playing with loose strands of hair. She recognized something in it, an understanding that had been waiting for her to catch up. Sometimes, the wisest thing was to release your hold, to trust that the world would shape itself without constant direction. Stillwater had done exactly that, growing into something both recognizable and entirely unfamiliar.

She remained there, watching the lanterns sway overhead, the glow casting uneven patterns on the ground. Voices from the festival carried through the warm night, fading but not yet gone. In that quiet space, with the evening pressing close and the sight of Ashley and Laura touched by soft gold, Miriam felt a kind of stillness settle inside her. It wasn't profound. It didn't change anything. It simply was - steady, enduring, like the town she had always known.

She reached back, closing the door, the soft creak of the hinge breaking the silence. "Goodnight," she whispered to no one in particular, though perhaps the town itself heard her. She didn't need a reply.

As she turned to leave, Miriam's thoughts drifted to the small cottage nestled just beyond the edge of Silver Birch, the place she now called home. The cottage was modest by any measure - a single-story building with shutters that had softened over time and a roof that sloped gently, showing its age - but it was home. Tucked into a grove of birch and maple, it seemed to belong more to the trees than to the world of people. Mornings there were quiet, broken only by the rustle of leaves or the tentative call of birds testing the dawn. Inside, the rooms were small, the furnishings humble: a well-worn armchair by the fireplace, a bookshelf half-filled with well-loved books from the store, and a kitchen table where the light always fell just right in the late afternoon. It wasn't grand, but it was hers. And in its simplicity, she had found something she hadn't known she was looking for - a sense of peace, a life that asked for nothing more than what she could offer.

The drive back to the cottage unfolded slowly, her old station wagon making its way along the winding road that cut through the heart of the town before slipping into the quiet of the woods. The festival's sounds followed her at first, laughter and fragments of conversation carried on the warm evening air. The distant notes of a fiddle hung in the air like the final strains of a song, fading gradually as she turned away from the lanterns and the buzz of the crowd.

The solitude of the road suited her. It gave her space to think, though tonight her thoughts were less pressing and more like the meandering course of a stream. She thought of Ashley and Laura, of their laughter and the easy way they moved together as if they were already part of Stillwater's fabric. She thought of the bookstore, its shelves alive with new ideas and voices, the way it had transformed into a gathering place not just for books but for people. And she thought of the town itself, resilient in ways she hadn't imagined, finding its way back to life not through some grand gesture but through a series of small, steady steps.

As the road climbed gently toward Silver Birch, the festival sounds gave way to the chorus of crickets and the occasional rustle of unseen creatures in the underbrush. The air grew cooler, and Miriam rolled down her window, letting the night breeze sweep through the car. It carried the faint, earthy scent of the woods, grounding her, reminding her of where she was headed - not just to the cottage, but to the quiet life she had carved out for herself, a life that had been waiting all along.

When she reached the cottage, she paused for a moment at the gate, looking out at the small garden she'd started. It was a humble thing, just a few rows of herbs and vegetables, but it felt like a beginning. She stepped inside, the floorboards creaking underfoot, a sound she had long since grown familiar with. She crossed to the window, pulled back the curtain, and watched as the last slivers of sunlight washed over the trees. The faint glow of festival lights twinkled in the distance, a quiet signal that life continued beyond her small world, pressing onward.

Miriam stood there for a moment, the dying light casting long shadows across the room. She thought about the years that had passed since she first arrived, the days that seemed to vanish one after another without her noticing. At first, she had believed time was something solid, something she could grasp, but now it felt slippery, slipping through her fingers in ways that didn't make sense. So much had changed in the quiet corners of her life - some things lost, others discovered - but the garden, the cottage, and even the familiar creak of the floorboards, were what remained. The world outside might have continued on its relentless march, but here, in these small, quiet spaces, she had found a rhythm of her own. Time didn't wait, but maybe, just maybe, there was something in the passage of it that made all things meaningful in their own way.

Laura and Ashley were exhausted. The first day of the festival had been a whirlwind of activity, drawing crowds from neighboring towns and keeping the little bookshop bustling from dawn to dusk. Now, in the calm that followed, the two worked through their closing tasks with the ease of those who had done this countless times before, their movements slow but purposeful.

"I think my feet have declared independence from the rest of my body," Laura groaned, leaning against the counter as she counted out the day's receipts. Her hair, usually neatly braided, had come loose in wisps around her face, giving her a charmingly disheveled appearance.

Ashley chuckled softly, her own fatigue evident in the slump of her shoulders. "I'm pretty sure mine seceded hours ago," she replied, straightening a display of books. Her fingers lingered on the spine of *Men at War*, a collection of short stories curated by Ernest Hemingway. "I don't know if the shop has ever been this busy."

"Probably not," Laura said, closing the cash register with a satisfying click. "I think Miriam and your father would've loved it, though. All those people, all those stories."

Ashley nodded, a familiar ache rising in her chest at the mention of her dad. His presence filled every corner of her thoughts, like a shadow she couldn't escape. "I think you're right," she agreed.

With the day's tasks finally complete, they made their way to the narrow staircase at the back of the shop. The wooden steps creaked under their feet, a homey sound that never failed to make Ashley smile. It was one of the many quirks of the old building that had initially charmed her.

The small apartment above the bookstore had become their sanctuary, a cozy nest that bore witness to their growing love. As they entered, both women let out a collective sigh of relief, the tension of the day beginning to ebb away.

"Shower?" Laura suggested, already peeling off her festival t-shirt.

Ashley smiled gratefully. "God, yes."

They shuffled into the tiny bathroom, shedding clothes like weary travelers discarding heavy backpacks. The shower was barely big enough for two, but they had long since mastered the art of sharing the space. Warm water cascaded over them, washing away the dust and fatigue of the day.

Ashley leaned her forehead against Laura's shoulder, letting the steady rhythm of the water lull her into a state of peaceful semi-consciousness. Laura's hands moved gently over her back, kneading away knots of tension.

"You're amazing, you know that?" Ashley murmured, her words nearly lost in the sound of running water.

Laura pressed a kiss to her cheek. "So are you. The way you handled that crowd today . . . your dad would've been proud."

She met Laura's gaze. "You really think so?"

"I know so," Laura replied. "You've breathed new life into this place, into your life."

Ashley nodded, unable to speak past the sudden lump in her throat. She let the water wash away the few tears that escaped, grateful for Laura's steady presence.

When they emerged from the shower, they quickly cocooned themselves in the comfort of soft, well-worn towels that carried the faint scent of lavender and time. The bedroom awaited, its quiet promise of rest impossible to resist. They fell into the bed with twin sighs of relief, bodies instinctively seeking the familiar curve of each other, a choreography as old as their love.

Moonlight, unfiltered by curtains, pooled through the window, spilling silver across the walls and floor. Ashley let her eyes trace the light as it danced over Laura's face, softening the sharpness of the day's edges, smoothing away years. In this light, Laura looked impossibly young, her features rendered almost ethereal, a vision that Ashley wished she could hold onto forever.

"What are you thinking?" Laura whispered.

Ashley was quiet for a moment, gathering her thoughts. "I'm thinking about how different my life is now. How I never expected to end up here, in this town, in this bed, with you."

Laura's hand found hers under the covers, their fingers intertwining. "Do you regret it?"

"No," Ashley said, the word coming out more forcefully. "No," she repeated, softer this time. "I just . . . sometimes I can't believe how much has changed. How much I've changed."

Laura hummed thoughtfully. "You know, when you first came back to Stillwater, you were like a caged bird. All ruffled feathers and sharp edges, ready to fly away at the first opportunity."

Ashley winced at the accuracy of the description. "Yeah, I was pretty awful."

"You were scared," Laura corrected gently. "This place represented everything you'd run away from. Your mother's leaving, your father's intransigence, your brother's resentment, the smallness of this place. But you faced it all, Ashley. You stayed when it would have been easier to just leave again."

Ashley turned onto her side, propping herself up on one elbow to look at Laura more fully. "I stayed because of what I learned about my parents at first," she admitted. "But then . . . then I stayed because of you."

Laura's smile was soft in the moonlight. "And now?"

"Now I stay because this is home," Ashley said. "This town, this bookstore, this life we're building together. It's everything I never knew I wanted."

They lapsed into comfortable silence, each lost in their own thoughts. Ashley's mind drifted back to the early days of her return to Stillwater, the reluctance and resentment that had colored her every interaction. Then she thought of the first time she'd met Laura, at the library on campus.

"Do you remember the day we met?" she asked.

Laura chuckled. "How could I forget? God, I was so bold. But I knew what I wanted."

"And this? You wanted this?"

"I love it," Laura said. "I love knowing that Willow Garner will always have the ratty purple hat sitting atop her head. That

Edgar McDowell will always be searching for a secret tunnel under Main Street. And Eleanor Kimball will still be selling her over-priced apple turnovers."

Ashley laughed. "I guess we've become two small-town girls."

"I guess we have," Laura mused. "Do you think your father would be shocked?"

"I don't think so," Ashley said. "He knew I'd find my way back here eventually. "I think he thought that I was out there, collecting stories. That one day, I'd come home and share them all." Tears pricked at her eyes. "I wish I'd come back sooner. I wish I'd had more time with him."

"Hey," Laura said softly, pulling Ashley closer. "You were here when it mattered most. And now you and your brother are carrying on his legacy."

Ashley nodded against Laura's shoulder, allowing herself to be comforted. They lay like that for a while, the moonlight slowly shifting across the room, the distant sound of crickets filtering through the open window.

"Laura?" Ashley whispered, unsure if the other woman was still awake.

"Hmm?"

"Do you think . . . do you think my father would approve? Of us, I mean. Of . . . everything."

Laura was quiet for so long that Ashley thought she might have drifted off. But then she spoke, her voice clear and certain in the stillness of the night.

"Ashley, I think your father loved you more than anything in this world. He wanted you to be happy, to find your place, to build a life that fulfilled you. I think if he could see you now - see us - he'd be overjoyed."

Ashley let out a breath she hadn't realized she'd been holding. "Yeah?"

"Yeah," Laura confirmed. "You've reconnected with your brother, passed the antique shop into his capable hands, and now it's thriving. You're home, here in Stillwater, where you belong. And you've found love. What more could a parent wish for their child?"

Ashley thought about her father, back when things were simpler, before her mother left, before she kissed Sarah at school. He was different then. His eyes held a softness, and his smile was always patient, gentle. He had a way of pulling stories from even the most quiet, reluctant person. She remembered the lessons he'd shared, not through words, but through the way he lived - quiet and steady, showing her more than any lecture could.

"You're right," she said finally. "Dad always said that the measure of a good life was in the connections we made, the stories we shared. I think . . . I think he'd be happy to see how many connections we're fostering here."

Laura yawned, snuggling closer. "He'd be proud of you, Ashley. So proud."

As sleep began to settle over them, Ashley's thoughts meandered toward the day waiting on the other side of dawn. Tomorrow, they would unlock the doors of the bookstore once more, welcoming the rhythm of the festival. There would be shelves to straighten, books to recommend, and familiar faces to greet as the town pulsed with its celebration. Community events would hum with small joys, the moments stitched together like a patchwork quilt of ordinary happiness.

It was a life so far removed from the sleek and hurried existence she had once known, the airports and the boardrooms, the endless rush of somewhere to be. But here, with Laura beside her in this small apartment above a small-town bookstore, Ashley had found something she'd been searching for all along - a sense of belonging, of purpose, of home.

As she teetered on the edge of sleep, Ashley sent a silent thought out into the universe, hoping somehow her father could hear it: "I'm home, Dad. I'm finally home."

ABOUT THE AUTHOR

Philip Mazza is a novelist with a boundless imagination, captivating readers with the epic fantasy series *The Harrow Saga*. Born in New York in 1959, he earned a degree in Business from LeMoyne College and an MBA, later holding leadership roles in human resources and operations. Now a professor at the Madden School of Business and Economics, Philip dedicates his time to his students and writing. *The Road to Stillwater* is his tenth literary work. He and his wife enjoy travel and continue to live in upstate New York.